LEFT TO DIE . . .

Another quick burst angled into the room from beyond the door, jolting the general back to reality. The terrorist was in the middle of his second stride within the room when Ritter placed the muzzle of his revolver against the base of the man's skull. But it was too late. Under the force of the attack, the experiment was raging irrevocably out of control!

In about thirty seconds, the whole building was going to vaporize. On his way out of the lab, Ritter turned and looked back at the unconscious Lt. Rogers strapped into the chair. *Those Guardians are cool customers*, Ritter thought, and he was glad of it. Because there was just no time to save him . . .

THE GUARDIANS
DEATH CHARGE

RICHARD AUSTIN

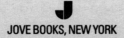

JOVE BOOKS, NEW YORK

THE GUARDIANS: DEATH CHARGE

A Jove Book / published by arrangement with
the author

PRINTING HISTORY
Jove edition / August 1991

ISBN: 0-515-10409-4

Jove Books are published by The Berkley Publishing Group,
200 Madison Avenue, New York, New York 10016.
The name "JOVE" and the "J" logo
are trademarks belonging to Jove Publications, Inc.

PRINTED IN THE UNITED STATES OF AMERICA

10 9 8 7 6 5 4 3 2 1

PART
ONE

PROLOGUE

Tom Rogers felt more than just uncomfortable, strapped into the chair like a 1930's Sing Sing criminal waiting for some sneering warden to throw the switch. He also felt stupid. He asked himself over and over again why he had been such a damn fool to volunteer for this duty in the first place. But then the answer always shot back to pierce his forehead like a diamond bullet, "Marta." The name screamed in his brain, and he winced at the thought of her. The image of her face seared into his imagination and knotted his intestines. Had he not been strapped down he would have doubled over in pain.

"Everything all right, Lieutenant?" a white-coated technician droned through the intercom connecting a glassed-in control booth with the test lab. Rogers was wired with sensors, and his reaction had registered on the instruments arrayed on a panel before the two scientists monitoring the experiment.

"Yeah, sure thing." He grimaced. "Let's slice this turkey."

Rogers forced that haunting Mediterranean face which filled his mind's eye to distort into a blur. He concentrated on an imagined spot on the wall a few meters in front of him. The whitecoats had told him to relax, and even had offered some drugs to help him in that direction, but he had refused them. He thought it somehow unprincipled that the U.S. Army would offer mood-alterants to one of its own. He was a Green Beret, after all, a Special Forces officer, and a Guardian. So he would push her out of his mind by the force of his own granite will.

He wasn't quite sure what this was about, the experiment and all. The scientists had explained it to him, but he didn't understand much of what they'd had to say and he really didn't give a damn. All he knew was that he'd had to get out of Washington, and the assignment offered him an escape. Duty in Hawaii was just the respite he needed, even if he was stationed at a secret base on Niihau, the westernmost of the major eight-island chain in the Pacific.

At least here, he reasoned, there was no way to see Marta again, though that was what he wanted more than anything. The thought of meeting her by accident somewhere around Washington had paralyzed him with terror. He snickered to himself, and a needle moved slightly on a gauge on the control panel in the next room. It was ludicrous to think that, after all the combat he had survived in his thirty-five years, a five-foot-four-inch brunette could freeze him with fear. One of the whitecoats, the one with the thick horn-rimmed glasses, pushed the intercom button to speak, but noticed Rogers's expression and thought better of it.

The procedure had something to do with magnetics, Rogers vaguely remembered. It involved the reversal of polarities in a magnetic field. If the oscillation could be maintained at a rapid enough rate, this could cause the alteration of the very matter constituting the field itself, and thus produce enough energy gain to support the whole process. Rogers rattled off this explanation in his head like the military litany that it was. It was the official Army interpretation as dictated by General Elmo A. Ritter, Commander, Special Scientific Detachment, and leader of Project Dynamo. Rogers never quite understood what that designation had to do with the actual project. He assumed that it was supposed to generate energy of some sort, though he was never told what kind. But what the hell. He'd volunteered anyway.

The device itself was called a Magnetic Enhancement Device (M.E.D.), and consisted of two cylindrical tubes that ringed the lab in descending circles along the walls. The chair was bolted to the floor in the exact center of the room.

Rogers caught a green flash out of the corner of his eye, and turned toward the glass to see General Ritter swagger into the control room. The commander was a large man, nearing sixty, with a great shock of salt and pepper hair combed straight back. He always dressed in full uniform, tunic replete with theater ribbons, regardless of the occasion. He had incorporated jodhpurs and knee-high riding boots into his outfit, exercising the leeway given general officers to personalize their uniforms. It was not uncommon to see him in an old-fashioned helmet liner emblazoned with the three stars of his rank. Rogers thought the general was the most ridiculous man he had ever seen, and called him "Patton" behind his back.

"How are we doing today, Rogers?" Ritter leaned over one of the technicians to speak into the microphone that goo_senecked out from the control panel.

"Oh, just fine, General," Rogers answered as politely as he could. "And how are you, sir?"

"Brimming, Lieutenant. Just brimming with enthusiasm. This is going to be a great day." The general flashed his capped smile through the glass, then to everyone in the booth.

Rogers wondered at the remark. After all, he was just supposed to sit in the chair and provide the scientists with a warm body upon which the effects of the experiment could be studied. His hair might stand on end, he thought, but other than that he couldn't imagine what excitement could possibly be derived from watching him sit in the middle of a magnetic field.

"Are we ready, gentlemen?" Ritter's massive brow swiveled as he surveyed the whitecoats. A chorus of "yes, sir" echoed in the booth, and the technicians began their pre-experiment drills. The control panel and its built-in computer terminals blazed as lights flashed and chunks of data materialized on the amber screens. The order to seal the lab came over the intercom, and the giant steel door which separated the two rooms automatically droned to a close. One of the technicians indicated that the preparations had been completed and that the M.E.D. was ready for ignition.

"Fire that mother up!" Ritter ordered with a flourish.

CHAPTER
ONE

Uli Kanina motioned for his men to stay low as he crouched against the seawall thirty meters beyond the crashing surf. His squad, a dozen strong, helped one another unharness their scuba tanks. Then they discarded their masks and fins. Kanina hoped that the reef-runners would suffice as shoes for the advance to the laboratory compound. They had to travel over loose coral most of the 300 meters to the target building. He plugged in his earpiece to the transmitter he had carried in a watertight bag during the half-mile swim from the trawler. The boat, now two miles offshore, would be well within range of his signal.

He raised his ten-power Zeiss binoculars and focused on the compound. The three low buildings were aligned in a T. The long building in the middle contained the object of today's mission. The other two housed the staff, including a security contingent which had been estimated at platoon strength. The intelligence reports also indicated that two-thirds of the force, having worked all night when the perceived threat was at its greatest, would be asleep in the two buildings that formed the cross of the T. He turned to see two of his men busy setting up the mortar. That should take care of the sleepers. "You snooze, you lose," Uli said to himself with a chuckle.

A sudden jolt of static blasted his eardrum, and Kanina clawed the tiny speaker out of his ear. "Shit!" he said under his breath. He turned down the volume on the receiver mounted on his diver's belt and re-inserted the earpiece.

"Typhoon calling Rainbow, come in, Rainbow." It was that familiar Arabian accent again, the one Uli hated.

"Typhoon, this is Rainbow. We are ashore and in position. Repeat. We are in position," Kanina lied through his throat mike.

"That's a roger, Rainbow. Good luck and remember: I must have those disks. Don't fuck it up! Typhoon out."

The transmission snapped dead in Uli's ear. "Piss up a rope," he mumbled, then wondered if foreigners were all born presumptuous or just became that way after years of diligent practice. Of course he wouldn't forget the goddamn computer tapes. Although he had no idea what information they contained or why it was considered so valuable to the world of Islam.

He looked at his watch. It was 6:51, nine minutes until he was to commence the attack. Kanina unzipped the watertight pouch and unpacked his Uzi, checking the weapon for any signs of moisture. He motioned to his men to lock and load and fan out to their respective flanks. He checked his watch against those of the mortar crew, then at 6:52 gave the signal to move out.

The coral, broken into large chunks, had been placed around the perimeter to discourage just the sort of activity that was now occurring. The heavy-duty rubber and nylon reef-runners proved insufficient protection against the razor-sharp rock that sliced into Uli's right foot just below the ankle bone. He left a trail of blood as he sneaked towards the chain-link fence which bordered the grounds one hundred meters out from the buildings.

The pain was worth it to Kanina. He would today strike a blow for Hawaiian independence, even though he realized his cause was considered insignificant by the Arab interlopers who'd organized and financed the mission. But Uli didn't care. He was Hawaiian—pure Hawaiian—born and raised on Niihau. The last refuge for the unspoiled Polynesian stock that had left the Marquesas in the Middle Ages and sailed thousands of miles north through the Pacific to this land.

His small band of Hawaiian separatists, the "Lono," were

young men who were as brave and committed to destroying the compound as he was. The facility was in direct violation of the special status which governed Niihau, the last island reserved for those of pure blood. Today, the sacred land would return to its intended use with the removal of a spiritual contamination, an American military installation. And tomorrow? Well, tomorrow anything could happen. Even a free and independent Hawaii.

Seven minutes later the ten-man team arrived at the fence. There were no guards and no towers, their absence a testament to American arrogance. Unfortunately, the fence was also electrified. Uli used the remaining minute to work his fingers into the heavy rubberized gloves which, with the special wire cutters made of a synthetic, non-conducting metal, would protect him from the lethal voltage. He would wait another twenty seconds until the first mortar shell struck before he made his cuts. Then it would not matter if the breach was noted by the security computer inside the compound. After the first round landed, the team would have approximately thirty seconds to cut the fence and reach cover behind the center building directly ahead. From there the group's small-arms fire would polish off the survivors of the mortar attack as they scrambled dazed from the barracks. At least that was the plan.

Uli looked at his watch. The seconds flashed away until the Casio digital read 7:00. Then the building closest to him erupted in a tangle of splinters, smoke, and flame. The squad flattened to avoid the fragmentation of the blast. Then Uli was up and furiously cutting his way through the fence. He had just ten seconds before the mortar crew fired the second round. The metal sparked and hissed with each snip, but his hands remained safe within the protective gloves. After eight seconds the first man slithered through the fence, and Uli ordered his crew down again.

The next round caught the back of the second building, which meant another shot would be forthcoming. Ten seconds later Uli went through the fence after holding the wire open for his comrades. By then the first man was in position behind the trucks, and was rattling off a spray of 9mm parabellums into a group of G.I.'s who managed to stagger out of the demolished barracks.

When Uli arrived at the trucks the second building was ablaze. His team was hosing down any survivors who thought they were lucky enough to escape the blast and fire. Within seconds the defenders had been sufficiently thinned so that Uli could approach the back door of the long central building and fire a burst into the steel lock. The door popped open like a toy, and two of his Lono swept inside.

A curtain of hot steel greeted the pair and cut them down in the hallway. Uli popped the pin on a baseball grenade and wristed it as hard as he could around the doorjamb. The building quivered from the concussion, and smoke belched out the door. Kanina leapt through the opening and dove down the hall, his Uzi blazing. But the only enemies he saw were two blackened bodies already shredded by the grenade. He crawled over his dead friends, then over the G.I.'s, and snaked his way down the hall.

He knew the resistance would stiffen now that their attack was no longer a surprise. Almost a third of the security troops were stationed in the building, and even now might be between him and his objective. But Uli was resolved to make it to the laboratory and secure the computer disks for the Arabs. Their money, after all, was much needed by the movement. Beyond that his mission was to kill everyone in sight.

The alarm clanged through the control room, deafening those inside. General Elmo Ritter clapped his hands over his ears and stared at the control panel.

"What's happening, sir?" one of the technicians, a young captain, yelled.

"Probably some sort of damned drill, son. Just go on about your business. It'll stop directly," Ritter bellowed back. He was sorry the sound had prevented him from using his crisis-neutral tone. He had been practicing it lately. He did have genuine cause for worry, however. He knew the alarm was not the result of a drill, at least not one that he had scheduled. Still, he could not believe they were actually under attack. Not in *Hawaii*, of all places.

Ritter noticed a blinking light on the panel, and finally recognized it as the visual indicator of an incoming phone call. The general snatched up the receiver and stuck a finger in his other ear.

"Sir, we've got a breach of the perimeter, and the system reports both barracks destroyed," the security officer shouted through the receiver.

"Jesus! Who are they? Wait a minute. Turn that goddamn

noise off," Ritter barked. The alarm suddenly stopped, but its effect continued to echo in the general's head. "That's better. Now, what the hell is going on?"

"The staff barracks have been destroyed, and laboratory security has been compromised, sir."

"Shit!" Ritter bobbed his head as he spat out the word. "How many of them?"

"Sir, we haven't been able to ascertain that yet."

"Any idea who are they are?"

"No, sir," the young officer replied. "We're running the only segment of video we have on the intrusion through the computer now to see if we can come up with a visual match."

Compromised? Ascertain? Intrusion? Ritter thought. *What kind of goddamn language is that to fight a battle with?* The general was miffed that the young lieutenant's crisis-neutral tone was more effective than his. "Where is it now?"

"What, sir?"

"The fucking attack, boy. What do you think?"

"Oh, yes, sir," replied the disembodied voice. "From the sound of the gunfire I would estimate that it was—" A sudden blast sent a shrill scream through the phone, and Ritter jerked the receiver away from his ear, wincing. Then the line went dead.

"Damn!" Ritter understood all too well that the security command post was located a mere twenty meters down the hall, and that the sound which had come over the line just before it went dead was that of an explosion, probably a grenade. He sucked in a deep breath as he estimated that he had no more than a minute to live. Then he drew his .45 revolver from its hand-tooled leather holster and took comfort from the smooth ivory grip.

A whitecoat swiveled away from the control panel. "What should we do, sir?"

After a pause, which was perfectly timed for dramatic effect, the general replied, "Pray, Captain. Pray."

"No, sir. What I mean is, what do we do about the experiment? Should we shut it down?"

Ritter stared blankly at the young technician.

"Sir?"

The general slowly turned toward the large window which separated the control room from the soundproofed lab. He could see Lieutenant Rogers sitting in the chair, blithely unaware of what was about to happen. *So much the better*, Ritter thought. *No point in alerting him. There is nothing he can do and nothing we can do for him.* He knew Rogers was safe behind the giant steel door, and that the window was made of a special translucent resin that was bullet-proof. Unfortunately, the door between the control room and the hall was constructed of more ordinary materials. "What is the oscillation velocity?"

"Approaching full capacity, sir. After it reaches that point, the process will be irreversible."

"How much time till then?"

"Sir, twenty seconds and counting."

Above the approaching gunfire, Ritter could hear the M.E.D.'s high-pitched whine. There was only one thing to do.

"Shut her down," Ritter commanded. "Now!"

The captain swiveled back toward the control panel. As he reached for the emergency termination button, a hail of gunfire sliced through the door and a deflected bullet crushed his outstretched hand.

Ritter turned to the door as it flung open and fired his revolver. The fat .45-caliber slug splattered the face of a young man in a black wet suit. Ritter watched dumbstruck as the youth, no older than twenty, lurched backwards through the opening and fell dead in the hallway.

Another quick burst angled into the room from beyond the door, killing the captain, who had huddled in the opposite corner. The two remaining technicians watched their friend twitch, then slump into a heap on the floor. For an instant they were transfixed by the sight of his lifeless eyes staring off into nothing. Then they both lurched for cover underneath the control panel.

The gunfire jolted Ritter back to reality. Moving quickly, the general hugged the wall next to the door and pointed the pistol temple-high at the bloodstained opening. He stood there for a long moment, staring at the emptiness and waiting for the inevitable. As his anticipation grew, so did the shrill sound of the M.E.D. Suddenly it registered in his mind that there was no one on the controls, and that the experiment had passed the point of no return. The energy was compiling at an exponential rate and the whole process was raging irrevocably out of control.

He looked down at his two technicians cringing under the panel. Their expressions of caged terror confirmed his worst nightmare. They were holding their ears now against the high-frequency whine as they glanced furtively at the door. All three in the room knew the M.E.D. was marching toward its own destruction and theirs. Finally, the youngest, a lieutenant, bolted for the opening. "Don't shoot," he pleaded as he disappeared through the doorway, his hands held high. "We're all going to be—" A volley of submachine gun fire cut him short. An instant later, Ritter heard his body smack the floor in the hall.

Suddenly a stubby gun barrel appeared in the doorway, and Ritter forced himself to wait for its owner to follow it into the room. But the man didn't. Instead, he spoke from just beyond the door. "Where are the computer disks that control your work here?" he asked in a loud but even voice.

The owlish young technician pointed to a bank of computers on the side of the room opposite the general. "Over there," he said. Ritter noted with admiration and relief that the sergeant's horn-rimmed glasses never looked in his direction.

The gun barrel finally probed its way into the room. Its owner was Polynesian. And he was not very careful. He seemed preoccupied with his objective instead of his safety, and was in the middle of his second stride within the room when Ritter placed the muzzle of his revolver against the base of the man's skull. The general glanced quickly out the door to make sure no one performed the same trick on *him*. The hall was clear, though he didn't know how long it would remain that way.

"Back up while you drop the weapon," Ritter sneered in his best Clint Eastwood imitation. That and the pressure of the gun barrel against the back of the head did the trick. The man dropped the Uzi and backpeddled slowly beyond the edge of the door. "What the young man you just murdered was trying to tell you is that in about thirty seconds this whole building is going to vaporize and we will all die," Ritter snarled. "Do you understand?"

The man nodded.

"So you and I and the gentleman under the panel are going to walk out of this place and seek whatever shelter you haven't destroyed. And if we encounter any of your friends along the way, you will instruct them to lay down their arms or I will drastically rearrange the few brain cells you have left. Do you understand?"

The man nodded again.

"After you, sir," Ritter snarled. "Let's go, Sergeant." The whitecoat scrambled out from under the control panel, picked up the Uzi, and started for the door. But Ritter stopped him.

"Get the disks," he commanded. The sergeant returned to the console, pressed a button, and two 3½-inch computer disks popped out of the control panel. Ritter marveled at how tiny they were, and hoped that their ejection would somehow terminate the experiment. But he knew that their data was already loaded into the machine and that the process would grind on to its conclusion.

At that moment he stopped and looked through the window into the lab. There he saw Rogers strapped into the chair with his head lolling back and his eyes closed. The general noted with astonishment that his experiment's subject had apparently fallen asleep. *Those Guardians are cool customers*, Ritter thought, and he was glad of it. There was just not time to save him. The general sighed and walked out of the room.

"What's your name, son?" asked Ritter, using the gun barrel to prod his prisoner down the body-strewn hallway.

"Uli Kanina."

"Hawaiian, huh? Well, unless you want to become a *puka* head, I suggest you keep your buddies off us so we can all walk out of here safe. You got it?"

"I got it," Uli gritted through his teeth.

"Good. Then you can start right now. Sing out!"

"Brothers of Lono! This is Uli. Listen closely. I have been taken prisoner. I want you to use all your force to kill me and my captors. Do you understand?"

Ritter spiked his prisoner on the cheekbone with the edge of his revolver butt, and Uli cried out in pain. "Now let's try that again, son. Shall we?"

Before he had a chance, a wet-suited Lono appeared from around a corner directly ahead. Ritter pushed Uli to the floor just as the man fired a short burst that stitched the sergeant across the chest and sent him spinning backwards. Ritter got off a single supine shot. The terrorist dropped like a bag of sand. The general dragged Uli up to the corner, where he inspected the neat hole in the Lono's forehead. He placed the nickle-plated revolver into Uli's crotch and said, "Do it right this time, son. Please."

A look of abject desperation slipped across Uli's face. "Comrades! Evacuate the building. The place is going up any second. Do you here me, Lono? Get out of here, now!"

"You know, son, I'm beginning to like you," Ritter said. Then he poked him hard in the balls with his gun barrel.

The two made it to the back door of the building unmolested just as the high-frequency whine reached an excruciating pitch. A peculiar emerald glow enveloped the building. Ritter with Kanina in tow, both bleeding from the ears, looked about in a frantic search for shelter. Everything had been destroyed except for an industrial-size Dumpster twenty meters away. They made a dash for the iron box, and dove through the opening just as a loud clap boomed from the building. As he shut the sliding steel door, Ritter sneaked a look through the narrowing aperture, and saw soldiers and terrorists alike standing there, transfixed by the phenomenon. Then he watched as they erupted in a wave of brilliant flame.

CHAPTER
TWO ———————————————————————

Moheb Nazrullah squinted landward through the twenty-power marine binoculars. He couldn't believe what he saw, or rather didn't see, and so altered the focus once more. He had thumbed the instrument's adjustment three times now, and still he was astonished. He could make out the bodies, what was left of them, clearly enough, and the large steel box which had flanked the laboratory. But those were the only things left to see, except for the smoldering debris of the support buildings. The laboratory itself had vanished. Not a beam or a brick of the structure appeared in the binoculars' field of view.

But Moheb wondered if he could trust his own eyes. He was still seeing spots from that brilliant flash of green light that had been followed by what he could only describe as a sonic boom. By the time his vision had returned to almost normal, the laboratory was gone.

He turned toward the Hawaiian pilot, who had changed the trawler's course for Oahu and was racing out to sea. Nazrullah drew his pistol and sharply ordered the man to come about and proceed toward shore at a cautious rate. He had to get a closer look at what his binoculars had already told him was true. He

15

could not afford to radio Barcelona without visual confirmation. His master, after all, was not a man to accept conjecture as an intelligence report. And a message consisting of speculation was out of the question.

As the trawler moved at half speed toward the rocky coast, Moheb cursed himself for not disobeying orders and accompanying the squad on its mission. The Hawaiians were dedicated and brave, descended from a long line of courageous warriors, but they were hopelessly inept. That was why the mission was a failure and they were dead. It was Moheb's experience that ardor was always accompanied by amateurism. And amateurs never got the job done.

But Iskander Bey had radioed his rejection of Moheb's request to lead the attack. The Champion of Islam had deemed it unnecessary, and worried over the consequences of his best agent being killed or captured. But the price of too much caution was always failure. It was the first lesson Nazrullah had learned at the KGB academy years before.

As an Afghan orphan, he had been sent to Moscow to study the ways of the great Satan. He learned well, and eventually was posted back to his homeland, where he elevated the act of betrayal to the level of a fine art. Had it not been for the will of Allah, he would no doubt have remained an infidel.

While torturing a *mullah* during the last desperate days of the Afghan War, Moheb saw the light of God in his victim's eyes. Each broken limb seemed to increase the old man's strength and peace. His indifference to pain was inhuman, and the forgiveness in his eyes was so terrifying that Moheb had burned them out to preserve his sanity. But hidden in the sound of the ocular fluid sizzling against the glowing iron was the cry of the All Merciful. Had it not been for his comrades, who pried the knife from his trembling hands, Nazrullah would have killed himself on the spot. His conversion to Islam and inevitable service to the *mujahadeen* followed rapidly. Then, after the One-Day War had restructured the world, Moheb joined the Bey's Army of Light in its grand *jihad* against the murderers of the earth.

With the Muslim thrust into southern Russia and his complete control of North Africa and the Middle East, Iskander Bey held the vast majority of the world's oil supply. This not only fueled his armies, it also denied energy to his enemies.

Word of a troubling new discovery had then reached the Bey, and he had dispatched Moheb to Hawaii to verify its existence.

Stored on computer disks just over a kilometer away were the plans for a machine which supposedly could produce the nonnuclear conversion of matter into pure energy. From the demonstration Moheb had just witnessed, he was inclined to believe that the information was true.

The trawler approached within 300 meters of the reef. It was as close as Nazrullah could possibly get without launching an inflatable and going ashore himself. He contemplated that idea for a moment, but decided against it. If he encountered anyone in authority he would have to explain his presence. And what would an obviously affluent and educated Afghan be doing on a fishing trawler in the Pacific? Besides, his capture would only reinforce the initial failure of the mission.

Perhaps, Moheb thought, there was another way. He could send the first mate, also a member of the Lono, ashore. He was Hawaiian, after all, and could pass as a local fisherman. It wasn't as good as a first-hand reconnaissance, but would be better than nothing. Moheb ordered the inflatable prepared, briefed the sailor, and sent him over the side. He watched the raft skim above the reef and bounce toward shore. *Maybe something will materialize*, he thought, smiling at the pun.

"I adore you, Tommy," she purred in a voice that was part whiskey and part child. He could feel the palm of her hand lying flat over the center of his bare chest, right above his heart, and the heat of her breath upon his shoulder. Even when they lay apart, she would crowd him with her hips, almost pushing him off the bed, just to be near him—just to touch him. Then she would explode with a laugh that croaked of joy and mischief, and the sound of it filled him with delight. All that mattered was that they were together and, for the first time in his solitary life, he was in love. "I adore you, Tommy," she purred.

Then he woke up. Tom Rogers had all the symptoms of a hangover. He was sick to his stomach, and his head throbbed. If he got any dizzier, he would fall off the face of the earth. He had been drinking too much lately. Well, for about six weeks, ever since Marta left. He had been promising himself that he would quit, but somehow he hadn't quite gotten around to it. If one more drunk caused him to feel this bad, he would stop today.

He opened his eyes slowly against the sunshine and looked around. Then he sat bolt upright. "Jesus Christ!" he sputtered. He was sitting on a slab of concrete in the middle of an open field about a quarter of a mile from the ocean. "That must have been one helluva drunk." He had no idea where he was. He noticed the smell of burning flesh and rubber, and turned to see some charred bodies strewn over the ground and, further away, a large truck engulfed in flames. He recognized the area.

"Holy shit!" He leaped to his feet and pressed his hand to his forehead. Something was weird here. He was in the compound on Niihau. Only there was no compound anymore. The barracks had burned to the ground, and the lab had been completely blown off its foundation. That was where he was now, he realized, where the lab used to be. But if it had been blown away, why hadn't *he* been blown away with it?

He moved his hand over his eyes and froze. That was what had seemed so weird. His hand, he couldn't see it. "Shit!" he screamed. He couldn't see his arms either, or his legs, or the rest of his body.

"Well, this is it," he said out loud. "I'm dead." Only, he heard his own voice. And he felt his own hand upon his face. He leaned over and traced the outline of his legs with his fingers. According to his hands everything was there, and he could feel the sensation of each part. He just couldn't see it. If this was death, he decided, he didn't want any part of it.

He thought he might feel better if he walked around a bit. Maybe a turn down by the sea would make things clearer. He took four steps, and something hit him flush in the face, knocking him down. "Who's there?" he yelled. But he could hear nothing except a ringing in his ears. Then he remembered that high-pitched whine just before the explosion. He had been strapped into a chair during an experiment. If the force of the explosion had been enough to separate him from the chair, then it was also probably enough to separate him from himself. He could see no other alternative to the conclusion. He must be dead.

He touched his nose and felt a moistness there, like blood. He wiped some on his fingers and felt its sticky wetness. Then he held his hand up to what he thought was a position directly in front of his face, but saw nothing. "Hmmm."

He decided to try to walk again, but this time he would take it more slowly. He haltingly pushed one foot, then another out in front of him, and like a blind man he moved toward the surf. Then his foot touched something solid. He reached out his hand and felt a flat, perpendicular surface a few inches before him.

He knelt and dragged his hand down the plane toward his foot. He felt something reminiscent of a large tube mounted parallel to the surface, and below that, more level facing. It was a wall, he surmised. An invisible wall.

Then the thought hit him like a truck. "Good God almighty!" he screamed. "I'm not dead. I'm fucking invisible!"

Rogers could almost feel the concept rush over him, or in his case, through him. "If the reversal of polarities could be maintained at a rapid enough rate, it could cause the alteration of the very matter constituting the field itself," he repeated aloud. "Goddamn, you idiot. You *were* the very matter constituting the field!"

A wild rush of confusion coursed through his brain. He was delirious that he was still alive, yet baffled by his new condition. And what of the side effects? Had he been contaminated by radioactivity? No, the experiment had been non-nuclear, he remembered. Would his skin strip off, or his eyeballs fall out, or would he simply go insane and skip madly about like Claude Rains in that movie?

The thought of the film reminded him of clothes. Was he doomed to wisp about naked for the rest of his unnatural life? If so, he was certainly glad that the experiment had gone awry in Hawaii instead of Alaska. He touched himself all over, and indeed felt the presence of material covering his body. It was, of course, the same jumpsuit he had worn when he entered the experiment chamber. That was a relief. At least he wouldn't have to contend with the same situation that plagued H. G. Wells's protagonist.

Now that he had discovered his condition, it was time to kick in his military discipline and figure out what he was going to do about it. First he would have to get out of the lab. In order to do that he had to learn exactly where within the lab he was. He searched his memory for a layout of the room. There was nothing in it but the chair and the machine which lined the walls. He remembered that one wall, the one in which the door had been cut, also contained the control room window. The door was just to the left of that.

Rogers proceeded to search the walls by touch for the window. After a few minutes he found it, though not where he thought it would be. Then he felt the door. It was of heavy, impenetrable steel. "Great," he said. Then he remembered an emergency control hidden behind a panel built flush into the

wall. If he could find it, then he could escape. He seemed to remember that it was a short distance to the left of the door and
between two layers of tubes just above his head. He felt about
until he found the grooves that marked the rectangular panel.
He removed his dog tag from around his neck and used the flat
edge to pry open the small door. Inside he felt for the button,
found it, and pushed it. He heard the self-contained electric motor drone. Then he moved quickly backwards to avoid being hit
by the door. When the motor stopped, Rogers slid his hand
along the door and walked out of the room.

The journey through the halls of the building was more difficult. Several times he fell over what turned out to be invisible
bodies. He felt the corpses, and discerned that they had all been
shot. He surmised that one was a technician because of his long
lab coat and horn-rimmed glasses. He figured it was the young
sergeant who had operated the control panel. He couldn't have
been more then twenty-three years old, Rogers thought.

Surrounded by death, Tom suddenly grew paranoid and
longed for the feel of a weapon—of any kind—and decided to
search the body. As he patted the man down, he felt something
odd in the left lab coat pocket. He reached in and drew out two
thin rectangular slabs about $3\frac{1}{2} \times 4\frac{1}{2}$ inches. Rogers knew they
couldn't be anything other than computer disks. Something told
him to take them. He slipped the objects into his breast pocket
and zipped it closed.

The other bodies he searched were foreign to him. They wore
tight rubberized clothes that he guessed were neopreme wet
suits. There must have been an attack, he thought, by these men.
That was why the experiment had gone off track. Some details,
though no more than educated guesses, were beginning to make
some sense. And sense, Roger decided, was what he needed
most.

He found the back door, the closest exit to the laboratory, and
walked outside. He looked around. He could feel the trade
winds and see the surf, but could hear neither. He wondered for
a moment if partial deafness necessarily accompanied invisibility. Then he remembered the earplugs. Because of the unusual
sound of the M.E.D., he had been issued special hearing protec-
tors. He reached up and removed the plugs from both ears. The
wind whooshed and flapped past his face and he could hear the
surf. The best part was that everything outside was visible.

But everything was also dead. Buildings, vehicles, and peo-

ple all smoldered throughout the compound. The lab edifice itself was surrounded by a path of scorched earth. One smoking
body still stood like a carbonized statue. In spite of all the combat he had experienced, Rogers had never seen anything like
this before.

Suddenly, Tom heard something clang about off to his left,
and out of reflex, froze. Slowly he turned toward the sound in
time to see a small side portion of an enormous trash bin slide
open. Out tumbled a young Hawaiian in a wet suit followed by
General Ritter with a pistol.

"Don't try anything funny, kid. I'd hate to shoot you after
what you just lived through," Ritter snarled. The general burned
his hand on the scorched metal while crawling out of the huge
box. "Shit!" he yelled while falling to the ground. "Goddamn!"

It was the same old General Ritter, Tom noted. Without
thinking, he laughed out loud.

"Did you say something, boy?" Ritter barked.

The Hawaiian shook his head.

"If you want something to laugh at, think about the next fifty
years of your life. They tell me the federal penitentiary is a regular riot."

Ritter pulled himself off the ground and shoved his prisoner
toward the ring of blackened earth. Rogers had to move out of
the way or the pair would have walked right into him. The Hawaiian sensed the movement and looked quizzically into Tom's
eyes as he walked past him. It was the first time anyone had
ever truly looked right through him. The phenomenon gave
Rogers an eerie sensation.

"My God," Ritter sighed as he looked at the standing body
that used to be one of his soldiers. He looked towards the foundation slab that he thought was once his laboratory. "Jesus." He
just stood there and stared for a long moment. "Poor Rogers,"
he said finally. "He just disappeared."

No shit, Tom thought, *thanks for getting me out of there*.

Ritter walked towards the building, and Rogers thought
about warning him, but decided against it. Something told him
to keep his condition a secret, at least a while longer. So he just
watched as Ritter bounced off the building and fell to the
ground.

"Fuck!"

Rogers could barely contain himself, and had to bend over to keep from laughing. The Hawaiian, however, had nothing to hide and blurted out an astonished howl.

Ritter, bleeding at the forehead, scrambled to his feet. "What the hell?" He looked at his prisoner, who was equally as perplexed but was still smiling.

"One more time, Kamehameha, and it's a bullet in the brainpan for you." Ritter leveled the revolver at the man's head, and Kanina stopped smiling immediately. "Come over here." The general waved the pistol toward the spot where he had apparently bumped into solid air. "Walk in front of me."

The Hawaiian did as he was told, but he moved slowly with his hands outstretched. Rogers watched as the two felt their way to the door, entered the building, retraced his own steps down the corridor, tripping over bodies along the way, and eventually arrived at the lab. He could no longer hear what they were saying, so he decided to amble down to the shore until they returned.

He had walked a short distance when a police car roared up to the installation. Tom waited until the vehicle stopped, just in case it crashed into the building. He didn't want to miss that. But the car stopped short of the foundation. He figured it would take several minutes for Ritter and the Hawaiian to exit the building and set the cops straight, so he continued his walk to the sea. He was beginning to appreciate the unorthodox freedom which accompanied invisibility.

The sea crashed over the rocky beach and slid up to the retaining wall where Rogers sat contemplating his new status. He was developing a certain delight in the situation, and began to imagine all the ways he could turn it to his advantage. Perhaps he could even return to Washington and pay Marta a little visit, hang around her apartment and try to find out exactly why she had dumped him.

Maybe he had been moody, or hadn't talked enough, or had been uneasy in social situations. And he had to admit, he didn't have much experience with women. After all, he had spent the majority of his life in jungles and swamps in the company of men, fighting men like himself. He had always thought that he was gentle, considerate, and polite. Maybe that was the problem. Perhaps he was too accommodating, and Marta thought of him as somehow weak. He snorted once. He had been accused of many things in his life, but never of being weak. If it was strength she wanted, then he could show her strength. He could

take her neck in his hands and snap it like a twig . . . Rogers
caught himself and shook off the reverie. How could he possibly think of killing her, someone he had loved, still loved? It
wasn't the first time the idea had ricocheted around in his brain.

Suddenly he heard the hum of a tiny outboard approaching
the shore. On instinct he flipped backwards over the short retaining wall and crouched behind it. Then he remembered he
didn't have to do that anymore and stood straight up. He saw a
small raft fighting the surf towards the beach. A Polynesian,
perhaps Hawaiian, in his late twenties struggled with the light
craft through the waves. He killed the motor a few meters out
and walked the inflatable up onto a stretch of sand. Then he
pulled out a portable radio and turned toward the open sea. Rogers followed his gaze to a trawler anchored just beyond the reef.
Tom had been so engrossed in his thoughts before that he had
not noticed the craft.

The man spoke into the hand-held unit. "Rainbow calling Typhoon. Come in, Typhoon."

Rogers moved closer.

"Rainbow, this is Typhoon," a voice squelched over the small
speaker. "I read you five-by-five. What do you see?"

Rogers noticed a distinct accent that was not local.

The Hawaiian turned suddenly and stepped up to the retaining wall. The move caught Rogers by surprise, but his sharp reflexes allowed him to juke out of the way. The man withdrew a
pair of mini-binoculars from a fanny pack and raised them to his
eyes. "I see a police car and four people . . . two cops, an old
man, and . . . my God, it's Uli!"

"Say again," came the voice over the speaker.

"I said Uli's here. Repeat! Kanina is still alive."

There was a long pause, then finally, "Kill him." The command was matter-of-fact.

The Hawaiian stared at the radio as if it were a live grenade.
"What the fuck?" he said. Then he raised his binoculars and focused them on the trawler. "Say again, Typhoon. You want me
to kill Uli?"

The radio squelched. "Shoot him, now!"

The man, incredulous, turned back toward the installation.
Rogers could see that he was locked in a moral dilemma, and
guessed that the target was his friend. After several moments,
however, the Hawaiian returned to the raft and retrieved a long

Cordura gun case, unzipped it, and produced an M21 sniper rifle complete with scope and Sionics silencer.

So much for friendship, Rogers thought. Then he set about to decide how he was going to deal with this situation. Obviously the trawler served as the base for the morning attack that had leveled the compound and turned him into a leading contender in a poltergeist contest. It was executed by locals, but planned by a foreigner, who had sounded Middle Eastern. He guessed that the object of their mission was not to destroy the installation but to gain information about the project. But the whole thing had blown up in their faces, and now they were trying to cover their tracks as well as their asses. Ritter's prisoner would be the only link the government would have to the terrorists, so Rogers could not afford to let him be killed. There was only one thing to do.

The Hawaiian mumbled to himself as he set up the rifle on the retaining wall. He clearly did not want to do this, but he was going to anyway. Rogers, feeling more than just a little bit like God, was in a position to resolve the man's ethical quandary. Tom sneaked up behind the sniper and delivered a side-handed blow to the back of his neck. The Hawaiian, his dilemma solved, slumped unconscious to the sand.

Rogers found a short spool of gaffer's tape, an indispensable combat accessory, in the fanny pack, and taped the man's ankles, wrists, and mouth. Rogers was pleased to notice that, along with the tape, there was also a U.S. Navy S.E.A.L. survival knife in the fanny pack. He grabbed the knife, stowed the rifle in the raft, and climbed aboard.

He considered delivering his unconscious prisoner to Ritter, but thought the sight of a body floating in midair toward the compound might give the general a heart attack. Besides, it could very well draw fire from a couple of panicked cops. And the most important thing now was to get aboard that trawler and find out what the hell was going on.

Tom knew that the Guardians would arrive in a matter of hours, and would be available when he needed them. They had served as his family for over two years, and he could depend on them. It was a good feeling to be able to count on people, and he concluded in retrospect that he never should have left Washington in the first damn place.

Instead, he should have trusted his friends to help him get through his pain. But he couldn't bear to see the pity in their eyes. So when the Hawaiian opportunity had opened up, he'd taken it. So much for bad choices, he thought. He reminded himself of the adage that when things are at their bleakest, don't worry, they can always get worse. All of a sudden, heartbreak was beginning to pale by comparison to invisibility.

He cranked up the little Seahorse motor as the raft plunged into the surf. *Otherwise*, he thought, *this just might turn out to be fun.*

CHAPTER
THREE

Lieutenant Williams McKay sat on the satin-covered couch that fronted the fireplace in the Oval Office. Though he had been to the White House many times, he never felt at ease in the formal environment. Somehow he sensed it was more dangerous than all the battlefields he had survived. He looked across the famous carpet, the one which bore the presidential seal, and thought that the room was smaller than it should have been. But then he was used to open spaces.

Sam Sloan and Casey Wilson seemed even more ill at ease than their fellow Guardian. They sat in the stiff, early-American chairs and tried to appear relaxed, but it wasn't working. They scanned the traditional oil portraits of American heroes that decorated the walls, and waited for the meeting to begin.

Dr. Marguarite Connoly stood by the fireplace chatting aimlessly with Dr. Lee Warren. Both were presidential advisors, Warren on scientific matters and Connoly on everything else. Except for her legs, McKay couldn't imagine what the President saw in her.

"Hey Maggie," he interrupted. "When are you and me gonna have dinner?" McKay gave her a quick wink.

Connoly turned slowly away from the mantel and cocked her hip in a provocative pose. "At your funeral, Billy." Then she resumed her conversation with Warren right where she left off.

Women! McKay thought. *Tom was right to leave the continent just to get away from them.*

A door concealed in the wall opened, and the President of the United States strode into the room. Jeffrey MacGregor, as always, appeared casually elegant. His sweater and slacks of complementary tones matched his brown hair, which was turning gray at the temples and served as the only indication that he was past forty. His cordovan loafers and tortoise-shell glasses completed the preppy image. He carried his slender frame with an erectness that made him seem taller than his six feet, and his high cheekbones accented a broad face which was cinematically handsome. But today that face was troubled.

MacGregor sat at the opposite end of sofa from McKay, and the two Ph.D.'s joined the circle. "My thanks to all of you for coming," the President said, looking at each in turn. "Especially on such short notice. I'm afraid, however, that I have some bad news."

What other kind is there? McKay wondered.

"There has been an accident, of sorts, in Hawaii," MacGregor added.

McKay, Sloan, and Wilson all moved to the edge of their seats.

"A scientific installation on Niihau has been destroyed."

"Oh, my God," Sloan said, rubbing his temples with his fingers. Casey inexplicably stood up. McKay, his face a mask, just stared impassively straight ahead.

"The initial reports are that there are only two survivors." The President looked at each of the Guardians. "And neither was Lieutenant Rogers."

Sam let out a long sigh, like a moan. Casey paced over to the fireplace, and McKay continued to stare straight ahead.

"I'm sorry, gentlemen." MacGregor looked down at the floor. Connoly and Warren, embarrassed, glanced at one another.

After a long pause, McKay finally spoke. "What happened?"

"We don't know for sure." The President nodded at Warren, who took his cue to leave and gather the facts. This was the first he had heard of the tragedy. "There was an attack on the facility during an experiment," MacGregor continued. "Apparently, the

staff was preoccupied with the attack and the experiment got
out of hand. The installation exploded."

"Who was responsible for the attack?" McKay asked, still
staring.

"Hawaiian separatists," MacGregor said. "A group called
Lono."

"Hawaiian separatists?" McKay shot the President an incredulous look.

"That's what I was told."

"Are they certain Tom is dead?" Sloan asked. "Have they
found his body?"

"I know nothing more than what I've just told you, Sam.
We'll all have to wait for more details. Lee is trying to assemble
that information now. Sorry."

Casey stepped away from the mantel. "May we have permis-
sion to go to Hawaii and handle the arrangements?"

"Of course," MacGregor replied. "I was just about to recom-
mend it. The country seems calm at the moment, so take all the
time you need."

"Thank you, Mr. President." McKay stood. "We'll do that."
He extended his hand.

"Billy." The President rose and took McKay's hand, "I know
you and Tom were particularly close. I'm very sorry about this."

A slight crooked smile worked its way across McKay's lips.
It was a smile of irony, embarrassment, and concealed pain.
"Thank you, sir." The two shook hands.

CHAPTER
FOUR ————————————————

Moheb Nazrullah returned to the port gunwale just in time to see the raft buck its way toward the trawler. *Damn!* he thought. He'd missed the kill. He had always enjoyed a skillful display of shooting, and the first mate was an expert sniper. He silently cursed Iskander Bey for picking the precise moment of the marksmanship exhibition to contact him by radio, but his master could not be refused. It had been some time since Moheb had reported in, and the Bey was anxious for news. Nazrullah had been forced to stall over the radio. It was something he was reluctant to do, but the circumstances had necessitated it. Soon, however, he would have to reveal the awful truth that he had failed, and he did not look forward to the punishment.

The Afghan raised his field glasses toward the compound, but he was unable to distinguish between the figures there. He aimed the lenses at the raft, but it was too close for a proper focus. However, the twenty-power instrument did provide a perfect view of the beach.

Moheb gasped in disbelief. He spotted his first mate, who lay motionless and hog-tied on a small stretch of sand between the rocks. He lowered the glasses, which hung by a strap around his neck, and squinted through the glare at the approaching raft. He could see no one, but then the morning sun glinted off the waves and made viewing across the water difficult. Besides, he already knew the occupant was no friend. Unless it was Uli, who had somehow managed to escape the Americans. He turned to order someone to fetch his rifle below decks, and realized there was no one aboard but the pilot who had the helm. Nazrullah scrambled below, retrieved the AK-47, and dashed back to the deck, smashing his shin against the hatch along the way.

By the time he returned, the raft was alongside the trawler and empty. But how could that be? Moheb wondered. Surely there had not been time for the small craft to cover the distance, tie up alongside, and rid itself of any passengers. After all, he had been below for less than a minute. What was happening here?

"Uli?" Moheb called out. "Kanina? Is that you? Where are you, for God sakes? Show yourself, immediately!" He raised and cocked his weapon.

But there was nothing. No sound, no movement, no appearance of anything or anyone, except for the sea and the inflatable raft which bobbed upon it. Nazrullah leveled the rifle and pivoted in a slow circle from the center of the deck. The trawler pitched and groaned as the pilot, who Moheb could see through the glass of the small cabin, nursed the wheel. Otherwise, there was nothing.

Then came a sound from the port, the same side to which the raft was tied. It was a thud, as if someone had jumped from the gunwale to the deck. Moheb spun and unleashed a short burst from the automatic. The rounds ricocheted off the deck and nailed the high gunwale.

"Shit!" It was a loud whisper from the right.

Nazrullah twirled forty-five degrees in the direction of the epithet and cranked off another burst. There was no one there. His shots stitched an empty deck and glanced off into midair. He saw the Hawaiian pilot staring through the glass as if he were questioning Moheb's sanity and contemplating his own safety at the same time. The Afghan returned the stare with a puzzled expression of his own. Perhaps it had been only the combination of the surf and the wind that had made a sound reminiscent of a human voice. Or perhaps Moheb was wound tighter than he realized. The stress of planning the attack, the depression accompanying its failure, and the anticipation over the consequences could have affected him. Not since his torture session with the old *mullah* had he been this jumpy.

He straightened from his combat crouch, took a deep breath, and nodded to the pilot as if to say, "It's all right, I'm back in control now." The Polynesian rolled his eyes toward the sky and resumed his duties at the helm. Moheb scanned the deck and the sea, not knowing what he expected to find there. He listened for a noise that would seem out of place on an empty deck, but his head swirled with the thousand sounds that accompany a ship at sea.

Nazrullah crept back to the port side and leaned over the gunwale. The raft was still there, tethered alongside. It was still empty. Moheb scratched his head. There was no one in the raft, and no one on board the trawler, except for the pilot and himself. Yet the raft was neatly tied up to the boat. Therefore, it must have motored out to the trawler all by itself. Therefore, he must be crazy. The Afghan groaned. The last time he felt like this had been after a weekend in Marrakech.

"Unusual, ain't it?" a voice breathed into his right ear.

Nazrullah almost fell over the side, recovered, then spun to his right, spewing gunfire as he turned. The leaden spray shattered the glass of the pilot house, exploding the head of the helmsman inside. "Fuck!" It was as close as Moheb could come to a lament.

"Kinda makes you feel like a dipshit, don't it?" the voice echoed from the other side of the boat. "You just killed the only friend you had on this tub."

"I will kill you next!" Nazrullah screamed as he flicked the adjuster switch to full automatic. Then he lashed the trawler with a hail of fire through which nothing could possibly live. The bullets dug splinters the size of spikes from the deck, ripped apart a storage locker aft, and like a chain saw cut down the short mast. A small fire sprouted near the engine hatch.

"You'd better put that out," the voice taunted, this time from directly behind Moheb. "We wouldn't want to burn up the boat, now would we?"

Moheb whirled and stared at the handle of a boat hook which floated in midair just above and in front of his terrified face. *"Allah akhbar!"* he shrieked, as he pulled the Kalashnikov's trigger. The metallic snap of the firing pin echoing through the weapon's empty chamber was the last sound the Afghan heard.

● ● ●

Tom Rogers took a moment to step back and look upon his handiwork. Like a painter admiring his canvas, he regarded the netted prisoner as a work of art. He could have been an Arab, though he looked more like a Pashtun native of Afghanistan to Rogers. Now he dangled in a fishnet pouch from the stubby remains of the trawler's mast. He would soon come to, and Rogers would learn all he needed to know about the morning attack.

Meanwhile, he decided to relax and enjoy the sea air. He had already dumped the bloody pulp that was once the pilot overboard, and had watched amazed as the shark fins assembled even before the body sank. The tigers and makos had ripped into the remains just a few seconds after it disappeared below the water's surface. Another vanishing act, Rogers had thought, as he marveled at the savage display.

He dabbed at the wound inflicted by the Moslem's first burst from the AK-47. He had field-dressed it, but the graze on his right shoulder had oozed some before it clotted. Tom wondered if that would be enough to attract the monsters circling below. He removed the bandage and returned to complete invisibility.

The sound of an incoming transmission suddenly crackled over the ship's radio and snapped his attention back aboard the trawler.

"Protector calling Typhoon, come in."

Rogers looked about for the radio, and saw a half-meter satellite dish mounted on the roof of the wheelhouse. He followed the sound of the squelch, and found the electronic equipment below decks in the main saloon. He instantly recognized it as a sophisticated device compatible with a satellite hookup. He investigated the control panel, which was labeled in English, and determined he would have little trouble operating it.

"Typhoon, this is Protector calling. Come in. I say again, come in Typhoon, now!" The speaker's accent was Middle Eastern.

Tom rushed on deck, skinning his shin against the top step of the hatch during his ascent. He drew the S.E.A.L. survival knife from the first mate's fanny pack and hopped in pain about the deck, brandishing the blade like a Comanche warrior dancing before battle. When the sting subsided, he cut down his prisoner, taped his hands, and slapped him into consciousness.

"Wha . . . who . . . what?" The Pashtun was coming around. Rogers slapped him twice more, once for the reviving effect and once for the fun of it.

"Typhoon! This is Protector calling. Come in, Typhoon. And if you know what's good for you, you'll answer!" Then, in a lowered, singsong voice: "The master is getting pissed."

"Wake up, sleepyhead." Rogers hit him again. "Pappa's calling."

The Moslem opened his eyes and stared all around for his assailant. He covered his face to protect it. Then his expression twisted in confusion and terror when he found no one delivering the blows. He whimpered like a child when he saw the knife suspended in midair and remembered how he had gotten in this situation in the first place. "Allah be merciful," he cried. "Protect me from this Satanic curse!"

"Watch it, pal. I'm a Methodist," Rogers said. Then he hit him again. "And you're coming with me or I'm going to make you convert." Tom couldn't remember when he'd had so much fun. He snatched up his prisoner by the collar and dragged him out of the net and down the stairs to the radio. The man bobbed his head incessantly while mewling some Moslem prayer every step of the way.

"Typhoon?" Rogers thought it was a different voice coming over the speaker. "This is your Protector. Answer me, my son." The prisoner cowered in front of the speaker as if it were an icon.

"Answer it," Rogers commanded. "Or you'll enter heaven through the mouth of a shark."

The Moslem stared at the speaker, then at the floating blade with equal terror. Rogers recognized the I-don't-know-whether-to-shit-or-go-blind-look pasted all over the prisoner's face, and decided it was time to add a little physical incentive. He flicked the black blade and sliced off the lower lobe of the man's left ear.

The Moslem screamed as he writhed against the pain. The bindings prevented him from clutching the wound with his hands and added frustration to his agony. "Okay, demon, okay," he yelled. "I'll do whatever you wish." He turned toward the microphone on the table, and fought to control himself before he spoke. After several seconds, his hysteria finally subsided, and his breathing returned to even. Rogers reached over and flipped on the transmitter switch.

"Protector?" the man said hesitantly into the microphone. Rogers gigged him gently with the knife as a reminder to normalize his delivery. "Protector, this is Typhoon. Typhoon calling Protector. Come in." It sounded okay to Rogers.

"Typhoon, this is Protector," came the transmission over the speakers. "Why was your response delayed?"

The Moslem shot a desperate look at the knife, as if it were his captor.

"You were up top," Rogers said.

The prisoner cocked his head quizzically, and Rogers gestured upward with the blade. "Oh," the man said, then turned toward the microphone. "My humble apologies, Excellency. I was on deck and had to come below to answer."

"Very good," Roger said, wiggling the knife.

"A probable excuse, my dear Typhoon, but somehow I doubt its veracity," the voice oozed over the speaker. "Instead I believe you've been avoiding me because you have bad news. Well, out with it."

The Moslem stared blankly at the microphone, then at the blade.

"What is your name?" Rogers asked politely. The man continued to gape at the knife. "Let's try that again." This time Rogers placed the knife under the prisoner's chin. "What . . . is . . . your . . . name?"

"Moheb Nazrullah!" he bleated.

"Well, Moheb Nazrullah, do as the man says—out with it!" The blade moved to within a centimeter of the man's eye, and he whirled back to the microphone. Rogers hit the toggle.

"We . . . rather . . . I have failed, Your Excellency. The installation was destroyed during the attack, and I do not know why." He waited for some reply but there was none. "Excellency, are you there?"

"I am here, fool!" the voice boomed through the speaker. "And I would have thought your extensive training would have taught you to dispense with any insipid obeisance over the wireless. A simple code name will suffice for communications purposes."

"Yes Excellency . . . I mean, Protector." Rogers could see that the prospects of confronting two adversaries, one of them invisible, had rattled an otherwise consummate professional.

"You mean the package was destroyed?" the Protector asked.

"Yes, I mean the package was destroyed," replied Nazrullah.

"And so too was the gift?"

"Yes, Protector . . . I mean, I think so. I am not certain." Rogers noticed that Nazrullah was trembling now.

"Did you reconnoiter the remains of the package?"

"Protector, there were no remains. The package was totally destroyed. It vanished!"

"Impossible, Typhoon," the voice snapped through the speaker. "The gift was obviously well protected. It must have survived. Your job is to find it. Do you understand?"

"Yes, Protector."

"I'm sure you do, Typhoon, but do you truly . . . *understand*?"

Moheb gulped and closed his eyes. Then he looked at the blade, which flicked once toward the microphone. "Only too well, Protector," he said quietly.

"Then I will leave you to your work. The next time I hear from you I expect to learn that you have secured the gift. Protector out."

"Typhoon out," Nazrullah almost whispered.

Rogers reached over and turned off the transmitter. He gave his captive a short respite to recover his composure, then asked, "What's all this package and gift shit?"

Nazrullah turned slowly toward the blade and looked at it with lifeless eyes. "Kill me now, devil. You'll be doing me a favor."

Rogers was tempted. "I asked you about the code words, package and gift."

Nazrullah turned away in silence.

"Okay, I've got package pretty well figured out. That's the installation, or rather the laboratory."

Moheb remained expressionless.

"Now, what is the gift?" But the prisoner was like a stone. "Okay, have it your way." Rogers placed the point of the knife at Nazrullah's crotch. "The gift?" From reading his face, Rogers figured that Moheb was prepared to die, but not prepared to suffer castration. He jabbed the knife a millimeter closer, and Nazrullah's eyes widened. "The gift!" Rogers repeated.

"The computer disks which control the experiment," Moheb sighed. "There are two of them."

Rogers patted the invisible disks in his invisible pocket with his invisible hand. Then he smiled an invisible smile. His intuition had told him to pocket the disks back at the lab, though he wasn't sure why he had done it then. Now he knew. They were the prize after all. He moved the knife still further. "Who carried out the attack for you?"

Moheb scrunched up his face in thought, then shrugged. "A group of local revolutionaries—amateur fools!"

Rogers had trouble swallowing that one. "Local revolutionaries?" He punctuated the question with a quick jab of the knife.

Moheb flinched. "I swear before Allah, it is true. They are a collection of Hawaiian separatists who call themselves the Lono."

Rogers searched the Moslem's eyes for the lie, and decided he believed him. "Hawaiian separatists, huh." He relaxed the knife. "Who were you just talking to?"

"I cannot tell you that." Moheb shook his head. "It would mean a horrible death."

"Would that be worse than a horrible life?" Rogers twisted the blade.

Nazrullah sucked in a quick, deep breath, and thought harder about his predicament. "Iskander Bey," he said, rolling his eyes.

Rogers was glad he was invisible because he could imagine how the expression on his face would look. He was dumbstruck. By all accounts from every intelligence arm of the government, the Bey had fried at the point of the Cygnus laser back in the spring. "I thought he was dead."

"Like all great leaders, the Protector of Islam is resourceful." It was Moheb's turn to smile. "Now I would like to ask a question. Who *are* you?"

"You wouldn't believe me if I told you."

"You are no demon, though? No, of course not. You are from the laboratory. You were there during the attack. What happened to you?"

"I'll leave that to your imagination."

If Nazrullah's hands had been free he would have slapped himself in the forehead. "Aiyee, the equations on the disks are more important than even the Bey realized," he said, grasping the concept for the first time. "You are an invisible man!"

"And you ain't no brain surgeon," Rogers said dryly. "What did you think I was, some sort of gargoyle from hell?"

"The experiment did this to you?" Moheb was still incredulous. "Your own people did this to you? You must harbor great resentment. Let us join forces and I will help you wreak your revenge."

Tom disregarded the Moslem's nonsense. He did not blame

General Ritter or the Army or anyone. He just considered the whole situation a mistake, a weird accident that would eventually be rectified. But what if it wasn't? What would he think then? He realized he had let Nazrullah plant a seed. "Let's get some air!" He grabbed his prisoner by the arm and jerked him towards the gangway.

"You should consider my offer," babbled Moheb as he was wrenched toward the hatchway. "We could each shake off the yoke of our masters and create a force formidable enough to command the respect of the world. Do you not see?"

"Shuddup, raghead, and get up those steps!" Rogers decided he had grown tired of this game.

"Ow, shit!" Nazrullah pounded his shin against the top of the gangway again. "Allah!" he swore, stumbling out onto the deck.

Rogers laughed to himself as he watched his prisoner endure the pain. He remembered that same awful feeling from his last trip up the steps, and this time decided to be more careful. But it was difficult not being able to see his own footfall. He took his eyes off Nazrullah for an instant to better gauge the position of the top step. This time he found it without repeating the Moslem's mistake. But when he looked up again he saw that he had made an even greater error. Coming toward him in a blur was the sole of Moheb's boot, which caught him across the mouth and sent him reeling down the stairs. *Nice move, raghead*, he thought as he tumbled backwards down the gangway and smashed his head on the lower deck. Then, for an instant, he reflected on how stupid he had been to underestimate his enemy. It was the last thought he had before he drifted off into unconsciousness.

CHAPTER
FIVE ─────────────────────────────

Great folds of scorched flesh heaped over the sides of the special bed. The patient groaned periodically against the pain and fidgeted from the long periods of confinement, but generally he took his situation well. Of course he would have been happier directing his generals on the battlefields of southern Europe instead of wallowing on his enormous belly waiting. He allowed himself to reflect on the tediousness of the healing process, and didn't notice the young nurse who wisked into the sterile room.

"It's time for your shot, Excellency," the woman said behind her surgical mask. With her white nurse's headdress and covered mouth she appeared the very picture of Moslem womanhood.

The huge man tried to move his hand to gesture her away, but the pain was too great. "Not now," he gasped. "I wish to think." He had just dismissed the radio technician who had handled the communications hookup, and the man had wheeled the sophisticated equipment out of the room. The simple job of speaking over the microphone had proved excruciating. But he had suffered through the conversation because he needed to know how his Hawaiian operation was faring. He was sorry he had bothered.

"It's so dark in here." The nurse scowled. Then she opened the curtains with a flourish and let the Spanish sunlight pour into the room.

With great effort the patient turned his head toward the windows and saw the harbor of Paseo Marítima glistening beyond the cathedral's sixth-century basilica. Scenes such as these had endeared Barcelona to him. It was a city so odd yet so beautiful.

"Oww," he groaned. The movement created a wave of pain that undulated from his toes all the way to his scalp. The skin along the entire back part of his body, almost fifty percent of his total surface area, had third-degree burns. His survival alone had, for many of the faithful, been a testament to his divinity.

"Are you sure you don't want any relief, Excellency?" The nurse smiled pleasantly with her eyes as she brandished a hypodermic.

Had he been able, he would have smashed her in the face. He was in no mood, after all, for pleasant smiles. "Get out!" he bellowed, then winced. He wanted relief, all right, but it was not the kind she offered. He would have preferred to have the German actress knead his tired shoulders while the French twins gobbled him below. But that was not to be, at least not for a long while, and perhaps never. "Allah be merciful," he moaned.

Deep inside he knew that God showed mercy only to the benevolent, and the Protector of Islam had not led a good life. From his early days as a dashing tank commander in the Turkish Army, through his career as a general officer who had risen to deputy commander of NATO, Hafiz Tülül had smashed enemies and friends alike. The One-Day War had offered him the opportunity to revive the glory of the Ottoman Empire through the pretense of a *jihad*, and for that a spiritual leader was needed. So General Tülül had become Iskander Bey, Defender of the Faith, Chosen of Allah, the leader of the Moslem religion and general to its eight hundred million followers.

He still held all of those titles, of course, but his real power was slipping away. Every day that he lay incapacitated the grip on his dream loosened. He knew that the younger generals who took the field in his stead would some day supplant him. For now, however, they were occupied with the much-delayed thrust into the soft underbelly of Europe.

In two days' time his Armies of Light would launch an attack the likes of which the world had never seen. It would make Hitler's heralded Operation Barbarossa of sixty years before pale by comparison. The Satanic hordes controlled by Yevgeny Maximov, chairman of the Federated States of Europe, would reel before his fury. And when they were destroyed, then he would deal with Maximov personally!

It had been Chairman Max, after all, who had ordered the attack in the spring that had put the Bey in his bed. A laser beam, fired from a cannon aboard the Cygnus space orbiter, had carved up his hideaway on the beach at Arenys de Mar just north of Barcelona. But Allah had been with his prophet that day, and had instructed his Defender to move at the last instant to escape the full frontal force of the laser. The intense heat had liquefied the sand, which then blasted the back portion of the Bey's body. He shuddered as the horror of that moment flooded over his memory. He visualized himself writhing beneath a blanket of molten glass. Soon the circumstances would reverse, and then the good chairman would be at *his* mercy. And everyone already knew how lacking the Bey was in that department.

For now he turned his attention back to the problem on the other side of the world. He had been dismayed to learn that Moheb Nazrullah, ordinarily his best agent, had bungled his latest assignment. Not only was the Bey unaccustomed to condoning failure, but the price for this particular defeat could prove too steep to pay. After taking great pains to secure nearly all of the earth's petroleum resources, the Champion of Islam could not afford to sit by while the infidels created an alternative energy source. Whatever this process was, it must be secured and eliminated before the Americans could share it with Maximov. He knew that the two were sworn enemies, but he also understood the precepts of *realpolitik*.

Beyond this fear, however, lay something else, something the Bey could not quite pinpoint. It was something that Nazrullah had said, or perhaps the way he had said it. It could even have been something he had *not* said. The Bey wasn't sure. Something more than the original objective was somehow at stake here. He didn't know what that was, but it existed. *It always pays to listen to one's intuition*, he thought. And about such things, the Chosen of Allah was almost never wrong.

CHAPTER
SIX ─────────────────────────────

Lieutenant William McKay paced the length of the cargo bay of the Hercules, staggering as the C-130 pitched over the Pacific. He was glad that Mobile One was still under repair, and they hadn't been able to take it along. The absence of the behemoth allowed for more room in transit. The V-450 Super Commando Armored Personnel Carrier had taken a shellacking from Junior Gaithor's Ag-Cat in the Arkansas river bottoms, and would be laid up at least another week. But that was all right. For this mission they didn't need the machine anyway.

McKay couldn't stop thinking about Tom and the irony surrounding his death. *His death*, he thought. The phrase sounded alien when applied to Tom Rogers. Countless times McKay had shared the possibility of a swift death with Rogers, but had never thought he would outlive the Green Beret. The notion that his end had come as the result of an accident, or whatever . . . well, that was just too weird to contemplate.

Ultimately it was the girl who McKay blamed. Although she hadn't fired a weapon, she had killed Tom Rogers nonetheless. She had buried him with her rejection as effectively as if she

41

had used a spade. But then he expected nothing less from someone who worked for Maggie Connoly.

It was funny, he had never thought of her as a woman, but always as a girl, though she was easily Tom's age. Still, she was a bona fide looker, with those high cheekbones that perfectly flanked a wide, sensuous mouth. The fine dark hair complemented her olive skin, and her almond eyes gave her an exotic look. She had the long legs of a dancer and a lean, ropy body to match. The only reason McKay had never jumped her himself was because she had no tits. That and because he respected the "Code of the West": *Thou shalt not fuck thy friend's woman.* He knew that Tom probably would have cut his balls off if he had even looked at her funny.

But McKay sensed that there was something odd about her, a certain stiffness, an artificiality that bothered him. It wasn't an overt thing, but an elusiveness that quivered just below her surface. He was pretty sure she had no awareness of it, and that made her the most dangerous kind of all.

The result of this, McKay knew, was that Tom was dead before he ever left Washington. It just took awhile for his body to catch up to his soul. After Marta dropped him, Tom had wandered around in a daze, unable to concentrate on the slightest details.

McKay had been glad when Rogers decided to take the Hawaiian assignment. It seemed safe, and it would get Tom the hell out of Washington. A change of scenery was the best cure, and besides, McKay had depleted his repertoire of ways to avoid looking his friend in the eye. *I actually encouraged him to go*, McKay thought. He rested his forehead on his hand, as if he were praying, and listened to the drone of the engines.

Major Miles Gentry bounded down the steps from the flight deck. "Hey, are you guys the Guardians?"

Casey Wilson, stretched out on a pile of duffles, groaned once and rolled over. This was his first flight in memory during which he had not taken a turn in the cockpit. The shock of Tom's death and the fifteen hours in the air had simply worn him out.

Sam Sloan didn't look up from his round of liar's poker. "That's us, compadre. At least most of us."

Gentry strode over to the group crouched in a circle studying their dollar bills. "You the guys who made the L.A.P.E.S. drop in Arkansas?"

"I'm afraid so," Sloan said smoothly, but inside he churned. The memory of that event iced him with panic.

"You boys actually rode down in an A.P.C. during a drop on the water?" the major said.

Sloan thought he recognized that voice, and glanced toward the man. Sam did a double take. What he saw had to be the most dapper officer in the United States Air Force. Even in a flight suit, the major cut a figure of a *beau vivant*. He wasn't large, perhaps five-foot-ten, and slightly built, maybe 160. His black hair was parted on the side, and receded just enough in front to give him the look of a corporate attorney or a successful investment banker. But it was the paisley ascot, the rakish shades, and the cigarette holder that added panache. "Who are you?"

"Me?" the major asked, touching his chest with his fingertips. "Why, I'm Major Miles Gentry. The pilot and commander of this craft as well as the official spokesperson for Grab-Your-Ankles Airlines." He punctuated his introduction with a broad smile. "I'm glad, and frankly a little surprised, to see that you guys didn't perish down South."

"Did you say Grab-Your-Ankles Airlines?" Sloan's expression switched now from bemused confusion to angry recognition.

"Yep." Gentry grinned. "Fly Grab-Your-Ankles and get fucked every time."

Sloan lurched off the floor. "You son of a bitch. I'm going to kill you!"

McKay watched with a detached amusement. He too recognized that distinctive voice. It was the same educated Carolina drawl that had oozed over their headsets while the Guardians, buttoned up inside Mobile One, had waited for their L.A.P.E.S. drop a few months back. Their nerves had been raw enough with the anticipation of a maneuver that was considered the most dangerous performed by the Military Airlift Command. Gentry had sadistically magnified that anticipation with his pre-op commentary which had come dangerously close to pushing Sloan over the edge.

Gentry's two loadmasters prevented Sam from turning the major into a quadriplegic, so McKay never had to move from his seat. One of the crewmen, Animal Bukowski, was able to restrain Sloan almost by himself—*almost*. Finally, Sam cooled down, and Bukowski was able to walk him back to the front of the ship.

". . . they don't call him Mad Miles for nothin', sir," McKay heard Bukowski say when they returned.

After several minutes, the major carefully approached the others. "No hard feelings, Commander." He extended his hand. "We were just trying to kill the boredom."

"No hard feelings, Major." Sam shook his hand. "I was just trying to kill *you*." They both laughed uneasily.

The sound of the engines changed as the plane started its decent into Lihue. Dr. Lee Warren staggered the length of the cargo bay toward the rest of the men. He had been hovering over the one tiny urinal that served the ship ever since their rendezvous with the refueling tanker 600 miles out. His face was ashen, and a thin stream of drool ran from the corner of his mouth. McKay snickered as he watched Warren weave toward him. "So, that's what Ph.D. stands for, eh, Lee? Doctor of pisser-hugging?"

The plane dipped suddenly, and Warren fell into McKay's lap. "May your mutant children grow up to devour your flesh, Billy."

"Thanks for the sentiment, Doc," McKay said, holding him like a baby. "Now, you want to get off my lap before I get a hard-on?"

Warren struggled to his feet. "I'm surprised to hear you still can." He lurched off toward the flight deck.

Take one jarhead, one greenie beanie, one swabby, and one jet jockey, make them heroes (you know: give them good P.R., put them up in the best hotels, get them laid, and pick up the tab), then send them out to the desert and train them like banshees until they can eat dirt, repair a mainframe, and kill a tyrannosaurus rex with their bare hands. Then tell them their job is to wait until the world turns into a supernova, then escort the President of the United States to a secret base buried deep in the Iowa cornfields. Then fill the base with enough giant computers to turn a smoldering ruin back into the great nation it once was.

Only the President drops out of the sky over Canada and takes the master plan with him. So the boys are left to guard a stand-in, still wet behind his vice-presidential ears, and a lot of hardware with no programs. Then the real President reappears, after a miraculous escape, with the master plan along with the idea of selling the whole show to a Russian maniac who just happens to be running a united and unscathed Europe.

Next send the boys after the essential components to make the master plan work, then tell them to survive an invasion and cruel occupation by the mad Russian. Add a presidential advisor who's a twisted bitch and thinks the Russians are okay, throw in a one-eyed major who was tough enough to train the boys, then make them kill him, and ram more firefights and betrayals through their lives in two years than rounds through a minigun in an hour. And what you've got after all that is a grim, burnt-out crew that would rather eat shit and die then say, "Have a nice day!" What you've got after all that is the Guardians.

The copter's twin turbines whined as the UH-60A churned through the darkness above the Kaulakahi Channel. General Ritter had ordered the transport to ferry the Washington contingent from the airport at Lihue on Kauai to the lab site at Kawaihoa Point on Niihau. Lee Warren slumped in the rear of the ship and contemplated how much worse air travel was by helicopter than by plane. Casey and Sam, each thinking about the nature of the mission, sat solemnly nearby. McKay was trying to hear General Ritter above the engine noise.

"This is simply unbelievable, Lieutenant," Ritter shouted. "The installation just disappeared!"

McKay strained through his semi-permanent earplugs to hear the general, but he could make out only a few words. He wished the man would just shut up until they landed. And he was a little surprised that Ritter's attitude displayed such a lack of respect for the death of a fellow officer.

"Did you hear what I said, McKay?" the general bellowed. "The whole goddamn thing *vanished*!"

McKay just looked at the man as if he were speaking Swahili, gestured that he could not hear, and turned away.

"Shit!" Ritter mouthed.

The Black Hawk snapped on its searchlight and circled a makeshift helipad illuminated by automobile headlamps. The helicopter settled to the ground with a slight jolt, and everybody groaned in relief as they disembarked.

"Follow me, boys," Ritter commanded as he marched off to a cordoned area several meters away. "You won't believe this shit!"

McKay and the others trudged dutifully behind until they arrived at what appeared to be the foundation of a building. The slab was lighted by portable floods that turned the rectangle into a stark, white field. Men in protective clothing moved about eerily upon the concrete, picking their way from one point to another as if in a maze, and appeared to be performing tasks in pantomime. McKay had no idea what was going on. Then Ritter told him.

". . . and the bottom line, though we can't be sure, is that right now it looks like Tom Rogers is not among the dead and is nowhere in the building," Ritter said.

McKay almost missed the crucial conclusion to Ritter's monologue because he was still having trouble with the earlier part that included the word "invisible." After a long pause, during which the information seeped into his skull, McKay finally asked, "Did you say Tom is *alive*?"

"We can't be sure," Ritter answered, "but there is certainly that possibility."

"What else could it be?" McKay asked.

"We don't know," Ritter said, then he paused. "Perhaps he was vaporized."

"Vaporized?"

"You know," Ritter explained, "the matter that constituted what we knew as Tom Rogers just dematerialized. Poof!" He snapped open his hand and fanned his fingers in an accompanying gesture. "He was right there in the lab surrounded by the machine, after all. If it did all this to the outlying area," he pointed out, "then just think of the forces he was subjected to."

McKay looked around. The building was there but was invisible, as were the several bodies now being toted outside. He looked at the scorched path which surrounded the scene and at the burned-out vehicles further out. A lot of power had been unleashed here.

Ritter motioned to McKay to accompany him around to the back of a deuce-and-a-half parked just beyond the lights. There, sitting under the canvas top with his hands and feet bound, was a young Hawaiian. Two guards, armed with M16's, flanked the tailgate of the truck.

"This is the one I captured," Ritter declared. "Says his name is Uli Kanina and that he leads a group of Hawaiian separatists called the Lono. Our intelligence people don't seem to know anything about them."

"I am being held illegally as a political prisoner by the imperialist forces of the United States," Kanina hissed. "I demand to be released at once!"

Ritter reached for his side arm. "Shut up or I'll give you a release you won't believe."

McKay just stood quietly and looked at the man. He pulled out his buffalo-hide cigar case, extracted two slim smokes, and offered one to Kanina. The prisoner brightened. "Unshackle his hands," McKay ordered the guards.

"Now wait just a goddamn minute, McKay," Ritter objected. "I—"

"General," McKay interrupted. "He's not going to escape. And if he tries, I will catch him and place a live grenade down the front of his pants." His voice was tinged with an icy calmness that both the prisoner and the general found menacing.

Ritter nodded his approval, and the guards helped Kanina down. McKay handed him a cigar and lit it. The prisoner drew deeply of the Indonesian tobacco and exhaled a long plume of smoke. "Thanks, man."

"Anytime, pal," McKay said. "Listen, maybe you could help me out. We seem to have lost somebody here today."

"You lost a lot of people here today."

"Yeah, but this one may still be alive." McKay took a drag. "And besides, he's special. He's my friend."

Kanina looked up at the big *haole*. The conviction in his sharp blue eyes told the Hawaiian that loyalty to a friend was something to which this man paid more than just lip service. Uli knew at once that this was a white man he could trust, even if he was the enemy.

"I saw no one, other than those they are carrying out, and I can't even see them now," Kanina said. "The general had a gun on me, and then the building started to blow so we ran for our lives. I didn't pay attention to nothin' else."

"How did you get here?" McKay asked.

"I used to live here."

"That's not what I asked," McKay said sharply. "I see you are wearing a wet suit so I assume you came in by sea. How?"

Kanina hesitated.

"What sort of craft?"

Again the Hawaiian stalled. McKay reached down to his ankle and drew a Tanto boot knife. Nonchalantly he began to trim his fingernails. With each quick slice the stainless-steel blade glinted in the light.

"It was a trawler," Kanina said rapidly.

"A fishing trawler?"

"Yeah. Registered out of Kona on the Big Island."

"The island of Hawaii? Where is it now?" McKay stopped the knife and looked up.

"I don't know," Kanina said. McKay resumed his trimming. "Honestly," the Hawaiian blurted out. "The fucking Arab left me!"

"Arab?" McKay said. Then he moved the knife to his own throat and started a dry shave. Before he finished, Kanina had told him everything.

After returning the prisoner to the care of the M.P.'s and supplying him with several cigars, McKay wandered about the area to give himself time to digest the new information. He went over it in his mind as he walked toward the sound of the surf.

An Arab planned, financed, and oversaw an operation to secure data from the lab computers. What data? Presumably about the experiment. McKay would have to grill the general for that, but if he ran into any security static he would just let Warren handle it.

This Arab had found Uli Kanina and a loose group of his ideological friends and hastily trained them for the mission. He had supplied the arms and equipment as well as the cash. And the Arab received his instructions over a sophisticated satellite communications system aboard the trawler. From whom the prisoner did not know. McKay had his own ideas about that, but they didn't jive with the most recent intel reports. He made a note to check this out with Washington.

"Halt!" A young M.P. braced his weapon and blocked McKay's path. "I'm sorry, sir, but you've reached the edge of the perimeter. And my orders are that nobody comes or goes."

McKay stopped. He realized he was out of what the Army referred to as standard uniform. The Guardians each wore a special jumpsuit, sort of a combination B.D.U. and flight suit, specifically designed for its all-purpose functionalism. The only insignia was a small shoulder patch of the American flag. "Do you know who I am, soldier?" McKay hated to pull the celebrity bit, but he sometimes found it useful. He hoped this would be one of those times.

"Yes, sir," the young corporal snapped. "But orders are orders, sir."

"I understand that, Corporal." McKay was both vexed and impressed by the young soldier's professionalism. "I'll go get the general, and we'll have those orders changed."

"Thank you, sir."

"Carry on, soldier." McKay skipped the salute, since he wasn't wearing a hat, and turned to leave.

"Lieutenant McKay?" the corporal called after him. "Where did you want to go, sir?"

"Just down to the beach," McKay replied. "I've got some thinking to do."

"All right, sir, but I'll have to escort you."

"That's fine, Corporal. Let's go." They both ambled off toward the crashing surf. "Have you people patrolled the beach area?" McKay asked.

"No, sir. We were just ordered to form a security perimeter two hundred meters out from the complex."

"Hmmm," McKay groaned. He stumbled upon a rock wall. "What's this?"

"Seawall, sir. It was built to stop erosion before the rocks were laid around the complex."

The tide had receded, and an open stretch of beach beyond the wall shone in the moonlight. It was studded with silhouettes of coral which stood out from the sand like clumps of coal. McKay focused on one of those outcroppings which appeared shinier than it should, and he motioned for the soldier to follow him down the beach.

The old warrior's instinct proved accurate. The coral turned out to be a pile of scuba equipment. This confirmed the arrival by sea as well as the trawler's relative position during the attack. McKay had learned all this from Kanina, but it was always reassuring to have proof, especially when relying on the word of a prisoner. "Let's see what else we can find," McKay said, and he ambled off down the beach. The corporal popped a chem stick, laid it on the sand to mark the mound of gear, and followed the Guardian.

After they had covered a thirty-meter stretch, the soldier suddenly stopped. "What's that, sir?" he asked apprehensively.

"What's what?" McKay could hear only the surf.

"It sounded like a groan, and it came from over there." The corporal pointed off to the left.

Unable to remove his earplugs, McKay trusted the younger man's senses and drew his Model 1911 Colt .45 automatic. Both men crouched and moved off to investigate the sound. Fifteen meters later they stumbled on a young Hawaiian bound and gagged with duct tape.

"What have we got here?" McKay snickered. He holstered his .45, fired up his brass Zippo, and yanked the tape from the man's mouth.

"Shit!"

The M.P. trained his rifle on the man's forehead while the Guardian squatted nearby holding the lighter above the man's face.

"Hi there," McKay chirped. "You don't look so good. Been out here long?"

The man groaned and struggled to sit up. McKay helped him into a supine position, and motioned for the corporal to share his water. The Hawaiian gulped until the soldier pulled the canteen away. McKay produced a handkerchief and wiped the sand from the man's face, then dabbed at his blisters. "I hope these are just from the sun and not from any beach creatures," McKay commented.

The Hawaiian, shivering, struggled to speak. After some effort he managed to whisper a thank you. Then he asked to be cut free.

"I don't think we're quite ready for that," McKay said. "Not yet, anyway. Now, if you can supply me with some answers to a few questions, then we'll see what we can do about restoring you to the world of the quasi-normal."

"What questions?" The man coughed.

"Well, for starters, how about you tell us how you got in this embarrassing situation in the first place?"

"I don't know."

"Is it getting chilly out here, Corporal, or is that just my imagination?" McKay asked.

"It's definately cold, sir," replied the M.P., playing the game. "And when the tide comes in it's going to get even colder."

"Somebody hit me from behind," the man bleated. "I never saw who it was."

"What were you doing here in the first place?"

"Uh . . . fishing."

"I see. Where's your tackle?"

"It got washed out to sea."

"Really?" McKay arched a brow. "How come your attacker didn't steal it?"

"I don't know. Maybe he did."

"How did you get here?"

"I walked."

"From where?"

"Puuwai."

McKay knew for a fact that Puuwai, the main town on Niihau, was on the opposite side of the island several miles away. "Fuck this shit! Corporal, tape him up, and let's get out of here."

"Wait a minute," the man cried. "You're not going to *leave* me here?"

"Yes, I am," McKay answered matter-of-factly.

It took the man approximately a tenth of a second to blurt out the word "trawler."

"Was there an Arab on board?"

A furtive look raced across the man's eyes while he hesitated. McKay could almost see the alternatives clicking through his brain. Finally his prisoner nodded.

"That was a sound decision, mister. Now, where did he go?"

"I don't know." Then the man added quickly, "I really don't. I was knocked out, for God's sake!"

"Then where did you come from?"

"Port Allen, but he won't go there."

"Why?"

"Because he knows that's where you'll go."

McKay cut free the man's feet but left his hands bound. Then, on a hunch, he decided to check the tape. It was wrapped counterclockwise around the Hawaiian's wrists, indicating that the man who wrapped it was left-handed.

McKay ordered the corporal to take the prisoner back to the compound. The soldier obeyed, ignoring the regulation that prevented McKay from remaining beyond the perimeter alone. The Guardian watched the two men disappear into the darkness, then turned and looked out into the black sea. With each crashing wave the crustaceans sparkled in the moonshine like liquid jewels. To McKay the sight represented both life and death in one movement, and he wondered where on that water Tom Rogers was right now. God only knew what he was up to, but McKay was certain that his heartbroken, left-handed friend was damn sure up to something.

CHAPTER
SEVEN ———————————————————

Jeffrey MacGregor sat in the leather executive chair behind the presidential desk in the Oval Office. He had his back to the room, so he could look out the windows and enjoy the natural scene beyond. But the panes were glazed with a special bullet-proof plastic that distorted the view. The outdoors appeared like an image seen through one of those exterior automobile mirrors that make the traffic look farther away than it really is. For the next few moments he pondered the relationship between distortion and safety and wondered if it was all worth it.

He swiveled back to the desk, opened the folder marked FOR THE PRESIDENT ONLY, and reviewed the text printed on a single white page inside. The message, received just minutes before, had caused the young President to seek solace in the pastoral view of the White House lawn in the first place.

The summary stated that the experiment, which supposedly had killed Tom Rogers, might have rendered him invisible instead. The President's first reaction had been relief that the Guardian might be alive, but this invisibility business would take a little getting used to. If the news proved to be true, then this startling process could open up a Pandora's box of bizarre possibilities with grotesque consequences.

On top of this, the message indicated that Iskander Bey might also be alive. This revelation came in spite of the latest intelligence reports, now admittedly a few months old, which had declared that the Bey had been killed during an attack launched by the laser cannon aboard the Cygnus X-1 orbiting vehicle. McKay had learned that an Arab had masterminded yesterday's terrorist mission against the Hawaiian lab. This Arab could be an agent for the Bey, or his successor, or he could be a freelance who was working for Yevgeny Maximov. MacGregor secretly hoped it was Maximov. The President's record against the chairman was red hot at the moment, thanks to the Guardians.

The door leading to the corridor opened, and Dr. Marguarite Connoly slipped into the room so quietly that MacGregor barely heard her. She never made an appointment, but came and went as she pleased, treating the Oval Office as her private conference room. The President looked up from his reading and smiled a welcome.

"Good afternoon, Mr. President." She approached the desk. "May I have a word with you?"

"Certainly." He leaned back in his chair and motioned for the woman to sit. "What's on your mind?" he asked, knowing full well why she was there.

"The same thing that's on yours, unless I miss my guess." She crossed her silky legs and smoothed her skirt.

"I'm afraid I don't know what you mean," he lied.

"Then open that folder on your desk and read some more. When you get to the part that says Rogers is both alive *and* invisible, then we can start talking." Her smile was barely noticeable.

MacGregor's frown, however, was painfully obvious. He thought he had replaced all of Maggie's contacts in the White House communications room following the arrest of her assistant for espionage. Though Maggie had been duped, and was eventually cleared of complicity in the incident, the President had initiated a systematic program to insure that such a potentially damaging circumstance would never happen again. This included ferreting out as many of Connoly's moles as he could find. Evidently, MacGregor concluded, he had missed one.

"Why don't you save me the trouble, Maggie, and tell me what's in the folder marked for my eyes only."

"I thought I just did." Her smile broadened. "Oh, yes, there's also the conjecture that Iskander Bey is alive and well and living in sin somewhere. Let's not forget that." For a long moment the two strong-minded people stared at one another. "How am I doing, so far?" Maggie said finally.

"Better than I had hoped." He returned her smile. "So what's your analysis and recommendation? I might as well ask since I know I'm going to get your opinion anyway."

Dr. Connoly uncrossed her legs and leaned forward intently. During the maneuver her stockings made a swishing sound that MacGregor found surprisingly stirring. More than once he had noticed her lavender eyes, golden hair, and trim figure, and had even wondered what it would be like to have those stunning legs wrapped around him. Then he caught himself. There was no future in allowing Marguarite Connoly to elicit a normal human reaction. Especially if it was sexual. That would be a hook which would prove too sharp.

"I think someone has laid the golden egg right in our laps," Maggie said. "And we should definitely go for it."

MacGregor's brows knitted as he wondered how someone would "go for" something which was already in his lap. Or in this case, *her* lap. "What exactly are you saying, Doctor?"

"My God, Jeffrey, don't act so dense." Her smile disappeared. "Just think what we could do with an invisible army, for crissakes!"

"Oh, shit, Maggie!" MacGregor threw up his hands. "Not again."

"What do you mean?"

"I thought that last episode involving your assistant—what's her name?"

Maggie winced. "Mary Beth Wilson."

"Right—Mary Beth Wilson—would have squelched your appetite for anymore harebrained power schemes."

"Someone has just handed us a new and vital technology, Jeffrey. There's nothing harebrained about it."

"Look, the last time you meddled it almost cost us the Guardians. And the time before that, you actually went on television to advocate my overthrow. Jesus Christ, Maggie! Not only could I have imprisoned you, I could have had you shot!"

Maggie rose from her chair as if it were an ejector seat. "I re-sent that! You know I was not advocating revolution but an alliance. And as for Mary Beth, I'm the one who blew the whistle on her. So you can take your insinuations that I am a traitor and stuff them up your presidential ass!"

"Are you quite finished?" MacGregor said calmly.

"No. As a matter of fact, I've just begun. Just think of it, Jeffrey. The power to make one man or a thousand invisible is an unfortunate but, as of yesterday, incontrovertible fact of life. It has inexplicably happened, so whether we like it or not, that power is now a reality. The only remaining question is whether we are going to harness it against our enemies or are they going to use it against us." She nodded and sat down in one quick motion.

There was a long pause. "Now, are you finished?"

"For the time being, yes."

"Good, because I am sick of the mentality that insists on rushing after the newest, most diabolical edge. If the One-Day War taught us anything, it was that there is no such thing as an edge."

"Please, Jeffrey, spare me the flower-child crap. It doesn't play."

For the first time the President stood. "If we develop a 'stealth' man or whatever you want to call it, then it is only a matter of time until Maximov, or the Bey, or someone else develops one too. Don't you see that? Then they will send theirs to assassinate me and we will send ours to assassinate them, or worse. There is conceivably no limit to the damage just one of these, these *things* could do."

Maggie shifted her eyes from side to side as her mind raced. "What are you suggesting?"

MacGregor sat down. "I don't know." He stared at the closed folder on his desk for what Maggie thought was several minutes. She didn't dare say anything. Finally, she could stand it no longer.

"Jeffrey, you're not seriously thinking of . . ."

"Of course not!" he snapped. "It's just that I keep remembering what it was like to come above ground for the first time and look out these windows. The Washington Monument was gone. The city was in flames, and our very own people stormed the White House with blood in their eyes. All because we, you and me and others like us, insisted on developing the newest, fastest, cleverest, most powerful instrument to insure our safety.

"But we missed the whole point. The secret always has been that there is no human contrivance that will guarantee perfect safety. Never was, never will be. Yet there is another way. And it's always been right there in front of us. It's called trust."

Jesus Christ! Maggie thought. *He's finally gone off his nut.* "So what are you saying, exactly?"

"I'm saying we must end this mind-set of technological aggrandizement once and for all. It simply does not work. And beyond that, it just isn't right." The President reclined in his plush chair, his clasped hands on his forehead.

"What are you going to do, Jeffrey?"

"There's only one thing we can do."

Maggie took special note of the word "we." "What's that?"

"My God, Maggie. Are you going to make me say it?"

"Yes, Mr. President, I am."

He sighed and swiveled his chair around toward the windows, turning his back on Connoly. The distorted lawn appeared before him, and for an instant, he thought he saw a mob of desperate citizens hurling themselves into a curtain of machine-gun fire. He could see chunks of crimson flesh exploding from their bodies as they swarmed over the fence and crossed the lawn en route to certain death.

He twitched once, and the image disappeared. Then he sank deep into the soft leather, closed his eyes, and placed his fingertips lightly against his temples. "Who will free me from this turbulent priest?" he said, finally.

Maggie leaned against the door of her inner office. Her heart was pounding, and she found it difficult to breathe. She rested her head against the polished wood and closed her eyes, grateful that she had made it to the sanctuary of her private office before she threw up, passed out, or did God knows what. She had always thought of herself as a strong person, especially for a woman, but this newest development would prove a test even for her iron resolve.

She waited a few moments for her heart rate to stabilize. Then, slowly, she crossed the carpeted expanse to her desk and sat down with the exaggerated caution of a drunk. She repositioned the folders and messages on her desk until they were arranged by priority, then looked about for some other trivial task to perform. She found none. Finally, she forced herself to face the problem.

The President of the United States had just indirectly ordered her to arrange the murder of Tom Rogers. *That is what happened, isn't it?* she asked herself. Or had she misunderstood? Could this be some sort of elaborate game the President was running in order to test her loyalty? Especially in light of her recent gaffes? No, she concluded. He wasn't that devious. Or was he? Finally, she decided that MacGregor had reached his limit.

The President was nothing if not an honest man, so he must truly believe it was possible to prevent more slaughter by eliminating this new weapon. And ironically, he was willing to murder a man to accomplish this. The poor deluded fool, she thought, reminded of Jimmy Carter over twenty years before. *Doesn't he realize that until all men are like him, it is best to keep our swords sharp?*

Next, she had to figure out what she was going to do about this bizarre situation. Perhaps she could just ignore it, and it would go away after a day or two, enough time to let Jeffrey come to his senses. But what if he didn't? What if he really meant what he had said? Oh, the phrase had been cryptic enough, but the meaning was unmistakable. He wanted Rogers—she couldn't bring herself to say the word—"taken out." What if the President expected immediate action from her? What if he called her tomorrow for a report? My God, she thought. It was all too confusing.

Maggie took a deep breath and concentrated on composing herself. She mentally listed the criteria for her decision.

Do it. 1. To get back in the good graces of the President. 2. It would at least prevent the specimen—she couldn't say his name—from falling into the hands of an enemy. 3. Perhaps by *pretending* to do it she could gain some control over the situation and save Rogers along with the concept of invisibility, then worry about explaining her actions to the President later.

Don't do it. 1. She didn't quite know how to go about it. 2. The only compelling reason—it was murder!

Though Maggie suspected she was thought of as a ruthless woman, she had never even considered killing anyone, let alone somebody she knew.

Of all the Guardians, she liked Tom Rogers the most. He was quiet, strong, and sweet. It was a shame what Marta had done to him, kissing him off without so much as a word. It was something a teenager would do. If she hadn't wanted to see him again, she should have told him to his face and in private. Instead she chose to humiliate him in public. This was not the thing to do to a man who was both proud and sensitive, not to mention capable of killing you with his bare hands. And Maggie harbored some guilt over the breakup because Marta worked for her as a liaison between the White House and the Central Intelligence Agency. It was Maggie, in fact, who had introduced the couple. No, Marta Ryan was the one who was ruthless, Maggie concluded, not her.

Suddenly she had an idea. She swiveled around to the credenza behind her, slid open a panel, and dialed the combination to a small safe hidden there. She retrieved a file marked MARTA RYAN and spun back to her desk. She opened the folder and began to read.

Personal. Born: Coal Hill, Kentucky, 1962. Age: 35. Hair and Eyes: brown. Height: 5′ 4″. Weight: 110 lbs. Build: slender. Education: Julliard, School of Dance, NYC, 1983. Hobbies: flying.

Professional. Employer: President of the United States. Job Description: Liaison, White House/CIA. Supervisor: Dr. Marguarite Connoly. Duties: Coordinate interchange of information between the administration and the intelligence community. Background: field operative, CIA, 1988–93; operations staff, CIA, 1993–95; White House, 1995 to date. Performance: excellent.

There was more, but Maggie had seen enough to confirm her decision. The words "field agent" leaped off the page at her. It had been over two years since she had read Marta's file, and that particular entry had long since been forgotten. She closed the folder and punched the intercom button on her phone panel.

"I want to see Marta Ryan," Maggie ordered her secretary, "immediately!" *Perhaps*, she thought, *I really am as ruthless as people think*.

CHAPTER
EIGHT ———————————————————

Moheb Nazrullah looked at himself in the shaving mirror
and could not believe what he saw there. "The infidel actually
cut off my earlobe," he explained to his reflection, which stared
back at him incredulously. "The pig!" His anger built as he finished dressing the wound. He lurched out of the cramped head.
"I will now cut off his balls—if I can find them."

He climbed the steps and emerged on deck. He chuckled at
the sight of the net swaying from the shortened mast. It must
have been a very uncomfortable place to spend the night, he
thought. He poked the invisible bulge with the S.E.A.L. knife
just to make sure he still had a prisoner. After all, this invisible
warfare would take a bit of getting used to.

But what a wonderful weapon, he mused. Then he thought of
all the incredible things he could do with such an advantage and
how it would have altered all of his previous missions. *Altered,
hell!* he thought. *It would have reduced them to child's play.* He
jabbed the net again, just for the fun of it, and heard a groan.
"Wake up, sleepyhead," he mocked, "time to die!"

"Argggh." The net moved.

"Awaken, blasphemer, and prepare to serve me in paradise."

Nazrullah twirled and thumped the net with a vicious round-house kick, just for practice. The net jerked and roared at the same time, creating an effect so amusing that the Moslem decided to repeat the maneuver.

"Oww, goddamnit! What's your problem?" the net snarled.

"I believe you meant, 'What's your problem, *raghead*.' That is the pejorative term for those of my faith, is it not?"

"Yeah, you're right," said the net. "So what's your problem, raghead?"

Nazrullah delivered another kick. "I like you, infidel. You have great courage. No brains, of course, but great courage. I shall regret killing you."

"Go fuck yourself!"

"See? That's exactly what I was referring to. Only you would say such a thing in your situation." Moheb smiled, and his lips slid at an angle across his face, stretching the mustache that flowed over the corners of his mouth. "By the way, what is your name?"

"What's it to ya?"

"Nothing, except I would like to know who I am about to dismember."

"Kicking me out of the club, eh? Gosh, I'm mortified."

"If you persist in this idiotic banter, it will only increase the agony of your death. Now, what is your name?"

"Indiana Jones."

"Of course you are," Moheb hooted, "and I'm Steven Spielberg. Now what is your name?" He waved the knife menacingly, but the net remained silent.

"All right, Mr. Jones, or should it be Doctor—no, you haven't the intelligence for that—you may have your little jokes, but I have the computer disks." He patted his shirt pocket. "If you don't believe me, check your own pocket, if you can reach it with your hands bound."

The net thrashed about. "You son of a bitch!" it bellowed.

Nazrullah flushed a bright crimson and lurched toward the net. "You dare to insult my mother?" He grabbed at the webbing and thrust his fingers through the holes, probing for a vital spot. "What have we here? An eye? Perfect!" He brought the knife to bear and jabbed it into the net.

"Shit!"

"Now, what is your name?"

"Tom Rogers, goddamnit!"

Nazrullah sighed deeply and retreated from the swinging bundle. "There, that wasn't so difficult, was it? I certainly feel better. Don't you?"

"No."

"Too bad. I hope I didn't impair your vision. The way you impaired my hearing." Nazrullah touched his bandaged ear. "But no matter. For now I simply have to decide what to do with you."

The net wiggled. "I thought you'd already planned to disinherit me, or exclude me from your membership, or some damn thing!"

"You mean dismember?" Moheb started to laugh. "I'm afraid the separation I had in mind for you is a bit more drastic than you imagined. Perhaps, however, I should rethink the situation. It could be that you will prove more valuable alive than dead. What do you think?"

"Alive sounds good, but I still think you're a piece of shit!"

Nazrullah started for the net with his knife raised, but regained his self-control at the last instant. Grimacing, he turned and walked slowly to the port gunwale. From there he watched the waves undulate across the sea. The mesmerizing effect slowly restored his composure. As he stared, he noticed several dark fins cutting the boat's wake.

"What's the matter, camel jockey, lose your temper?" Rogers called out.

Moheb turned and leaned against the railing. "I've decided to take you back with me," he snickered. "The master will enjoy seeing you, or in this instance, *not* seeing you. In any case, I can assure you that his sadistic imagination is infinitely more developed than mine. Which means that you can look forward to an extremely creative death."

"So you and the master are real chummy?" Rogers said, tossing off the remark. "Funny, from the radio conversation, it didn't sound like you two were all that close."

"The master and I are as one," Moheb proclaimed proudly, holding up two intertwined fingers as an example.

"It couldn't be that the two of you are doing the dirty deed, now could it?"

"What?" Moheb yelped.

"What's the matter, gone deaf already?" Rogers pushed. "I said it sounds like you and the Bey are doing the ol' humpty-dumpty." He grunted twice for effect.

Nazrullah's face stormed past crimson, and was approaching purple by the time his knife reached shoulder-high. "You are the entrails of Satan, and I must cut you out. Aiyee!" He charged the net. But to his astonishment, the bundle spun in midair at the last instant, and the surprised Moslem took an unseen, crushing blow to the chest. Stunned, Nazrullah reeled across the deck. He struck the gunwale at the base of his spine and his momentum flipped him backwards over the railing. As he plummeted toward the icy Pacific he heard the invisible devil calling to him from the deck of the trawler:

"Seen *Jaws*, raghead?"

Marta Ryan sat over the wing of the 757 near Runway Four at San Francisco International Airport and slugged down the last of her gin and tonic. She peeked through the porthole at the three aircraft, all military, that preceeded the old Boeing on the taxiway. She wondered why her flight, one of the few civilian routes reinstated since the One-Day War, hadn't received special consideration from the traffic controllers. Then she remembered the CIA I-REP which explained that Frisco International was booked solid by the Air Force for transport traffic that ordinarily would have used surrounding bases.

She glanced beyond the runway at the lights of the bay bridge that twinkled in the summer night, and thought how lucky that her favorite city had escaped the fiery destruction of the nation's other metropolises. She knew it had been spared because of a direct hit on the Soviet missile guidance complex at Vladivostok during the opening minutes of the thermonuclear exchange two-plus years before. That bit of American marksmanship had forced many of the Russian birds aimed at the West Coast to fly off course. Ironically, that also meant that several small towns in Nevada, Oregon, and even old Mexico had been consequently erased. *Oh, well*, she thought.

A perky young stewardess strolled down the aisle and handed Marta another drink. The flight had originated out of Washington with both women on board, so by now the stew was familiar with the older woman's regimen. As she picked up the empty glass and soiled napkin the young attendant thought how attractive the woman had been when she first got on board. Now after nine drinks she had dissipated into another sloppy juicer. She knew that the woman had drunk herself clear across the United States, and intended to drink herself halfway across the

Pacific. She wisked away down the aisle to tell the other stewardesses not to serve her anymore.

Marta bristled at the officious attitude of the stew. Pretty young girls with tight asses, good tits, and no failures could be so tiring, she thought. The stewardess's stiff body language had also told Marta that she was holding her last drink of the night. *Just as well, I'm probably going to pass out soon anyway.* She set the glass down on the seat-back tray in front of her and lit a cigarette. She took a deep drag, reclined, and exhaled a long bluish cone into the cabin.

"I'm sorry, ma'am, but federal regulations prohibit smoking on board." It was the same perky stew. "You'll have to extinguish that immediately."

Marta turned slowly toward the voice and measured the girl with her bloodshot eyes. "Fuck off," she said.

The stewardess stood there for several seconds, gaping, then turned and stalked up the aisle toward the cockpit.

Marta took another hit off the brown-wrapped cigarette and blew several smoke rings. She fingered the glass on the tray before her and realized it would be her last taste of alcohol until the mission was completed. Mission, she thought. She was actually back out on a mission in the field. She started to tingle again with a mixture of excitement and apprehension—and something else—but she was too drunk to discern what that was.

She closed her eyes and thought of Tom Rogers. Poor Tommy, only he would volunteer for such a precarious assignment. It didn't take a rocket scientist to figure out that the experiment was potentially dangerous. But Tommy never thought about consequences. He just lowered his head and charged, then paid the price later. And now he was either dead or invisible. She tried to imagine which was worse. *You're such a fool, Tommy, such a strong, generous, brave, simple fool.*

A large part of her hoped that he had been killed in the experiment. At least then she would not have to face the dilemma if he turned out to be alive. After all, her orders were explicit enough. Find him, then report for instructions. Marta had served in the field long enough to know what that meant. The simplest translation was: "By then we'll know if he is expendable."

But could she kill him? she wondered. Ten years ago it would have been no problem, but now it was a different story. She was not the same blindly obedient drone she had been in her youth.

Somewhere along the way, Marta had changed. Maybe it was just the years, she thought, or maybe it was Tommy?

"Ms. Ryan?" She looked up into the face of the young copilot who leaned from the aisle over the arm of her seat. He held a slip of paper in his hand. "You have a message from Washington." He smiled.

"Thank you, Captain," she said, taking the folded note. She leered into his handsome face and wondered what it would be like to clutch his lean, hard body while he plunged deep inside her. She licked her lips at the thought.

"Ma'am?" the man said, and the word pierced her ego like a sword. "The stewardesses are complaining about your smoking. I'd appreciate it if you would refrain. Okay?" She watched, nonplussed, as he turned and walked back to the cockpit.

"Welcome to reality, Marta," she mumbled to herself, realizing that she was pushing forty and beginning to look it. She still had a good body, thanks to the hours she spent monitoring its reflection in the giant mirrors that lined the dance studio. She'd been good enough to turn pro in her younger days, but had given it up without really trying. Why had she done that? she wondered. She could no longer remember.

She unfolded the paper and read the message. "Gang approaching Port Allen. MAC." Marta read the message again, then ignited it with her cigarette lighter. *Wait'll the crew gets a load of this,* she thought. Smoke billowed up from the flaming paper. *Fuck 'em.* She realized that the message had come in uncoded, except for two words, and that the communications officer plus the copilot had already read it, but she burned it anyway. After all, it was procedure, and besides, she thought she'd piss off the entire plane.

"Gang" stood for the Guardians, naturally, and "MAC" was the acronym for Marguarite Connoly. Otherwise, the message meant just what it said. Marta shuddered at the unprofessionalism, then realized that Maggie had no background for this kind of work and obviously was no stickler for security. This was just one reason why she anticipated the assignment would prove to be the most difficult of her career. Another was that she had just come out of retirement and was unpracticed. Then, of course, there was Tommy.

The improbability of finding someone who had been rendered invisible was one thing, but the prospect of dealing with that someone when he had also been her recent lover was another. The whole situation was just too bizarre to contemplate, and Marta wondered why she had undertaken such an assignment in the first place.

She pondered the question as the plane rolled to the end of the taxiway, turned onto the main runway, and stopped there. For several moments the fuselage strained against the huge jets that roared at full throttle. Just when Marta imagined the wings would be torn from the plane, the pilot released the ground brakes. The 757 jerked forward and gradually built up speed until it rushed headlong down the tarmac. The great bird tilted back, then seemed to lift off the ground with a little hop. Marta felt the slight G-forces as the ship climbed above the sparkling city and peeled off toward the ocean.

She looked out the porthole and noticed her own reflection staring back at her against the black water below. The distorted image appeared so twisted and mean in the double glass that Marta finally turned away in disgust. "Why did I do this?" she said. Then she dropped her head onto the seat-back tray and passed out.

Tom Rogers kept waiting for the splash as he twirled around in the cotton net, but the sound never came. Or he never heard it. He cursed his earplugs for causing more problems than they eliminated. He decided that the reason he hadn't seen the splash was because he probably had been facing the opposite side of the boat when Nazrullah hit the water. Besides, he was nearly blind in his right eye from the gash carved in his eyebrow with the Moslem's blade. *The fucker*, Rogers thought, *he came within a centimeter of gouging my eye out.*

But Rogers had gotten his revenge. Nazrullah had had more pride than brains and had been an easy target for Tom's insults. All the Guardian had had to do was jack up his adversary's rage index and let him do the rest. The trick had been to maneuver himself into position. Not an easy task considering Tom was suspended in a free-swinging pouch, and his hands were taped behind his back. But the years of special training in the martial arts had endowed Rogers with extraordinary body control, and he'd used that skill to time the slow spin of the net with his own verbal barbs. When Nazrullah rushed him, Tom had been able to draw up his knees and kick the man full in the chest with both feet. The impact had thrust Rogers the short distance backward against the stubby mast, which gave him the resistance he needed to push his attacker across the deck. Gravity had taken care of the rest.

Tom was sorry the disks had gone over the side with Nazrullah. He would have preferred to return them along with the Moslem to General Ritter, but he decided his ego could live without that display. The important thing was that the Army had copies of the disks and Iskander Bey did not.

Now he had to get free. Nazrullah had bound Tom's wrists using tape from the same spool Rogers had used on the Hawaiian at the beach and on Nazrullah himself. *I guess we're just about out of tape*, Tom thought. He struggled with the bindings, but the two-inch adhesive strapping held fast.

Next, he looked about for some way to get out of the snare. The netting was gathered at the top and looped over a winch hook secured to a makeshift boom which Tom had rigged himself. His own weight in the pouch formed the resistance which imprisoned him. Without the use of his hands there was no way to work himself free. He was caught, and that was that.

He wiggled about looking for something that would give him an idea, but nothing that qualified as a stroke of genius presented itself. "Ouch!" Tom's movement did scrounge up something sharp, however, that poked him in the butt. He fiddled around with his fingers and managed to get a tenuous grip on the object and pull it out of his flesh. From the feel of it, Rogers judged that the prod was a fishhook which somehow had gotten embedded in the net. *"Voila!"* he said. If not genius, Tom concluded, then certainly he had been struck with good luck.

"*Voila* indeed."

Tom stiffened at the sound. On his next rotation toward the port side he saw the unmistakable figure of Moheb Nazrullah curling up over the side of the gunwale. *Oh, shit!*

"So, unbeliever, you thought you'd seen the last of me," Nazrullah said with a smirk as he perched on top of the gunwale. "But Allah was by my side, strategically placed you might say, and so too was the raft you tied to the side of the boat. Thank you, my friend. I fell right into it." He threw his head back and roared at the irony. "I'm afraid, however, that you will have no such luck. After all, infidel, Allah does not sit upon your shoulder."

Rogers watched, stunned, as Nazrullah slid from his seat and carefully approached the net. He noticed the black hilt of the survival knife protruding from the waistband of the Moslem's trousers. Moheb circled behind the net, grabbed a boat hook, raised it, and began pushing the boom to port. Within a minute, Rogers dangled in his pouch over the Pacific Ocean like goods in a cargo net. He looked down at the bright yellow raft still tied to the trawler and cursed himself for forgetting about it earlier. Not that it would have mattered much. Still . . .

He felt the fishhook with his fingers and clumsily tried to turn it so that the barb was extended upward. When he thought he had judged its position correctly, he began to move it back and forth in a frantic attempt to saw away at the tape. Ultimately he knew there was no time for the tiny strokes to do the job.

Nazrullah climbed atop the gunwale and steadied himself against the boom. With his free hand, he withdrew the knife and, one by one, began cutting the heavy strands from the winch hook. Rogers felt the net sag as each cord popped free. Then, suddenly, Nazrullah stopped.

"What is this, Tom Rogers?" Nazrullah sneered. "Do I see blood upon the netting?"

Rogers momentarily had forgotten about his wound, but Nazrullah's mention of it caused the pain to return. With his clear eye, Tom saw the bloodstained webbing and the crimson fluid that dripped into the water.

"I think you are about to become extremely popular with the marine life, my friend. Look!" Moheb pointed at several fins that cut the water's surface near the stern. "I hope you're not squeamish." Then he dropped to the deck, leaned over the gunwale, and cut the raft free. "To prove that I am a fair man, I will give you an incentive, which is more than you gave me." He turned and pitched the knife into the raft. It landed flat on the wooden floorboard and clattered to the back of the tiny craft.

Nazrullah leaned nonchalantly back against the gunwale. "Did I forget to thank you for the computer disks? How rude of me." He patted his shirt pocket. "The Bey will be very pleased."

"You'd better hope I die today, raghead, 'cause if I don't, I'm gonna find you and fuck you up!"

The Moslem's mustache slid into a patronizing smile. "I am surprised that the two strands I have left uncut have supported your weight for as long as this, infidel. The net is stronger than I thought."

Just then a strand gave way, and Rogers looked up to see that he was suspended by a thread. As if in a daze, he continued to peer upward at the last fiber until it snapped. Though he couldn't be sure, Rogers thought he heard the Moslem call out to him as he plunged into the cold sea.

"Good-bye, ol' *chum*."

PART
TWO

CHAPTER
NINE

Billy McKay ambled down the road that bordered the docks of Port Allen's bustling harbor. If it hadn't been for the Remington 1100 auto shotgun propped on his hip, the Colt .45 holstered on his belt, and the K-Bar sheathed upside-down over his heart, he would have looked like any other dockworker. At six-three, 225, he was certainly big enough to handle the heavy work, and his massive chest looked like it was accustomed to straining against bulky cargo.

He wasn't on the docks to unload anything other than his weapons. Through the barrels, if it came to that, and he hoped it wouldn't. He was there, along with Sam and Casey, because the Kauai location was one of the only leads they had that might point to where Tom Rogers had gone and lost himself.

The Hawaiian who McKay had found on the beach had mentioned the place, and had even narrowed it down to a warehouse. It was a gathering place for those of his political persuasion, pure-blood Hawaiians who wanted the split with the mainland to include more than just twenty-five hundred miles of ocean. *Ho hum*, thought McKay, *another goddamn political trip.*

The Guardians had also tried to track the trawler that both their prisoners had mentioned, but they came up empty. Much of the Coast Guard's Hawaiian contingent had been ordered back to the mainland because of the instant shortage there after the One-Day War, so no vessels were available in the area. McKay had tried to commandeer Elmo Ritter's big Black Hawk for a sweep of the area, but the general had other priorities in mind for his copter. None of which McKay thought were nearly as important as finding Tom. So as usual, the Guardians had to do it the hard way.

Kanina and his buddy, both handcuffed, walked ahead of McKay, who was flanked by Casey and Sam. Ritter, who'd insisted on accompanying the Guardians, trailed a few paces behind. He poised a hand over his ivory-handled revolved like a gunfighter from the Old West. McKay just smiled and shook his head.

Sam and Casey tried to ignore the man. They were still pissed because he wouldn't let them use his helicopter to search for Tom. "He's dead, boys, and you might just as well accept it," Ritter had told them. McKay knew better, and that was good enough for Sloan and Wilson. They were all on the verge of forgetting about the general when suddenly they heard his voice boom over the bone-conduction receivers taped behind their ears.

"Boys? I forgot to tell you—"

"Sir!" McKay interrupted. "You can speak in a normal voice or even subvocalize if you need to. These receivers are highly sensitive," McKay said through his throat mike. He already regretted loaning the general Tom's set.

"Yeah, I see what you mean," Ritter said, but he was still too loud. Then he added meekly, "Sorry."

It was Sloan's turn to shake his head.

"Anyway, the report on Sergeant Thibidoux came in just before we left Niihau," Ritter continued, "but I forgot to tell you about it. There were no tapes in his pockets."

"Disks, General," Casey said, without thinking.

"Yeah, disks, whatever. They weren't there. What do you make of that?"

"And the disks didn't show up on any of the other bodies?" Sam asked.

"Oh, right. I mean, no, they didn't."

"So, whoever has the disks," Sam added, "retrieved them *after* the explosion and—"

"That's enhanced magnetic eruption, Commander, not explosion," Ritter corrected.

"Of course," Sloan remarked sarcastically. "Therefore, we can deduce that whoever acquired the disks did so after the *enhanced magnetic eruption*. And that person either came from outside the lab or inside the lab."

"No one came from outside the lab!" Ritter stated emphatically.

"Then he must have come from *inside* the lab," Sloan concluded.

"Which means that Tom Rogers is alive, and you should have let us use the Black Hawk to find him." What the hell, McKay thought. He had never been known for his tact anyway.

"Horseshit!" Ritter bellowed. "No one could have survived that blast."

"Enhanced magnetic eruption, sir," chirped Casey.

"Yeah, right, whatever," the general mumbled.

McKay and Sloan grinned at Casey. The fighter jock returned their looks with a wink as if to punctuate the collective revenge. After all, they felt stupid and frustrated wasting their time on a wild-goose chase on Kauai when they could have been forcing the missing trawler to heave to under the guns of Ritter's giant helicopter. Besides, everyone but the general had figured out that the Arab aboard that boat was the key to the whole situation. In the regular Army, however, perception and reality were often two different things. The best they could hope for was that today's little escapade might at least give them the boat's destination. If this lead turned up dry, they would proceed to Kona on the Big Island, where the trawler was registered, and try their luck there.

Some faint static crackled in McKay's earpiece, and grew until it was broken by a familiar voice. "Mr. Wizard calling Cromagnon. Come in, Cromagnon."

"This is McKay, Doc. I thought we'd gotten rid of you." They had dropped Lee Warren off at the airport in Lihue before taking the short hop on Ritter's UH-60A over to Port Allen. Warren was scheduled to hitch a ride back to the mainland aboard Gentry's C-130.

"Yeah, you did," Warren replied. "We're in the air now. And you'll be proud to know that I've only puked once so far."

"Congratulations, Doc. We'll make a man out of you yet." McKay heard the microwave echos fade in and out as the satellite transmission was patched through the communications equipment aboard the Black Hawk just a few hundred meters away.

"Listen, Billy. I've got an interesting piece of news for you," Warren said. "Marta Ryan is flying into Lihue this morning."

"What?" McKay was stunned.

"Yeah. Curious development, don't you think?"

"How do you know this, Lee?"

"Maggie's not the only one with assets in the White House. I just got a phone call."

"Well, fuck!"

"That's exactly the type of succinct, articulate, and sophisti-cated response I would expect from you, McKay."

"You know how I hate to disappoint you, Doc."

"She's working for Maggie, of course. Under what orders I'm not sure yet. I'll let you know as soon as I find out."

"Thanks, Doc. I owe you one."

"You owe me several, Billy. By the way, keep your thick skull down. Wizard out." The transmission went dead.

For several moments McKay thought about what he'd just heard, but he still couldn't believe it. He knew that Marta was a former CIA field operative and had the necessary skills to be dangerous. What he didn't know was what she had been in-structed to do with those skills. But for Tom's sake, he had to as-sume the worst. "Did everybody hear that?"

"Yeah," answered Sloan. Casey nodded that he understood, and the general just looked bewildered. "Marta Ryan's flying into Lihue?" Sam added sarcastically. "Tom would just be thrilled!"

"Who's Marta Ryan?" Kanina turned to McKay.

"What do you care, asshole?" Billy needed someone to take his frustration out on, and the Hawaiian presented a perfect tar-get. "Turn around!" He slammed the prisoner between the shoulder blades with the butt of his Remington.

"Maybe we'd better speed this process up," Casey proposed. "What do you think, Billy?"

"Right!" McKay ordered the group to fan out across the blacktop as they continued their approach to the warehouse. When they arrived within twenty meters of the closed double doors, McKay signaled for the others to halt.

"I think I'll let you do the honors, Sam," McKay said, and he took Sloan's position on the right flank, prodding Kanina in front of him. Casey pushed the first mate over to the left flank, and Sam took up his position in the center. He loaded a 40-millimeter round into the M203 grenade launcher slung under the barrel of his Galil SAR.

"What are you doing, Commander?" Ritter blared.

"I'm getting ready to blow the doors off this warehouse, General," Sloan said in a tone that invited the follow-up *What the hell does it look like, dipshit?*

"That's not the way, Commander. Better let me handle this." Ritter swaggered over to McKay and relieved him of his prisoner. The surprised Guardian just looked at his mates and shrugged. Then the general marched Kanina out in front of the group and placed him before the warehouse doors. He took his position directly behind Uli and, being several inches taller, looked over the prisoner's head at his objective. Then he drew his nickel-plated pistol and placed it at the base of Kanina's skull. "You in there!" he called. "Come on out and let's pow-wow!" He turned to the Guardians and flashed a wide grin. The instant he turned back toward the warehouse, a shot rang out, and Ritter's brains blew out the back of his head. The general, already dead, just stood there for a moment with an astonished look on his face, then he fell over backwards like a ladder.

"Scatter, boys!" Sam yelled just as he fired the grenade launcher. The doors of the warehouse were instantly replaced with smoke and flame, and two blackened bodies slapped the concrete floor inside. Since there was nothing that provided cover outside, the Guardians had little choice but to march straight ahead, which they did behind a curtain of lead.

Casey cut loose with his MAC-10 that spewed .45 slugs like a garden hose while Sam reloaded the M203. McKay pummeled the impromptu entrance with his Remington 12-gauge. He figured that if he didn't kill anything, at least he would cause a nervous breakdown or two. In just this manner the Guardians shot their way into the building, where they finally took cover behind anything that wasn't burning, and some things that were. When the smoke cleared, McKay counted six bodies, all Hawaiian.

For several minutes nothing moved, and there was no sound except the crackle of the few fires that dotted the warehouse. Toward the back of the building a white stepvan sat flanked by scores of crates stacked several meters high. Numerous large boxes and crates occupied the near section of the building. A wide balcony, with an enclosed office built against the back wall, ringed the upper portion on three sides to form an open second story.

McKay looked through the gaping hole that was once the front of the warehouse and saw Uli Kanina and his comrade, their hands cuffed behind them, lying face down on the blacktop outside. McKay noticed there was no blood around them, and after a few seconds he saw them move. "Right where you are is a good place for both of you," he shouted. He drew his model 1911 and planted a .45 slug a few inches from their faces. Afterward, it appeared that both men tried to burrow into the asphalt.

"Billy," Sam whispered through his throat mike. "Maybe we'd better bring them inside where we can keep an eye on them. I don't like having anybody behind me in a fight, even if they're cuffed."

McKay realized that Sloan was right. Then McKay saw that he was slipping. Tom's predicament had affected him, and he was losing his concentration. This could prove dangerous, not only for him, but for the entire group. McKay vowed to knuckle down and get back his professional edge. "Good idea, Sam. Bring 'em in," he subvocalized. "Anybody see anything?"

A couple of no's echoed in his earpiece while he turned to check on the prisoners' progress. As the two men entered the building at Sloan's command, a lone shot from the rafters cracked the silence, and Kanina's companion collapsed on the concrete floor. Like a captive rat, Kanina scurried behind the first available crate.

"Shit!" Sam hissed.

"Where did it come from?" McKay asked.

"Up top somewhere," whispered Casey. "From the office, I think."

"Okay, dust her off, college boy!" McKay ordered.

Sloan shouldered the Galil, then rocked from the recoil as he touched off the M203. The upstairs office blew apart, catapulting shards of glass, fragments of furniture, whole file cabinets, and chunks of wall toward the front of the building.

"Oh, shit!" McKay shouted. He dove behind the biggest crate just as huge clumps of debris showered the area. After several moments the dust and smoke began to clear, and McKay contemplated raising his head for a quick look. Just then he heard Casey over his earpiece.

"Something's cooking at twelve o'clock, dudes."

McKay peered up over the crate just as the stepvan roared out from under a pile of ripped lumber and sheet rock that moments before had resembled an office. "What the hell!" Muzzle flashings, like little bolts of lightning, sparked from both sides of the truck as the vehicle crashed through the warehouse. The automatic fire splintered the crate tops and sent Casey and McKay lurching for cover.

"What's happening?" Sloan yelled from behind a box.

"It's the truck, Sam," McKay answered. "Pulverize the damn thing!"

"I'm not loaded!" he explained frantically.

"Shit!" McKay spat. He was sitting with his back propped against a crate. From that position he aimed the Remington at the spot the van would occupy when it passed. The cacophony created by the engine, revved to the max, plus the thunder of the automatic fire, climbed to a deafening peak as the truck approached. Suddenly a flash of white appeared, and McKay snapped off two rounds. The shotgun blasts peppered the body just behind the driver. "Damn!" McKay lowered the barrel for a potshot at the tires, but then stared at the flash of a machine pistol in the hands of man standing in the back of the open van. "Christ!" He rolled to his left as fast as he could. The 9mm rounds ricocheted off the concrete and stitched the crate where McKay had been crouching.

In all the confusion, Billy thought he saw something that he just couldn't believe. Right after his roll to safety, he looked toward the vehicle and was pretty sure he saw Uli Kanina chasing the damn thing. Then the man in the back of the truck extended his arm, grabbed Kanina's hand, and pulled him aboard. There was nothing the Guardians could do but watch as the van swerved onto the road and disappeared around the corner.

Finally, McKay couldn't stand it any longer. "Didn't we handcuff that son of a bitch, or have I lost my mind?"

Sam and Casey just looked at one another, then they turned toward the big Marine. "Both," they said in unison.

CHAPTER
TEN

"Things could be worse," muttered Tom Rogers, though offhand he couldn't imagine how. He knew that any normal person would be hard-pressed to discover a set of circumstances more depressing than the one he faced at that very moment. But no normal person would find himself deposited in the middle of the Pacific Ocean with his hands bound behind his back and gushing blood from two wounds as he waited for the inevitable school of sharks to approach. And anyone who did would probably shit through his eyeballs and just say "Good night!"

But there was nothing normal about Tom Rogers, not when it came to impossible situations. After all, the Guardians were trained for the impossible. It was their meat and drink. It was their stock and trade. It was their . . . *Ah, horseshit!* Tom thought. *Let's face it. I'm fucked!*

The giant swells rolled over him like mountains on the march. He fought to kick his way to the surface for the brief lungfuls of air he could snatch before the next wave engulfed him. He had managed to kick free of the net immediately after plunging into the sea through the hole in the top formed when

78

Nazrullah cut the bundle from the boom. One down, two to go, he thought.

He tried to float on his back with his mouth toward the sky and kick his way toward the bright yellow raft. Without the use of his hands the task was virtually impossible.

It was also more difficult to see the shark fins from this new position than it had been aboard the trawler. He knew the monsters were there, and the realization filled him with a mixture of hatred and terror. The fear was for the sharks, but the hatred was for the periodic glimpses he stole through the swells of the shrinking craft that loped its way east by southeast. Just the sight of it filled Tom with a terrible resolve. He vowed somehow to find a way to escape his fate and wreak vengeance on the Moslem for his incomprehensible cruelty. He reached deep to his very core and found there the strength to press on.

He hadn't seen the sharks since he hit the water, but he knew the blood that oozed from his face and shoulder would soon draw them to him. Between quick breaths he frantically searched the wave tops for any sign of the menacing dorsals. So far he hadn't seen any, but he realized the dark fins would be difficult to spot against the rolling surface of the gray water.

Tom knew he had to free his hands if there was to be any hope for his survival. He still clutched the fishhook he had freed from the net before he was dumped over the side, but the old iron was rusted and weak, and he feared it would be no match for the soggy tape. Still, he sawed away at the bindings, making little strokes with his thumb and index finger, realizing all the while that his effort was futile.

Then he spotted the first fin. The dorsal was smaller than he expected, and brighter. It shone almost silver in the sunlight as it approached from the left. From the color and the quick zigzagging motion with which it spliced the water, Tom knew instantly the fin belonged to a mako. At least he no longer felt quite so inept. Even with free hands he realized he would have been no match for an animal that could compete successfully in the water with a bullet.

The mako sped in a wide circle. Tom tried to swivel with it, treading water with a steady bicycle motion of his legs. He knew that sharks were attracted to quick jerks, so he fought to keep his movements as rhythmical as possible. The fact that he was scared shitless didn't help any.

Every other thought now was aimed at fighting the panic. He

had heard that sharks could actually smell fear in the water, and he wondered if that was true. If so, he imagined, then the mako probably thought he was circling a skunk.

He knew there was no question that sharks could scent blood from great distances. However, he could no longer distinguish whether the gash over his eye was still gushing. The ocean had a way of liquifying everything, he mused. He tried to steal a glance at his shoulder between swells, but was unable to tell if it too was still bleeding. He figured that water would only intensify any hemorrhaging, though. He wondered if he might be able to feel the sting of the salt in his wounds. But the cold and the fear shut down his senses so all he could feel was the steady approach of the mako in shrinking concentric circles.

With every pass, Tom thought of the pilot he had dumped overboard and the sickening fascination with which he had watched the sharks shred the man's body. Though the Hawaiian was past any feeling when he hit the water, Tom imagined the pain for him with every wound, every tear, every chunk of flesh the sharks ripped from his corpse. But it was the violent shaking motion which accompanied the gnashing that froze Rogers at his marrow. The sharks had tossed and thrashed the body as if it had never been anything more than a slab of soulless carrion, and he knew that was what they would do to him. Only he would be alive when it began.

He worked frantically with his fingers now to cut through the three layers of tape that bound his wrists. The adhesive had grown soggy in the water and was even more difficult to cut than before. As he sawed away he noticed another, darker fin sliding toward him from the right. The black dorsal was much larger than that of the mako and, unlike its shiny counterpart, headed right toward him. Tom stopped all motion, took a deep breath, and allowed himself to sink slowly into the sea.

Through the salt sting, he saw the huge striped animal glide past him in the murky water. He recognized it as a tiger shark, about a sixteen-footer. Rogers froze as the beast slid by and brushed him on the hip. The rough, sandpaper skin tore through his jumpsuit and scraped his flesh raw. He fought the impulse to cry out, realizing that any gasp would emerge only as a pathetic gurgle and would probably just cause him to drown.

Through his pain, Tom was still able to marvel at how detached the monster appeared as it went about its work. He noted with curiosity the professionalism reflected in its black, lifeless eyes. There was a slight reaction when it bumped its prey, but it amounted to little more than a brief annoyance. The shark swam on while Tom continued to sink toward the floor of the Pacific.

It was then that Rogers remembered he was still invisible. Through all the anxiety he had momentarily forgotten that one overwhelming fact. His condition had shielded him from killers on land. Why then shouldn't it perform the same function in the sea? Then he remembered that sharks relied less on vision than their other senses, which some scientists claimed included a type of sonar. Still, the tiger had sideswiped him and then had drifted right on past. *Humph*, he thought.

Perhaps if he couldn't cut through the tape, he could at least position his arms in front of his body. He wasn't sure what good that would do, but at least it would make him feel better. He decided to tuck his legs against his chest and try to slide his tethered wrists under his feet. It was worth a try, he concluded, but there was no time for that now. He was almost out of air.

He kicked hard for the surface, recognizing that with each stroke he sent out a homing signal to the sharks. But death from the predators was still questionable while drowning was a certainty. He could see the missile-shaped bodies gliding above as he pushed for daylight and realized he was heading right toward them. But they lay along the shortest route to the surface, and he needed oxygen desperately.

He felt as though his lungs would burst, and he thrashed harder with his legs, forcing them to perform the double duty necessary without the use of his arms. The movement attracted the attention of the sharks, and they twisted their boneless bodies in his direction. Before the animals could converge, he pierced the water. He gulped mouthfuls of the rich air before he crashed back into the ocean like a great, leaping fish. Then the sharks were upon him.

There were more than two now, though he didn't know how many. Five, he thought, three makos and two tigers, and none bothered with the pretense of circling. Tom no longer had the luxury of freezing dead still and drifting slowly toward the bottom. There was simply no time for that. The sharks were racing in for the kill.

A mako flashed in and jutted out its upper jaw, sliding its lip up and over a row of triangular teeth that glistened in the shallow water. The teeth were serrated on the edges like arrowheads. The animal's eyes disappeared behind an opaque membrane that rose from the bottom of the ocular cavity to shield the black orbs during attack. This demonic phenomenon added to the monstrous effect of the moment and pushed Rogers to the very threshold of terror.

Operating on instinct, Tom kicked upward, tucked, flipped over backward, then pushed with his legs as hard as he could. He plunged toward the bottom, and the mako gnashed into a mouthful of ocean. The animal broke two teeth when its powerful jaws snapped together.

Tom now had the time to try out his idea. Still pointed downward, he tucked again into a ball and stretched his arms to his heels. He scrunched and pushed at the same time, countering his own muscle movements. He threatened to dislocate one of his massive shoulders during the maneuver, and thought for an instant he tore something in his lower back. With his knees jammed under his chin, he fought to hold his breath a few seconds longer. Finally, the tape slipped over the edge of his heels, and his arms were on the proper side of his body.

His air supply grew short again, and he was forced to kick for the surface. This time, however, he swam with his arms outstretched before him. Consequently, he was able to swim away from the sharks that milled about aimlessly searching for traces of blood and snatches of movement.

His lungs ached, and his whole system cried out for oxygen. He accelerated his kicks with short, jerky motions. A large tiger, which had been swimming away from Rogers, picked up the vibration and suddenly reversed his direction. Still, Tom had no choice but to proceed upward as quickly as possible. He broke the surface thirty meters ahead of the shark and sucked in as much fresh air as his tortured lungs could hold. Then, treading water, he turned toward the animal to gauge its position while he frantically gnawed at the tape with his teeth. The other sharks sensed the anticipation in the tiger's sudden swift movement and joined in the hunt.

Rogers guessed that the approaching shark was the same tiger he had spotted minutes before. It appeared to be easily the largest shark in the neighborhood. Unfortunately, it was not the only one.

A smaller, faster mako flared in from the left side of the tiger with another on his tail. Tom was sure he could feel others approaching from the other side. Though highly disciplined, his emotions were dangerously close to racing out of control now.

If sharks were truly drawn to fear, then he imagined himself a giant magnet bobbing in the water. He had to figure out something, but there was nothing he could think of to do. So he did exactly what he had done before. After all, he concluded, that had worked well enough.

Tom kicked, tucked, and flipped, just as before, but this time when he pushed for the bottom, he struck something solid. He didn't have to be told what it was. He dove deeper as fast as he could swim and expected something to hit his feet at any second. To his surprise, he felt nothing but the soft resistance of the water. When he turned to look, what he saw astounded him. The whole head of the mako was in the mouth of the tiger while other sharks slashed chunks from the silver body. One mako, attached to his brother's side, spun furiously while another tiger twisted and writhed to rip a portion of the victim's tail free.

Tom figured he had kicked the mako right into the path of the approaching tiger. *Better him than me*, he thought, as he stole slowly away from the scene at an upward angle. He swam as "quietly" as he could until his air gave out, then he aimed straight up and breached the surface about sixty meters from his last position. The ocean roiled from the attack, and intermittently a dorsal appeared or a tail would thrash out of the water. A bright red bubble stained the foam, and bits of silver flesh popped to the surface. Rogers cringed at the sight and decided that sixty meters wasn't quite enough distance to separate him from the butchery.

He floated on his back and moved his legs just enough to propel him slowly through the water. He rolled once, carefully, over onto his stomach to get his bearings, and spotted the yellow raft riding high on a wave several hundred meters away. He pointed his body in that direction, returned to his back, and tore at the tape once again with his teeth. He scanned the wave tops for more dorsals as he worked. He was relieved to see none.

Finally, he ripped through the tape and freed his hands. Then he rolled and breaststroked easily through the swells. "Three down, one to go," he mumbled as he gained on the raft. Then he thought how viciously ironic it would be to have survived all this only to be cut in half within an arm's length of safety. He scouted the waves again, and this time his imagination projected dorsal fins everywhere. He quickened his strokes with the panic, then caught himself and returned to a slow, easy

movement. An hour later, he collapsed exhausted onto the teak
floorboard of the raft.

After several minutes of panting and thanksgiving, he rose
from the warmth of the sunbaked wood, then shivered for a few
minutes against the trade winds. He hadn't realized how cold he
had been. Indeed, he had never even thought of the Pacific
Ocean as a cold body of water. He supposed that was because of
the billboards advertising the South Pacific that had made such
an impression on him as a child. Every detail in the illustrations
had shouted of a warm sensuality. He would take away new images of the Pacific after this trip, he thought. That is, if he ever
got off the ocean alive.

He opened his eyes and saw the knife wedged between the
nylon fabric and the wood. It would not do to get this far only to
fuck up and puncture the raft. He curled his invisible fingers
around the hilt and drew the weapon toward him. "Four down
and one to go," he said, as he pointed the blade toward the
southeast.

CHAPTER
ELEVEN ─────────────────────

Marta Ryan walked unsteadily down the corridor of the Lihue airport and felt the oppression of the semi-tropical temperatures. A heat wave had pushed the thermometer to ninety-four degrees, and she was simply not prepared for it. Though D.C. was renowned for its sticky summers, Marta rarely ventured beyond the comfort of air-conditioning there. She felt a momentary wave of nausea sweep over her, and she wondered if it was just the humidity or the ill-effects of a hangover or both.

Offsetting the heat was the cool send-off she had received from the stewardess aboard the 757 upon her arrival in Honolulu fifty-eight minutes before. The young girl had flashed her a frozen smile, mumbled some inanity about a nice flight, and mouthed the word "bitch" just as she stepped off the plane. *Children*, Marta thought, *they take themselves so seriously.*

She was jostled by sweaty tourists in leis as she drifted down the crowded concourse and looked for a sign that announced the presence of a ladies' room. She searched above the straw hats and bald spots, but found nothing to indicate that she might be afforded the privilege of throwing up in semi-private. Finally, she noticed an empty boarding area and stepped around the velvet rope that cordoned it off. She found a chair next to a wastebasket and slumped into the seat. She could use some sleep, and vowed to nap as soon as she checked into the hotel and reported to Maggie. Then, just above the din, she heard her name announced over the airport paging system. She cocked an ear in the general direction of the sound and listened more intently.

". . . Ryan, please report to the white courtesy phone in the terminal lobby. Ms. Marta Ryan, you have a call on the white courtesy phone. . . ." *Terrific*, she thought, imagining the call must be from Maggie. Perhaps she had some sort of lead. *There goes my nap.* She collected her purse and merged with the traffic in the corridor.

When she finally found the phone and announced herself to the operator, the woman replied that the party had hung up. She returned the phone to the cradle, engaged a porter wearing an *Aloha* shirt to retrieve her luggage, and stepped outside to hail a cab. It was like walking into a blast furnace. She found a bench shaded by an overhang near the main exit and waited for her bags. *Maybe I can grab that nap after all*, she thought, exhausted.

A taxi pulled up to the curb directly in front of Marta at the baggage claim area, cutting in front of a long line of other cabs. A young Hawaiian jumped out from the driver's side and approached Marta. "Taxi, miss?" he asked politely. From the looks of his face, Marta guessed he had just been in some sort of scrape. It was a good face, pure Polynesian, and she was flattered that he had used "miss" as a form of address instead of that awful "ma'am," which made her sound so old.

"Yes, I would," she answered, and started to rise. Then several drivers from the other cabs approached.

"Hey, *puka* head, wha' da madda wid you? We in da taxi line heah," one of them said.

The porter arrived with her bags, and Marta motioned for him to load them into the young man's cab. After all, she liked people with initiative. She tipped the skycap and got into the car. "Sorry, boys," she said to the other cabbies. "I don't have time to quibble."

The young Hawaiian hopped behind the wheel. "Where to, miss?"

Marta gave him the name of her hotel, and the cab bolted into the late morning traffic.

After several minutes of travel, the traffic thinned, and the ride became more enjoyable. The fresh air blowing through the open window revived Marta and she no longer felt nauseous. The other symptoms of her hangover dissipated as well.

They had left the town now and were driving along the coast. Marta admired the view of the ocean and drank in the redolence of the vast array of flora for which Kauai was famous. She leaned back and, for the first time in days, actually relaxed. Just before she closed her eyes she noticed a sign which read, "Hanalei, 28 miles."

She was almost asleep when a large white stepvan roared past and cut sharply in front of the taxi. The driver slammed on his brakes, and Marta pitched forward. She braced herself with her arms against the seat back and cursed the driver for spoiling her perfect mood. The young Hawaiian just pointed at the stepvan and said nothing.

Less than a mile further on, the stepvan pulled off the highway, and the taxi followed. Marta was fully awake now and saw that something was wrong. "What are you doing, driver?" Again the Hawaiian said nothing and continued to drive. The two vehicles meandered up a one-lane dirt road for a few hundred meters, just far enough to get out of sight of the main road. Then they stopped.

"What the hell is going on, here?" Marta said. Before the driver could turn around to answer, both front doors of the stepvan flew open. Two men leapt out of the vehicle and approached the taxi. Then the back door rolled up, and Marta saw a young man standing in the bed of the van with an automatic weapon slung around his neck. "Oh, shit," she said.

The men approached the car, one on each side. Like the driver, they appeared to be pure Hawaiian. One leaned down to the driver's side window and stared at Marta. Then he turned to the driver. "Hey, Uli. She's not bad for an old broad, eh?"

For the first time, the driver turned around and looked at his passenger. "No," he said softly, and a hunger shone in his eyes. "Get her into the truck!"

The back right door opened, and a young man with a hypodermic needle leaned into the car. Marta slid along the seat away from him, only to encounter his comrade, who had opened the other door. Trapped between the two men, she could do nothing. The one on the right took Marta's arm, and gently rolled up her sleeve. He swathed a small portion of her skin with a ball of cold cotton and inserted the needle.

Marta understood that it was useless to struggle. Any resistance probably would have resulted in a botched job with the needle anyway. Besides, she knew that whatever they were injecting into her was not lethal. If they had wanted to kill her, they could have done it more easily with a bullet. And no one who is about to commit murder with a needle would go to the trouble of applying alcohol before the shot. She would live through this, she thought. All she had to do was ride it out.

She felt a slight prick when the needle entered her arm, then a more painful sting as the fluid rushed into her veins. The young man then rubbed the injection area with more alcohol. He offered her his hand, she took it, and he helped her out of the car. He was so gentle and polite that Marta was tempted to thank him.

The drug hit her when she stood. There was an initial jolt of euphoria followed by a delicious lethargy that crept through her system like a slow fire, and she partially collapsed. The young Hawaiian caught her and half carried her to the back of the truck. Then three men lifted her carefully into the vehicle.

The man with the machine pistol helped her up to the front behind the cab, where he deposited her on a large mattress stretched out on the metal floor. Then the taxi driver entered the van and lowered the door behind him. Everything went pitch dark.

Marta lay on the soiled mattress and fought her daze to understand what was happening to her. Her mind was so jammed with images and fantasies that she could only grasp the salient points of what she thought was her reality. She was in her own bed, in her own room, in the dark.

Then a shaft of light appeared, but she couldn't tell whether it shone in the room or only in her imagination. The light cut into her eyes. She felt the sensation of movement, as if her room was being transported. Then she imagined that someone was taking off her clothes.

Her dress suddenly disappeared from her body, then her slip was gone. Someone gently unclasped her bra and let it fall away. She could feel her nipples growing hard and pointed on the small mounds of her breasts. Someone carefully rolled down her stockings while someone else peeled her panties over her hips and slid them down her legs. The silky sensation aroused her, and she felt herself becoming moist.

She felt the touch of rough, calloused hands upon her. They were everywhere—on her face, her neck, her back, her breasts—hands everywhere. Strong fingers combed her hair, while still others parted her thighs. She opened her mouth and something long and hard filled it. Then she felt herself rise from the mattress, and turn over onto her knees as if she were straddling something that moved beneath her. She lowered herself onto a hot spike and threw back her head and moaned deeply.

More hands worked at her from the rear. They caressed and kneaded her buttocks, then roughly spread them apart. She felt another spike working its way up her back, and she cried out in a mixture of pain and pleasure until she was impaled on both.

For hours she imagined that she writhed between two dreams of flesh, peaking over and over again until she collapsed in a liquid heap of exhaustion. Then she slept, curled in a ball like a small child upon the stinking mattress, inhaling her own sweet shame with every breath.

She heard someone whimper. It was the unmistakable cry of a little girl calling out in the darkness. "Tommy!" the child's voice pleaded. "Tommy, where are you?" She jammed her fingers in her ears, but the voice continued. "Tommy," it cried. "Save me!"

CHAPTER
TWELVE ————————————

As he approached the north shore of Oahu, Moheb
Nazrullah hummed a melody he had learned while growing up
in the Afghan mountains. It was an appropriate tune, he
thought, considering how far he had come from that village. It
had once been his whole world, but now he thought of it as just
a primitive collection of stones and thatch. Besides, he now had
the entire globe to consider his own, thanks to Tom Rogers. The
computer disks would not only save him from his employer's
disfavor, but would actually catapult him into a position of pre-
eminence with the Bey. He patted his shirt pocket affectionately
and mumbled a prayer of thanksgiving to Allah.

He was disappointed that he would not have the American to
present to His Excellency. The Defender of Islam would have
loved that little show. After all, he was a man of wit who could
appreciate a presentation of the world's newest and perhaps
greatest weapon combined with a practical demonstration provided by the captured prototype himself. *What a spectacle that
would have made,* Moheb thought.

The American had long since been converted into shark
chum. It was too bad about Rogers, yet he had deserved his fate.

After all, he not only had insulted Moheb and the Bey, but Allah himself. And that was an affront no believer could tolerate.

Still, Moheb harbored a begrudging admiration for the American. He was perhaps the bravest man the Pashtun had ever met, and certainly one of the ablest. The fact that he had survived the experiment, then maintained the discipline, not only to accept his fate but to aggressively pursue the enemy as well, had been a remarkable exhibition of soldiering. One that commanded the Moslem's respect, if not fear. In truth, he was secretly glad Rogers was dead, because Moheb was not at all convinced he could have handled the invisible man.

Nazrullah checked his charts against the approaching coastline, and determined that the port of Haleiwa should appear beyond the promontory to starboard. He would refuel there and perhaps put up for the night before setting off for the Big Island. After all, what was the hurry? Rogers was dead. Kanina and the first mate had not betrayed him. If they had, he surmised, he already would have been killed or captured. Still he had to consider how long the Hawaiians could endure their interrogations. He decided to refuel, then be on his way, just to be safe.

Moheb guessed that he had under an hour before he would have to pilot the craft into the harbor. He decided to review the disks on the portable computer which served as an adjunct to the communications and navigational equipment. Besides, he needed to quell a fear that had periodically nagged him. What if, he shuddered, the disks did not contain the experiment's equations at all, but instead held the home version of *Wheel of Fortune*, or a similar inanity. Such a gaffe would fail to amuse the Bey.

Moheb set the automatic pilot, then retired below to use the computer. He uncased the laptop, inserted the nicad power pack, and carefully booted up the invisible disks. A fascinating array of mathematical symbols blazed in amber across the black screen. Nazrullah understood none of the equations, but that didn't matter. Above the cluster of numerals and Greek characters appeared the heading: "Project Dynamo." Then below: "Enhanced Magnetics—A Process for the Development of a Non-Fossil, Non-Nuclear Energy Source." That was all the Moslem needed to know.

He searched the cabin for blanks with which to copy the disks. Though the invisible originals were obviously easy to hide, they would be just as easy to lose. The only disks he could find were those containing the backup programming for the trawler's special navigational equipment, and he was reluctant to copy over those. He decided he would have to rely on the originals and take extra precautions to keep them secure.

Moheb checked the video display again, then started to eject the disk. Just as he reached for the button, he noticed a small flash at the top right-hand corner of the screen. At first he thought it was the cursor blinking, but then he saw an identical flash to the left. Carefully he pushed the button that controlled the cursor's movement, and the blink on the left scrolled downward. He returned the cursor to the top of the screen and repeated the operation. Curious, he thought. Although he was certainly no computer expert, he couldn't remember ever having seen a machine with two cursors. He decided the phenomenon must be some eccentricity intrinsic to the program, and ejected the disk. He would let the Bey's computer technicians unravel this mystery. His job was to deliver the goods. He carefully replaced the flat plastic rectangle in his right shirt pocket and buttoned the flap.

That movement subconsciously triggered his hand to move to his other breast pocket, from which he extracted a silver monogrammed cigarette case, a gift from the Bey upon Moheb's enlistment. There had once been a lighter to match, but he had lost that during his last mission, which had included an encounter with a beautiful agent under the employ of Chairman Yevgeny Maximov. She was now the proud possessor of his lighter, but she had been worth it.

He tapped the custom-made cigarette, an unfiltered cut of Turkish tobacco, upon the silver lid and struck a match. He was down to his last fifteen smokes and was forced to reduce his consumption. Since he wasn't quite sure when the mission would end, it was conceiveable that he might even run out. It would be a good time to quit. He closed the cover on the book of matches and smiled.

Waipio Valley Hotel, the cover read. Moheb noted with some irony that the printed matchbook was about the only amenity offered at that curious establishment. With five rooms, a single bath, and no restaurant, the hotel on the northern coast of the Big Island provided accommodations that barely surpassed those of camping. But the Moslem had found it charming and, best of all, isolated. The hotel and the surrounding valley held some sentimental value for him. It had been there that he had first met Uli Kanina and planned the mission. And it would be there that he would rendezvous with the seaplane for transport back to headquarters. He held the matchbook aloft in salute, then tucked it away along with his cigarette case in his left breast pocket.

Nazrullah returned on deck just as the trawler rounded the point which formed Oahu's Waialua Bay. He was glad it was summer because the waves were still manageable this time of year. During the winter, the surf of the famous North Shore stormed the bays along the coast with waves up to thirty feet tall. Sunset Beach and Waimea Bay, both famous for their suicidal surfers, were less than ten kilometers away.

He navigated the mouth of the Anahula Stream and slipped into the Haleiwa Harbor. The trawler blended in perfectly with the fleet moored in front of the old bridge that led to the pictur- esque fishing village. Moheb worked the throttles expertly, and the small trawler glided up to the fuel dock and stopped with a slight bump. Two dockhands leapt aboard to take the lines.

"Hey, there, young feller!"

Moheb froze for an instant at the wheel, then turned toward the dock. He saw a man in sea boots, jeans, T-shit, and captain's cap standing alongside the trawler. A medium-sized dog sat near the man's heel. "Looks like you had some trouble."

"Trouble?" Moheb asked.

"Yeah. Looks like somebody shot out your pilothouse." He tapped his pipe on a piling and stroked his white beard.

"Oh, that." Nazrullah smiled. "My last helmsman got drunk and put his fist through the glass. We had to tie him up. It ruined the trip, though. Had to put the crew ashore and head for repairs at Honolulu. Got any fuel?"

The man slipped his hand under his cap and, without taking it off, scratched his head. "Got all the diesel you can burn. If you got the funds, that is."

"Will cash do?" Moheb tried his best to affect an American accent.

"That'll do just fine, thank you." The man smiled. "Jump on down here, and I'll pour you a cup of the world's strongest cof- fee while the boys fix you right up."

Nazrullah looked around at the pilothouse. He had cleaned up the glass and blood during the crossing and had hidden the AK-47. He had also remembered to throw an old tarp over the satellite dish topside. There was nothing he could think of to do to disguise the mast, however. "Thanks, believe I will." He jumped to the dock.

He followed the man, who jabbered the full thirty-five meters to the harbormaster's shed, then preceded him into the small office. The dog circled a spot twice just outside the door and lay down. "Come on in, young feller," the man said, holding the door. "We don't get many foreigners up here."

Moheb stiffened. "I thought everyone in Hawaii was a foreigner."

"Just the opposite. Everyone in Hawaii is a native, regardless of what he looks like. Or better yet, what *she* looks like." He shot Moheb a sly wink as he poured the coffee. "I once knew a girl who claimed to be Eurasian. Actually, she was part Filipino, part Chinese, part Samoan, part German, and part Portagee—what I call a pure Hawaiian. Most beautiful bitch I ever saw." He offered Nazrullah a steaming cup. "What nationality are you, son?"

Moheb twitched and spilled some of the scalding liquid on his hand. "Shit!" He held the cup at arm's length while he did a little dance backwards. "Sorry about that, mister. Guess I wasn't looking at what I was doing."

"No problem," the man said, grabbing a mop from the corner. "That's what this is for." He gave the floor a quick slap, then turned to put the mop away. Over his shoulder he said, "What country did you say you were from?"

"I didn't, actually," Moheb explained, wiping his sleeve with his handkerchief, "but I'm an Israeli." There was no point in pretending that he had been born and raised in the United States, since the man had obviously picked up on his accent. Moheb guessed that all Middle Eastern speech patterns sounded alike to Westerners. "I grew up speaking Hebrew, though my parents were originally American."

"I see," the man said, but he didn't sound convinced.

Moheb sipped the hot brew and sighed. The coffee was strong and bitter. Suddenly, he was completely relaxed and even drowsy. Then he remembered he hadn't slept in over forty-eight hours.

"You look a little peaked, son. Have a seat over there." The man pointed to a chair beside an old rolltop desk. Moheb sat down. The Moslem watched as his host unlocked an oaken drawer and produced a pint of brandy, unscrewed the cap, and splashed some in the coffees. As the harbormaster put away the bottle, Moheb noticed that an automatic pistol disappeared along with the closed drawer. Then the man turned the key.

"Thank you." Moheb raised his cup. "By the way, my name is David Goldstein." He smiled as he extended his hand.

"Nice to know you, David. I'm Harvey Brubaker, the harbormaster around these parts." They shook hands, then each sipped at their mugs.

"That hits the spot," said Moheb, consciously leaning on the American cliches he had learned while training in Moscow.

"Yeah, it's pretty good stuff. V.S.O.P. The one vice I splurge on. I keep it around for when people go in the drink or I get depressed, whichever comes first." He took another pull. "So, how long you been fishing these parts?"

Here they come again, Nazrullah thought, *more questions from the prosecution.* He reminded himself that, though this Harvey person may have looked like a fool, he clearly didn't think like one. Moheb decided it would be best to stick as close to the truth as possible. "I'm not really a fisherman, Mr. Brubaker, though I'm pretty good with boats. The trawler belongs to a friend of mine who asked me to ferry it back to Honolulu. I am really just a glorified helmsman."

Brubaker deposited himself in an old swivel chair that matched the desk. "So, how did you get the bullet holes in the pilothouse?" he asked.

"One of the crew got drunk, like I said, only he didn't punch out the wheelhouse. Instead he shot it up with an automatic pistol." Moheb had expected the question, but not so soon nor so directly. Under the circumstances, he thought he was performing rather well. "The helmsman at the time was wounded, so they put in to Lihue at once. I flew over to bring the trawler back. None of the crew wanted to stay. They said something about a jinx." He shrugged his shoulders. "Go figure!"

"What about the mast?"

Moheb blanched. He had hoped somehow the man had not noticed that rather obvious detail. "The juicer also got a hold of an ax before we could subdue him. Crazy bastard." The Moslem gauged the man's eyes for a flicker of doubt, but found none. He sighed inwardly at the skillfulness of his own recovery.

The harbormaster smiled. "You'll pardon my questions, I hope, but part of my job is to check for stolen boats. You understand."

"Of course." Moheb nodded. He was secure in the knowledge that he had advanced Kanina the cash to purchase the boat.

"It's just routine," Brubaker continued. "Do you have the registration?"

"Oh board, yes," Nazrullah answered. "Would you like me to go get it?" He pulled out his silver case and tapped a cigarette on the lid.

"Not necessary. One of the boys will have the registration numbers on the fuel bill in here directly. Say, that's a dandy piece of work you got there, son. Can I have a look at that?" Brubaker reached for the case.

"Certainly," Moheb said, glad to change the subject.

"This looks like Spanish silver work to me. Is it?"

"Yes, I believed it is. My boss gave me that!"

"You must have done one helluva job." Brubaker turned the piece over and inspected the workmanship from every angle. Then he popped open the lid and gazed longingly at the Turkish cigarettes inside. "May I?" He pointed to the neat row of small white cylinders.

"Help yourself," Moheb said.

Brubaker selected one of the custom cigarettes and waved it back and forth under his nose like a connoisseur. "Got a light?"

"Of course." Nazrullah handed over his book of matches.

"Waipio, huh?" Brubaker remarked, looking at the matchbook. "I've never been down in there, though I was at the overlook once. A beautiful valley, isn't it?"

"Yes, it is." Moheb smiled. *And I'll be going there just as soon as you give me my fuel, you old fart!*

The harbormaster tapped the cigarette until a tiny recess formed at one end. Then he wiped his mouth, placed the cigarette between his pursed lips, and struck the match. He inhaled deeply, then sighed as he let out the smoke. "Ah, Christ, that's good. I'd forgotten how wonderful the taste of one of these goddamn things can be, and how much I missed it." He took another enormous drag and choked on the smoke.

"Are you all right?" Moheb stood and reached to pat the man on the back, but Brubaker waved him away.

"I'm okay." He coughed. "It's just been a long time since I had a real smoke. Turkish, aren't they?"

Moheb nodded.

"I've been on the pipe for more than twelve years now." He

made a face. "But nothing will ever beat the taste of a good cigarette. Too bad one of their side effects is death."

Nazrullah chuckled as the man took another draw though he was still coughing. Then, afraid that the conversation would die and Brubaker would return to the subject of the trawler, the Moslem looked about the small office for something—anything—to talk about. His eye fell upon a machete that was ceremonially mounted on a wooden plaque hung on the wall. "What is that?" He pointed.

"That?" Brubaker exhaled. "Oh, that's my old cane knife. I started earning a living with that thing over thirty years ago, right after I came back from Vietnam. I couldn't stomach going back to the mainland so I settled here, and cuttin' cane was a good way for me to work out my frustrations and make a little money at the same time. I eventually moved on to the mill up the road in Waialua until I retired to this job a year ago. Would you like to take a look at it?"

"I certainly would," Moheb said, happy to keep the man talking.

Brubaker rose and very carefully removed the machete from its mount. He offered it to Nazrullah with both hands, as if he were surrendering. "Here you go."

Nazrullah took the old knife and inspected it with the eyes of a soldier. The weapon's parkerized, carbon steel blade, once finished black, had long since turned silver with use. He noticed the barely discernible letters "Ontario Knife Company" stamped into the eighteen-inch blade and knew instantly the weapon had been a G.I. issue. The handle had been modified with a saberlike hand guard for cane cutting, he guessed, but his instincts told him it also had been used for other, more deadly work. "It's a beauty," he said. "But you didn't get this from the sugar company, did you?"

"You got a sharp eye, young feller." Brubaker smiled. "I liberated that from the U.S. Army about the time you were born. It saved my ass more than once in the jungle, so you might say I became sentimentally attached to it."

"You changed the handle after you began in the cane fields?"

"No, actually before. But the saber grip worked perfect in the fields so I kept it."

Moheb could only conjecture what sort of wartime work would necessitate such a modification. He concluded that this harbormaster, although about sixty, had seen some bloody days in his youth and perhaps should be regarded with more caution. Moheb decided he would contrive an excuse to hang onto the machete as long as possible.

The door flew open, and the dog that had been lying outside burst into the room, followed by an oafish dockhand. "Uh, oh," the man said at letting the dog in. "Sorry about that, Boss."

"Hey, old girl." Brubaker waved off the apology and lovingly cradled the animal's head in his big hands. The black and white dog beamed and twitched about in a combination of affection and anticipation.

The dockhand waited for the familiar ritual to run its course, then handed Brubaker the invoice for the trawler's fuel.

"Thanks, Jake. That'll do for now. Take Bonnie with you, okay?"

The dockhand grinned moronically and walked outside, patting his thigh to summon the dog. Bonnie looked at Brubaker, who pointed toward the opening, and reluctantly padded through the door.

"Okay, let's check the damage," Brubaker remarked dryly as he tallied up the bill. He handed the results to Moheb, then swiveled over to the wall and took down a clipboard that hung there on a nail. With his index finger he traced a column down the page until he came to an item that captured his attention. "Could I see that bill for a minute?" he asked.

As he handed over the paper, Moheb thought he detected a twinge of consternation ripple across Brubaker's face. An alarm went off in the Moslem's head.

"It says here that your boat has been stolen, Mr. Goldstein." He looked at Moheb with expressionless eyes.

Nazrullah's look of shock was genuine. He had given Kanina over a million dollars to purchase weapons and equipment, including a boat. He could only conclude that the little bastard had stolen the trawler and pocketed the cash. He might have preached revolution and independence, Moheb thought, but Uli was just a common thief. "There must be some sort of mistake!" he protested.

"Probably so," Brubaker said. "But your registration numbers appear on this hot sheet." He raised the clipboard. "I'm sure you can get it all straightened out with the Coast Guard."

"Coast Guard!"

"That's right. All marine theft reports are handled by the

Coast Guard. I'll just give them a buzz, and they can be up here in the morning. You did plan to stay the night, didn't you?"

Moheb had been aggravated often during his career. He had even been frightened and confused on occasion. This was the first time he had ever been completely flustered, and it showed in his face.

"Are you all right, Mr. Goldstein?" Brubaker was getting suspicious now, and the Moslem thought he detected the man eyeing the phone.

"Pardon me? I'm sorry. I was just running through the schedule in my head," explained Nazrullah, regaining his composure. "I really need to be getting along. I want to make Honolulu before it gets too late. I'll just check with the Coast Guard when I get there."

Brubaker looked at him quizzically. "I'm afraid that's not possible. You won't be able to leave the harbor until the Coast Guard arrives and checks this out. It's the law."

Moheb appeared sad as he fingered the machete lying across his lap. He had tried to talk the harbormaster out of contacting the authorities, but he wouldn't listen. He was insistent on doing things by the book, and Nazrullah regretted that that attitude would certainly cost the man his life. The Moslem's eyes narrowed as his fingers slipped through the hand guard and tightened around the handle of the machete.

Brubaker saw the hand movement and lurched for the drawer. *Fool*, Moheb thought, *did you think you could unlock a drawer and draw a pistol in the time it takes to wield a blade?* He decided he had been overly cautious about the harbormaster and that the man was just what he appeared to be, a weak old fart who long ago had seen his best days. Moheb leapt to his feet and raised the machete above his head. *"Allah akhbar,"* he said quietly, and swung the blade.

At the last instant, Brubaker pushed himself away from the desk and rolled in the office chair across the room. The machete fell and cut the telephone receiver in half.

Nazrullah was stunned by the old man's quickness, and wondered if his previous perception of him had been correct. "You move well for a geriatric, my friend, but I move better," he sneered as he pulled the key from the drawer lock and dropped it into his left shirt pocket. He raised the machete again.

Brubaker was on his feet now, and stood behind the chair in the corner. He flicked his eyes back and forth between his at-

tacker and the door on the opposite side of the tiny office, and
realized there was no way he could make it. He looked around
frantically for something to use as a weapon. The mixture of
desperation and panic in his eyes told Moheb there would be no
surprises in that department either.

Nazrullah approached his prey, who looked like a mouse
wedged in a corner. He waved the blade to get the feel of its heft
and to judge the reactions of his quarry. The older man juked
and dodged with each move and continued to surprise the Moslem with his reflexes.

After one more feint, Moheb whirled the blade at Brubaker's
neck. The old soldier ducked under the swing, surprising
Nazrullah. Then he pushed the chair into Moheb's shins, dou-
bling him over in pain. Still the Moslem kept his feet. Brubaker
used the time to reach into the corner and grab the mop he had
stored there earlier. The harbormaster used the mop handle as a
staff and skillfully blocked the next blow, but the razor-edged
carbon steel hacked through the handle, and left Brubaker holding two short sticks.

Moheb was furious now. His shins stung from the chair, and
time was growing short. If he didn't dispatch this man immediately, he would risk detection from the dockhands. And the pro-
longed racket from the fight might even attract their attention.
He steeled himself for one final lunge.

Brubaker appeared to dash for the door. Nazrullah cut him
off. But the old soldier had used the move as a feint, and quickly
reversed his direction to scramble for the desk, whipping the
chair across the floor in the same motion. This time Nazrullah
avoided injury, but still got tangled up in the chair and lost a few
precious seconds. Finally, he freed himself and wheeled on his
victim.

Brubaker gained the desk and frantically tugged at the top
drawer. To Moheb's amazement, it slid open, and he saw the old
Colt Model 1911 glistening in the wooden tray. As if in slow
motion, he watched Brubaker's fingers grip the pistol just as he
raised the machete. Then he saw the harbormaster's other hand
snap back the receiver as his own weapon reached the top of its
arc. The .45 automatic seemed to swivel toward Moheb in a lingering pivot while he began his downward stroke. Then the
muzzle of the huge handgun gaped directly at him. He thought
he saw Brubaker's finger tighten around the trigger. At that very
instant the big blade flashed, and the old soldier's hand, with the

gun filling it, leapt across the room. Brubaker stood for a moment and just stared at his handless arm as the stump relentlessly pumped blood onto the floor. Then he lifted his eyes to Nazrullah. "The lock on the drawer doesn't work."

"So I noticed," the Moslem said.

"You'll never make it, you know." Brubaker's voice was calm.

Like a samurai, Moheb hoisted the machete with both hands above his right shoulder. "Then prepare a place for me in paradise," he said. And he swung the blade.

CHAPTER
THIRTEEN

Tom Rogers stirred slightly under the soft press of her lips. Then he felt her tongue as she smothered him with good-morning kisses. It was another example of the new pleasures that accompanied the affair with Marta. It had been her way to introduce him to at least one different and exciting discovery every day. The cumulative effect was a gentle new world of tenderness and affection. A world Tom had never known before.

His universe had always consisted of harsh things. The scorch of a hot gun barrel cooking off rounds, the surreal menace of tiger-striped faces slipping into the jungle, and the sweet pungency of cordite mixed with gore. And the night had signaled danger or sometimes sanctuary, but never gentleness or passion.

Sex, when time and safety permitted, had always come hard and raw in the backwater brothels of the Third World. It had never involved the exchange of compassion or love. All his life he had been locked away in a cave of ice, his emotions frozen there. Marta had thawed those feelings and allowed him to grow. She had awakened his heart to the possibility of love, and for the first time there was a chance for him to live like other men.

Not since he had been an adolescent had Tom considered living like ordinary people. He had lied about his age and joined the Army before completing high school. Right out of basic training he went for his wings, then zipped through the Ranger program. The day he qualified for Special Forces, Tom got drunk and put three M.P.'s in the orthopedic ward of the base infirmary. It was his way of celebrating. Besides, they had misjudged his five-eight, 175-pound frame, and the young fireplug had simply defended himself according to his training.

He was a few pounds heavier now, sixteen years later, and his sandy hair was thinning in front, but the knowledge earned during those years had more than made up for any physical sharpness sacrificed to time. After all, he had prowled the rain forests of Cambodia and Latin America, endured the desolation of Iran, and even parachuted into Russia, but that information was classified. His innate right stuff had been honed by years of the real thing. His expertise as a cadreman had brought him to the attention of Major Crenna, the mastermind of the Guardian Program. Tom had been selected for his uncanny ability to live off his own resourcefulness and for his knack for getting along with people. His blend of skills had provided the perfect ingredient to balance the rest of the Guardian team.

That seemed a lifetime ago, back when he had a countenance. Now he was just a shapeless ghost, locked in a living death, wisping about like the wind. Still, there was always Marta, and her love would give him form, and her kisses would restore him to the man he once was and make him, someday, the man he was meant to be.

He sighed deeply as her tongue drew him from his dreams and coaxed him tenderly into a new day of infinite possibilities. Then . . .

"What the fuck?" he shouted. His eyes snapped open to the whiskered face of a cat that stood over him licking his nose with a sandpaper tongue. "Shit!" Tom bolted upright and hurled the cat, which bounced and rolled, squalling across the cluttered deck. *Damn!* he thought, scratching his head.

"What's all that commotion, Bullwinkle?" Tom heard a female voice call. "Where are you, rascal cat?" He judged it was an older woman who shouted from behind him. "Jack!" the voice continued. "What's happening with that cat?"

But instead of an answer, Tom heard what he thought was the sound of someone wretching in a cave. He turned toward the noise and saw a body draped over the lip of a battered oil drum on the bow decks of some sort of trashed-out craft. The body heaved and contorted as it hacked up what Tom guessed had to be at least half a lung. Then the man unhinged himself out of the barrel and wiped the drool from the corner of his mouth with the front of what was once a white T-shirt. The mosaic of stains included the red of fresh blood mixed with lung fluid.

"Goddamnit, Jack! Answer me!" the old voice roared. "What's Bullwinkle up to?"

Tom turned toward the stern and saw an old woman, about eighty-something, planted firmly at the helm of the boat. A red bandana protected her head, and a pair of soiled overalls under a leather aviator's jacket covered the remainder of her emaciated body. Tom could judge little from her face, which was hidden behind an enormous pair of black sunglasses that wrapped around her head explorer-fashion.

"Jack!" the voice boomed. "Answer me!"

Rogers looked back toward the bow and saw the man from the barrel weave across the deck to where Tom sat.

"I don't know where the cat is and I don't know what happened to him, Miz Hazel," the man brayed. He hacked up on last piece of lung and spat the dark chunk over the side. Then, still shaking, he lit a cigarette. "Maybe the damn thing fell overboard."

"Bite your tongue, young man," the woman bellowed. "That cat's got more sense than to fall overboard. And certainly he's got more sense than you do."

Tom saw the cat spring onto a grease-stained crate and shake its head several times in rapid motion.

"Here he is, Miz Hazel," the man announced. "Looks like he took a tumble, but he's okay now."

"Thank God," Hazel said. "Come on over here, Bullwinkle. Let me have a look at you."

Tom noticed that the woman groped the air in a petting motion, and it occurred to him that she couldn't see a damn thing. *Jesus*, he thought, *I'm on a garbage scow crewed by a deranged cat and a lunger and piloted by a blind geriatric. Perfect!* Then it dawned on him that this unlikely trio had found him floating adrift and managed to fish him out of the ocean. He rolled his invisible eyes toward the sky and thought that perhaps there was a God after all.

"Hey, you, mister? Are you awake yet?" It was the man whispering to a spot a few feet away from Rogers.

"Are you talking to me?" Tom whispered back. *What the hell,* he thought, *why not fuck with the man's mind for a while.*

The dissipated face swiveled in Tom's direction. "You over there?"

"Where?" Tom said.

The bloodshot eyes shifted a few centimeters to his left. "Right where I'm looking now?"

"Close enough," Tom answered. He had already determined that this man called Jack was incapable of posing any kind of threat.

"Say, who are you anyway? And how come I can't see you?"

"Trust me," replied Tom, "you wouldn't believe me if I told you."

Jack leaned closer. "You are human, right?"

Tom thought about that for a moment. "That's a good question."

"What I mean is, you're not from another planet, are you?"

"Not originally." Though Tom was playing with the man, he was beginning to find his questions interesting in light of his current situation. "I was born in the United States, if that's what you mean."

Jack drew away. "Then they came down and got you?"

"Who?"

"You know." Jack leaned in again. "Them." He pointed to the sky.

"You mean . . ." Tom hummed the four major notes from the old film *Close Encounters of the Third Kind.*

"Yeah, yeah!" Jack bobbed his head enthusiastically. Then he became stark still and dropped his voice to a whisper. "What was it like?"

Tom figured what the hell. Besides, he wasn't quite sure himself what had happened, but if it was what he suspected, then it would all be classified by now anyway. So . . . "I was on top of a high mesa in Idaho, or Montana, or someplace when this giant spacecraft suddenly appeared hovering over me. Then a beam flashed from its belly and washed me in a blinding light that transported me into the bowels of the ship." He was mixing a little bit of *Close Encounters* with a tad of *Cocoon* now, but all he knew about extraterrestrials was what he saw in the movies. "And the next thing I knew I was floating on a raft in the middle of the ocean."

Jack listened intently, drinking in every word as if each was a story point in the explanation of the meaning of life. "I knew it!" he said finally. "I knew it would be just like that."

Evidently, Tom thought, this man had seen the same movies. "Now let me ask you a question," Tom said. "Where the hell am I?"

Jack scratched his head as if he weren't sure of the answer. Then, abruptly, he said, "You're in the Kauai Channel just off the North Shore of Oahu in the Hawaiian Islands."

"What day is it?"

"Oh, yeah." Jack got excited again. "You could have been picked up a lifetime ago. What you really want to know is what *year* it is."

Tom groaned inwardly. "The day will do for now." Jack gave him the day, date, year, and time, just to make certain. Tom was relieved to learn that he had been out for just a few hours.

"Jack!" came a screech from the stern. "What you doin' up there?"

"Uh, oh!" He snapped to attention. "The old goat is calling. Don't go away, I want to hear more." He jumped up and disappeared in the direction of the stern.

"Where could I possibly go?" Tom asked himself. He looked around at the mounds of trash and concluded that he was either on board a garbage scow or a junk shop heading toward Oahu. At least his intermediate destination was on the right course. Tom remembered from the charts aboard the trawler that Oahu had been the general direction in which Nazrullah had been heading when he cut Tom overboard. He had verified that conclusion later when he watched the trawler chug off toward the southeast as it left him bound and bobbing in the Pacific. "I'm going to get that son of a bitch," he vowed out loud.

"Who?" Jack suddenly appeared over his shoulder.

"Oh, no one special," Tom said, "just someone I'm going to kill."

"I see." Jack blanched. "Anyone I know?" He was caught up in the intrigue now.

"I doubt it," answered Tom, "unless you happen to know a raghead who pilots a fishing trawler."

Jack's brow wrinkled in thought. "Can't say that I do. What do you want him for?"

"It's personal." Rogers's tone was cold and flat. "What did the old woman want?" he asked, changing the subject.

"Oh, she just wanted to make sure we were on the right course. We're due in at Haleiwa tonight."

Tom looked westward out to sea and saw the sun squatting on the horizon. The clouds had already turned a myriad of colors. "When do we get there?"

"Within the hour." Jack pointed in the opposite direction. "It's just beyond that point over there."

Tom followed Jack's finger and saw the landfall for the first time. He was surprised that the promontory loomed so large in the southeast and that he had failed to notice it before. But then, he remembered, he had been preoccupied with other visions at the time. His head had been so crammed with images of sharks and then thoughts of Marta when he came to that he hadn't even bothered to check the full circumference of the horizon. He shuddered once as his imagination flashed the picture of a giant tiger shark across his mind. He knew it had been mostly luck that had saved him from the monster. And it had been the kind of luck that he couldn't expect to see again, not in this lifetime. He forced the image from his head. "What's the story on the old woman?"

Jack shook his head. "She's a piece of work, ain't she?" Then he smiled. "She's my boss. We make the rounds on this tub stopping at each island to pick up trash or buy and sell junk. It ain't much, but it sure as hell beats gettin' a job."

"I can understand that," Tom said, thinking of the original allure of the Guardians' assignment.

"Of course, she couldn't see a mountain if she ran into one, and she can't hear thunder. Then too, she's meaner than a snake, but she picked me out of the gutter and gave me a place to live and something to do."

"I understand," Tom said sympathetically.

"Yeah, so anyway," Jack continued, "I'm sort of her eyes, when I ain't blind drunk, and her ears, when I stop coughing long enough to hear anything. It was me that spotted that yellow raft you was floatin' in. Hell, she'd a never seen it!"

"Glad you did," said Tom. "I'd hate to still be drifting out there."

"Yeah, and you're damn lucky the sharks didn't get you."

Tom winced. "Tell me about it."

"She don't even know you're on board."

"What?"

"That's a true fact," Jack stated. "I never told her."

Tom looked toward the stern. The old woman was blithely tugging away at the helm with absolutely no idea where she was steering.

"How about a nip?" Jack proffered a grimy half-pint with the words "Early Times" elaborately printed on the label. "It's the real stuff. E.T.! Appropriate, don't you think?" His grin showed a line of green teeth.

"What?" Tom was still fixed on the fact that they were sailing with a blind pilot, and had momentarily forgotten his earlier scenario of extraterrestrial bullshit. "Oh, yeah." Then, with difficulty, he reached for the bourbon. He was beginning to understand that hand-eye coordination required first a visible hand.

Jack fired up a Camel, then watched amazed as the bottle floated out of his grasp. "What did they do to you?"

"Huh?" Tom asked, taking a swig of the fiery liquor.

"How come you're invisible?"

"I don't know," Tom lied, sort of. "They zapped me, I guess."

The bottle floated on a return arc to Jack. "Wow." He pulled on the flask. "Must've been that beam of light, huh?"

"Probably." Tom burped.

Suddenly the boat lurched to port. "We're getting close, Jack," Hazel shouted. "You'd better take over."

"How did she know that?" Tom asked.

"She heard the surf."

"I thought you said she couldn't hear thunder?"

"She can't," Jack said as he rose from his haunches. "But she can hear the surf." He staggered off toward the stern.

Not since the first day, just after the accident at the lab, had Tom been around so many people. The dock where Jack had moored the scow was thick with warm bodies, all milling about in a swarm of curiosity and confusion. Rogers surmised that this was not standard behavior for the inhabitants of a tiny fishing village. Clearly, something out of the ordinary had happened.

Tom took advantage of the rapidly falling darkness to skirt the crowd of fishermen, dockhands, surfers, and villagers, all of whom appeared to be pressing toward a small shack at the landward end of the wharf. But to avoid the throng that bottlenecked near the shed, Tom had to climb a stack of cargo that lined the dock's back edge. If anyone had bothered to look up, they would have noticed the canvas drop cloths that covered the crates shift under Rogers's tread.

He moved over the plain wooden crates like an invisible thief sneaking across rooftops until, eventually, he arrived at the end of the stack a few meters from the small building. He perched there for several moments to reconnoiter the situation, and strained to hear any conversation that might reveal the object of the hubbub below.

"When did it happen?" he heard someone ask.

"Just now," another answered. "Didn't you hear the shot?"

"Why, no, I was just passing when . . ."

Rogers had heard enough to know there had been violence and it had happened sometime today. Everything else he discounted until he could get a chance to look at the scene, which he presumed was behind the door to the small shed, in front of which a uniformed policeman stood guard.

He looked down and saw that, while the pile of crates was staggered in an irregular fashion on top, the end of the stack was as sheer as a glass wall. The drop was only a few meters to the ground, but there wasn't a square centimeter of space that was unoccupied.

Then the crowd began to undulate, like a wave, and a narrow lane appeared at its center as several men pushed their way through.

"Step aside," a man in shirtsleeves with a tie said. "Police. Out of the way, please. Let us through."

The movement opened a small clearing directly below Tom, and he made an instant decision to capitalize on the disruption. He dropped straight down and landed perfectly on the spot with a faint thud. His hand, however, brushed a shoulder in front of him, and its owner swiveled a half turn in reaction.

"Excuse me," Tom said quickly, and the man stopped in midturn and nodded, then looked back toward the group of policemen. Rogers rolled his eyes in relief, glad that the man hadn't turned completely around to address an empty space. Then he thought he might as well take advantage of the situation and try to learn as much as he could. "What's going on here?" he breathed into the back of the man's neck.

"Harbormaster's been murdered," the man declared, tilting his head back slightly to reply.

"That's awful," Tom said. "What happened?"

The man's head tilted back again. "Don't know yet. The police won't let us in."

The small group of what appeared to be the local constabulary had wedged its way to a position even with Rogers, and their progress sent a ripple of displacement through the crowd that threatened to give him away. He decided he had better do something and do it quick. He moved toward the group. "Excuse me," he said with all the authority he could muster. "Pardon me, please. Police. Make way."

The people immediately to his right turned toward Tom's voice to see which way they should move, and flashed frowns of annoyance when they were unable to determine the source of the disturbance. Then, jostled by their neighbors, they grew downright testy.

"Hey, stop that," one woman complained.

"I didn't do anything," a man protested.

"Bullshit." She elbowed him hard in the ribs.

The man doubled over. "Fuck," he gasped.

Tom used the confusion to push his way past the people and fall in behind the cops, who were now almost to the shack. The guard opened the door as far as he could, and the group squeezed through the aperture. As he slipped in behind the rest, Rogers turned to see that he had cut a wake of bewilderment through the crowd.

Inside, he found himself in an even more precarious situation. Though he had judged from its exterior that the shed was small, he hadn't realized that it was tiny. Tom guessed the area was less than twenty-five square meters, and most of that was jammed with furniture, files, coiled ropes, and other articles of nautical equipment. The remaining space was occupied by four men who moved about at random. Two of the men, however, knelt over a body which lay almost in the center of the room. An ocean of blood saturated the floor and splattered the walls. A policeman moved out of Tom's view, and he saw that the corpse was headless.

Quietly and carefully, he took advantage of the others' preoccupation with the scene to crawl up on a file cabinet, and squatted there while the men went about their work. One opened a medical bag and, after waiting for another to snap some photographs, began his examination. Another drew an outline in chalk around the body.

"Check this out," one of the men said from a corner. Tom saw that he was kneeling over a severed hand which still clutched a Colt .45 automatic. "It's cocked and ready to fire."

"Jesus!" another said.

The man with the bag warned the others to be careful, that the reflexes might pull the trigger.

"Damn!" the kneeler muttered, and he backed away from the hand.

Then, in the leg space under the desk, the one in shirtsleeves probed tentatively at the head. At one point he choked, as if fighting off a wave of nausea, after which he back-crawled from under the desk, rose, and scurried to the door. He opened it and gulped deep draughts of air. Then, as if nothing had happened, the man closed the door and returned to his duties.

From his perch atop the file cabinet, Tom watched this gruesome scene in disbelief. He had surveyed the aftermath of scores of firefights in his life, but never before had he looked upon the scene of a single premeditated killing. Somehow he felt this was more malevolent.

"What about the murder weapon?" the one in shirtsleeves asked. Tom suspected from the man's necktie and bearing that he was in charge.

"Some sort of large knife or possibly a sword," the one with the bag said. Tom presumed he was a local doctor who doubled as a coroner.

Just then the door burst open and a large, stupid-looking man in work clothes was pushed into the room by two uniformed policemen. "I didn't do nothin'," he protested.

"What have we here?" said the man who wore the tie.

"We found him at the end of the jetty," one of the cops explained. "He had a dog with him."

"And this, Lieutenant!" The other cop raised his baton, which was inserted through the saber guard of a machete. "He had it in his hand." The policeman held the weapon so that it dangled in the light, and everyone saw that the long blade was stained with blood.

"Well, well," the lieutenant clucked. He carefully placed a handkerchief around the butt of the handle and, taking the machete, turned toward the one kneeling over the body. "Did you say something about a long knife, Doc?"

The coroner inspected the weapon. "That would do the job, all right," he confirmed.

"The A-rab did it!" the large man blurted.

Had Tom been an animal, his ears would have stood straight up.

The lieutenant turned. "What did you say?"

"That A-rab-lookin' fella on the trawler did it," the man repeated. "Me and Amoka fueled up his boat, then helped him cast off."

"He was alone?" the lieutenant asked.

"Yeah. Then I came in here and found Harvey just like he is now." He choked back a sob. "Oh, God! You don't think that *I* did this?"

"Where's the other dockworker?" the lieutenant asked the officers. Both men shrugged. He turned toward the suspect. "Where is this Amoka?"

"He was so freaked he just ran," the big man answered.

"Go find him," the lieutenant ordered, and the two uniforms disappeared through the door. "What's your name?" he asked the dockhand.

"Jake."

"Well, Jake, suppose you just have a seat and tell us all about it." The lieutenant reached for the swivel chair. "Are you boys through with this?"

The plainclothesmen nodded that they were, and he rolled the chair over to the suspect. The large man sat down.

Tom listened carefully as the man told his story, and within seconds Rogers had confirmed what he already knew. Moheb Nazrullah had committed this savagery. The color, name, and registration numbers of the trawler all matched. What he needed to know now was where the son of a bitch was headed.

"Which direction did this Arab go?" the lieutenant, reading Tom's mind, asked.

The large man lifted his head from his hands. "The trawler steered northwest out of the bay," he answered. "I watched it from the end of the jetty. That's where I found Bonnie."

"Bonnie?" the detective asked.

"Harvey's dog. She's dead."

"Dead?"

"Shot."

"Jesus Christ," the lieutenant exclaimed. "What's going on here?"

Tom wanted to tell the policeman that he was dealing with a

sociopathic fanatic who was even now in possession of top secret material crucial to the security of the United States. But . . .

"You said he was headed northwesterly," the detective repeated. He turned to the others. "Kauai, then." His colleagues
nodded their agreement.

Bullshit, Rogers thought. Nazrullah had come from Kauai, or
the same general direction, and was unlikely to double back into
the path of his own pursuers. He tried to visualize a chart in his
mind's eye and imagine Nazrullah's destination. But unless it
was a feint, a northwesterly course would take the Pashtun back
to Niihau or Kauai. Tom concluded that his enemy was aware of
witnesses on shore who could reveal his direction, and so had
chosen his departure course as a ruse. He was sure Moheb
would change his bearing once out to sea. But to where?

He had to somehow determine Nazrullah's destination. And
to do that, he either would have to stay put and hope to overhear
something that the cops might discover, or climb down off his
roost and hunt up some information on his own. He thought
about it for a while and decided he'd better stay put, at least until the one-room office thinned out. The last thing he needed
was to be discovered, or worse, captured.

The lieutenant looked around. "You fellas about through?"

"Yes, sir," one of the plainclothesmen answered.

"Almost," the other added. "I'll be finished fingerprinting
this last section in just a few minutes." Then he turned toward
the file cabinet upon which Tom sat.

Shit! Rogers freaked. He looked around desperately for a
way to escape. The policemen covered all four points on the
compass in the tiny room. Then the one who had finished his
work suddenly opened the door and walked outside. This created some evasion space, but did nothing about the cop who
was preparing to fingerprint Tom's lap. The man held his kit in
both hands, like an offering, and looked directly into Rogers's
face as he approached the cabinet. Then he abruptly stopped
and turned to his boss.

"Should I print this?"

"What?" the lieutenant asked.

"This file cabinet?"

"I can't think of a reason why not."

"Well, it's just that the crime doesn't look like a robbery," he
conjectured, "so why dust the files?"

"We don't know what the hell this is yet," the lieutenant explained, "so dust everything."

The young officer shrugged his acceptance, turned, and set down his kit on top of the file cabinet.

Tom exhaled his relief as quietly as he could. He stood in the only portion of the room in which he could turn around without bumping into anybody. He had slipped off the cabinet during the exchange in which the lazy fingerprinter had tried to con his superior, then tiptoed to his present position in the opposite corner. During the maneuver, he had come within a few centimeters of brushing the plainclothesman with his legs. He counted himself lucky that the conversation had covered the slight rustle of his jumpsuit, and that he had missed any creaky boards in the floor while traversing the room. He just wished he could have chosen another corner in which to "hide."

He looked down and saw that he was straddling the victim's severed hand, which appeared quite natural gripping the government-issue automatic. Then he noticed something else, like a smudge, on the appendage's wrist just below the cleft. He leaned over and squinted through the half light until he was able to make out a tattoo, faded with age, of a Screaming Eagle, the insignia of the 101st Airborne. The man, Rogers suddenly realized, had been a "brother" who probably had stalked the jungles of Vietnam when Tom was in kindergarten.

Suddenly, Rogers felt himself trembling with rage. He thought of how that fucking Moslem had hacked to death a comrade-in-arms, a forefather of duty. Tom silently promised his fallen compatriot that he would avenge his murder by inflicting on the killer an end so terrible that Nazrullah would beseech Allah himself for the sweetness of a swift death.

"Wait a second," the doctor, still kneeling over the body, said. "What have we here?" He raised his hand and flashed a pack of matches.

"Let me see that." The lieutenant reached for the book. "Where did you find this?"

The coroner slid his glasses down his nose and peered over the rims. "It was clenched in his fist." Then he added quickly, "The one still attached to his arm."

"Hmmm, Waipio Valley Hotel?" the detective read from the matchbook. "That's on the Big Island, no?"

"Yes," the fingerprinter said as he carefully blew on the top of the file cabinet, then brushed the surface lightly. "But I thought he was headed for Kauai."

"Yeah, me too," the lieutenant added. "I suppose those matches could have been left by anyone, anytime. Lots of boats move through this harbor." He returned the book to the coroner, who dropped it in a clear plastic bag and sealed the top.

Rogers witnessed this exchange from his safe corner. He projected an imaginary map of the Hawaiian Islands in his mind's eye, and thought how easy it would be for Nazrullah to shift his course from the northwest to the southeast. Once he was out of sight of land, no one would notice.

"But why would he have them clenched in his fist?" the lieutenant mumbled to himself.

"What?" the coroner asked.

"The matches." The detective loosened his tie. "Why would he have them in his hand?"

"Maybe he was about to light a cigarette when he was attacked?" the doctor offered.

"He wasn't surprised, Doc. He had a cocked weapon in his other hand, for crissakes!"

"Not for long," the fingerprinter honked, then he doubled over with laughter. The other men in the room just looked at him, stone-faced.

"Are you thinking that maybe Harvey was trying to leave us a clue?" asked the coroner.

"Perhaps," the lieutenant suggested.

"Do you seriously think that anyone would have the presence of mind, not to mention the courage, to spend his last few seconds before his own beheading securing a clue to his killer?" The doctor was incredulous.

"Harvey was pretty tough," the lieutenant maintained.

"*Nobody's* that tough," insisted the doctor.

After a long pause, the detective turned toward the dockhand. "You're sure the trawler was headed northwesterly?"

"I'm positive!" Jake answered.

"What's left of the Coast Guard around here is stretched too thin to search in both directions," declared the lieutenant. "We'll go with Kauai."

In the same instant, Tom decided to go with the Big Island. If the Waipio Valley Hotel was on the island of Hawaii, then that was where he was headed. He knew enough about the 101st Airborne Division to know what kind of men it produced, and he felt certain that his dead confederate had indeed left a clue. Although that clue wasn't meant to determine *who* the murderer was, but rather *where* he was going. That clue, Tom thought, was meant for somebody just like *him*.

CHAPTER
FOURTEEN —————————————————————

Marta Ryan sprawled upon the bed and sighed sweetly. The soft groan began deep in her chest and worked its way gradually up her throat until it emerged as a contented purr. She stretched once, then slid across the sheets to press her naked hips against Tommy, who had worked his way to the other side of the bed. *He always ends up over there*, she thought. Then she rolled over and curled up against his strong, broad back and felt the reassurance of his taut muscles.

She had always felt supremely safe with Tom Rogers. Not that she wasn't a capable woman. If she was anything, Marta knew she was that. But even she needed the feel of a rugged man to give her a sense of security. And the simpler the man, the stronger the feeling of safety.

Tommy was a simple man, impeccably simple, as she often described him to her friends. In fact, his simplicity approached that of the pristine, an extreme that proved both his greatest strength and his most telling weakness. In the final analysis, Marta found Tom sweet, strong, and boring.

His simple strength was reassuring to her now. She massaged his back, and the muscles quivered under her touch. She raked his skin with her polished nails, and he growled like a tiger. She kissed the nape of his neck, then traced with her tongue the bumpy ridge of his spine down to its base. He shuddered, signaling that he could stand it no longer. Then he rolled over, encircled her in his powerful arms, and squeezed tightly. She felt as though he might crush her, and a part of her wished that he would. But he wouldn't hurt her, she knew. That was not Tommy's way. He would be gentle, sweet, and attentive.

He made love to her tenderly, as though she deserved such consideration. Softly he rode her, pushing her closer and closer to the edge of delirium. Suddenly, his pace quickened and turned inexplicably brutal. Astonished, Marta stiffened as he thrashed away at her like a beast using another for its own sadistic pleasure. His thrusts were no longer plunges designed for pleasure, but stabs that threatened to rip her apart.

She opened her eyes and watched transfixed as his face metamorphosed into that of a demon. His head became two. The heads grew separate bodies that jabbed at her from the front and back, hurting her with each ruthless thrust. When she could take the pain no longer, she cried out for him to stop, for him to become Tommy again, the man she had loved. "Tommy," she whimpered, "where are you?" She heard no reply. Instead, there was only the pain, mixed now with a cruel pleasure. "Tommy," she cried, "save me!"

Then she awakened. She sat straight up on the mattress and fought to control her breathing. She looked around and saw nothing but darkness. She cradled her head in her hands and felt a clammy wetness cloaking her skin. Then she realized that her entire body was bathed in sweat. The recognition made her shudder, and suddenly she felt cold. She groped about in search of a blanket but found none. Then she raised her knees and wrapped her arms around her shoulders, as if she were holding herself, and rocked back and forth upon the bare mattress.

Of course the whole thing was a dream, she decided. Then as if the conclusion had exhausted her, she flopped back down on the mattress. She rolled over and inhaled the fetid mixture of semen and sweat. The odor suddenly made her realize what had happened. The reality of it came rushing back and threatened to engulf her in a flood of horror and shame. She bolted from the sticky pad and struggled to stand. She felt the cold metal floor beneath her feet. She was not in her own room, and she had not just left her own bed. She backed up against the side of the van and recoiled from the cold sheet metal against her flesh. She suddenly grasped that she was in the back of a truck somewhere in the Hawaiian Islands, and she had just been an involuntary participant in a savage orgy. "My God," she gasped, "I've just been gang-raped!"

She slid along the wall until she reached a corner, where she huddled for a moment, hoping that somehow the movement would shake off the images. Then she heard voices that filtered through the thin metal, voices that rang in laughter and celebration and were accompanied by music.

She inched out of the corner and felt her way along the wall until she arrived at a section that was recessed slightly. She groped beyond the indentation until she felt a handle and realized it was attached to a sliding door. She didn't dare hope that it was unlocked, but she gripped the handle and tugged anyway. The door moved.

A blade of light shot through the crack to bisect the bed of the van. The vertical beam sliced the black floor, and Marta stared at the partially illuminated mattress like a soldier gaping in shock at a fresh battlefield. Laughter and music poured through the crack along with the light. The clamor of the revelry rocked her, and she imagined the voices were celebrating her own shame. Her hands flew to her ears, but she couldn't shut out the sound. She wanted to scream, but fought the impulse, realizing it would only bring them to her. Then she heard something that sounded familiar, a voice she had heard before. It rang above the others and filled her with a mixture of terror and humiliation.

It was the voice of the taxi driver, the young handsome one who had flattered her into his cab. His face seemed to fill the darkness before her. Suddenly she was consumed with rage. She trembled at the vision of that mocking sneer that slid across his beautiful face just before it twisted into an orgasmic contortion. At that instant she vowed to wipe that sneer off his face and out of her memory forever.

She saw a bit of her own clothing at the edge of the light, and scrambled for the pile. She located her dress, slip, and shoes but couldn't find her undergarments or stockings anywhere. She rushed to dress as if the cloth could somehow protect her, like armor.

With her shoes in her hand, Marta crept back toward the sliver of door and peered outside. It was nighttime, though she

couldn't tell whether it was early or late. She carefully slid open
the door a bit wider, and saw a large fire banked in an open pit.
There were several vehicles and a few shacks in the background. About a dozen people milled about the fire, over which
a pig slowly turned on a spit. The familiar strains of Hawaiian
slack-key music quavered through the air.

Marta tiptoed through the door and into the cab of the
stepvan. The flames from the open fire danced off the oversized
windshield, and she could see her reflection in the glass. She
was shocked by her own image. She looked like a surreal crea-
ture, wild and mangled. Her mascara streaked down her cheeks
like long black tears, her hair was frayed and matted, and the remainder of her makeup was smeared comically all over her
face. Suddenly she laughed to herself as she thought of one of
Tommy's favorite phrases. "Marta," she said, chuckling as quietly as she could, "you've definitely been rode hard and put up
wet!"

Again she tried a sliding door, this one on the passenger side
of the vehicle, knowing it would be locked. Again the door slid
easily along its track. Perhaps, she thought, she should consider
herself lucky that the Hawaiians were more interested in
fucking than in security. *They will be sorry for that,* she promised herself.

She sneaked through the door and peered about furtively for
any guards. She found none. She conjectured that the fools must
all be celebrating, but celebrating what? She walked along the
side of the van, using the vehicle as a shield against the firelight
on the other side. When she reached the back, the protected
point furthermost from the crowd, she peeked around the edge
and froze.

There, several meters away, a shadowy form leaned against a
tree. Marta strained to see more, and spotted something glisten
against the man's body. It was something oiled and metallic.
She finally recognized it as a machine pistol slung about his
shoulder.

She retreated around the corner and pressed her back up
against the truck. She realized she had to get that weapon. She
began to tremble at the prospect of violence, something for
which she had been trained years ago, but something she had
never really had to perform. Once she had been forced to work
over a particularly obnoxious suitor who had been unable to
take no for an answer. That had proved an easy enough task.

The martial arts techniques taught by the Company had allowed her to dispatch that fool in short order. But then, he hadn't had an automatic weapon.

She heard the music abruptly stop, and a pervasive silence engulfed the grove. A familiar voice echoed from near the fire.

"Brothers and sisters of Lono, thank you for rallying to my aid today, and thank you for this *luau*."

Marta recognized the voice as the same one she had heard earlier. The one that had sent a chill shivering up her spine. She peeked around the back of the stepvan.

"I have cause for celebration," she heard the cab driver, or whoever he was, say. "I am alive and free. But seven of our brave brothers will feast with the ancient gods of our homeland tonight. Let us honor them."

A somber chant accompanied by declarations of praise followed his remarks. Afterward, the group cheered. Just then the man with the weapon moved away from the tree, and Marta recognized him as the "polite one" who had helped her out of the cab and into the van at the outset of her nightmare. He let the machine pistol hang at his side while he clapped along with the others. Marta wondered why he even bothered with the pretense of guard duty since he wasn't paying the slightest bit of attention to his job. She concluded that this would help her with what she now had decided to do.

"We must prepare ourselves for the ordeal ahead," the driver continued. "We must intercept this Arab devil and take from him what he has come for. I overheard the *haoles* mention computer disks that controlled the experiment. I'm not sure what it all means, but I do know that it is powerful and important. We must have those disks. Do you understand?"

"We hear you, Uli," someone shouted.

"Whatever you say, man," another piped in.

Uli, Marta thought. *That's an odd name.* But she compared it to the face glowing in the firelight and decided the two matched. *Well, Uli, now I know the name of the man I am going to kill.*

"This Arab, Nazrullah he is called, thinks he's a big shot. He's really just a fool. We took his money and gave him a stolen boat that the *haoles* will already have on their list. And if the Coast Guard doesn't get this coward, then we will. Because, my brothers and sisters, we know where he is going."

"All right, Uli," a follower spouted. "Lay it down, baby."

"Where's he goin', man?" another asked.

"Waipio, can you believe that?" Kanina answered. "He's going to our sacred grounds on the Big Island!"

"All right!" cheered a woman.

"That dumb shit!" a man howled.

"Really," Uli responded. "He's headed right into the jaws of the shark—our jaws!"

A collective cry went up from the group.

"How do you know this, Kanina?" shouted the polite one, now at the edge of the umbrella formed by the overhanging branches.

"The same way I knew to steal the handcuff keys from that idiot general's body, and the same way I knew about the arrival of the *haole* slut! I keep my eyes and ears open, man!" He leaned forward as he bellowed, and the veins in his neck bulged.

Marta fumed, stiffening as if the word "slut" had been a bullet. She glanced over at the polite one, who retreated under the branches, shaking his head. *Good*, she thought.

"It was at Waipio that I first met the Arab. During that time I noticed how much he appreciated the beauty and isolation of the valley. I took it as good sign, that the spirits of the sacred place had touched this man from the East. Only now I realize the truth. He saw it as a perfect escape route, and by now, he will have arranged transportation. We must get there before he gets away."

"Why do we need the *wahini*?" a girl asked, and Marta thought she detected a hint of jealousy in the voice. She eased a bit further around the truck for a better look, minding the man under the tree as she moved.

"We must have something to bargain with in case the *haoles* find the Arab first."

"What makes you think they'll trade for the bitch?" the girl hissed, and Marta saw that she was particularly beautiful.

"Because she is one of them, and these three *haoles*, the ones who search for their comrade, are men of honor."

"Men of honor?" the girl scoffed.

"Yes," explained Uli. "I discovered they are part of a group called the Guardians, an elite unit formed to protect the *haole* President during the One-Day War. I also learned that they did not come here for the disks, but for one of their own who was in the laboratory during the raid. They search for him, not the disks. So you see, they do not share our heritage of sacrifice."

Marta could sense that Uli was almost finished. If she was going to act, then she had to act now while the people were focused on the speaker. She squinted toward the tree and saw that the guard was sitting with his back against the trunk. She smiled. This would make her task easier.

"And, people, listen up," Uli declared. "It is just possible that this Guardian, the one the others are seeking, is invisible!"

"What?" The group was incredulous.

The guard was resting his head against the tree now, and his eyes were closed. Marta gauged the distance she would have to cover and estimated it at twelve meters. She dug into her memory for the training, and guessed that it would take her four seconds to reach the launching point and another second to complete the maneuver.

"I know it sounds like something right out of the *Twilight Zone*," Uli admitted, "but that's what I heard!"

Marta lifted up one foot, then the other, and removed her shoes. The moderate-heeled pumps would not do for what she had in mind. She hiked up her dress about her waist and took a stance like a long-distance runner waiting for the gun.

"So we have liberated a floatplane," Kanina continued, "and will fly to Hawaii tomorrow . . ."

Marta took a deep breath and leaned forward. Her toes bit into the soft earth as she launched her approach.

". . . by sunset tomorrow, we will have the disks and . . ."

She emerged from behind the stepvan, and hit her full stride halfway across the open space that was fully illuminated by the light from the fire.

". . . and then we can claim revenge for our seven dead brothers . . ."

She could see the machine pistol now as she approached the edge of the shadow formed by the overhanging foliage. The weapon rested in the lap of the guard, who sat cross-legged against the tree trunk. His eyes were still closed.

". . . but we must get some rest. Tomorrow is an important day for the history of Hawaii . . ."

She was almost there now. Just a few meters away from the cover of the shadow.

"Hey, what's that?" someone yelled from the direction of the fire.

Marta had just broken the plane of the shadow when she heard the shout. She saw the eyes of the guard flash white with astonishment just a few meters before her. His reactions were quick. It took him only a split-second to reach for the weapon.

"What's going on over there?" Uli called toward the tree.

The guard had both hands on the machine pistol now, and was lifting it into position when Marta left the ground. She jumped and leaned backward slightly, letting her momentum carry her forward. She cocked her legs into a semi-tuck, then when she was within a meter of her target, unleashed them, sending her feet toward the polite one's chin.

"Hey, what the hell is . . .?"

Marta's feet struck the guard in the mouth, and the force of the blow snapped his head into the tree, crushing the back of his skull. Somewhere inside she was exhilarated by her own precision, but there was no time to celebrate. She could hear the people scrambling from the fire as she untangled the sling from the polite one's body and retrieved the weapon. "Sorry," she said, figuring she owed him at least that much courtesy.

A large man wearing no shirt and carrying a baseball bat ducked under the canopy of branches and approached the tree just as Marta twirled. His enormous belly hung over the waistband of his surfing trunks and jiggled with every step. He drew the bat over his head. "Hey, bitch, what the hell do you think you're . . ." But before he could finish, Marta had cocked the bolt, gripped the handle safety, and fired.

The tiny weapon stuttered, and a short burst popped the man's belly like a balloon full of blood. Marta gasped as he toppled over. It was the first time she had ever fired a weapon in anger, and she was unprepared for the grotesque splattering and vile stench that accompanies a gut shot.

She forced herself to recover within a few moments and, her discipline kicking in, remembered to examine the weapon. It was a Mini Uzi, the scaled-down 1981 Israeli Military Industries version of the world's most famous automatic. She checked the clip and noticed it held thirty-two rounds, the largest production clip available. She was glad of that because she remembered from her weapons training that the little monster had a firing rate of 1200 rounds per minute.

She returned to the guard's body and quickly searched his vest for extra ammunition. She fumbled through the pockets and found two clips taped together. *Perfect.* She also felt a set of automobile keys, and took those too. Now she was ready.

Marta walked calmly out from under the tree and immediately encountered a young man with a .357 magnum in his hand. She cut him a new belt just above his navel before he could even raise his weapon.

Another man, whom Marta thought she recognized, shot at her from across the fire with a shotgun. His nerves were unsteady, and he missed with the double-aught buckshot. A look of amazement flashed across his face as he pumped a new round into the chamber. He still couldn't believe he had missed even while a spray of 9mm fire from the Uzi raked his face.

"Not bad for an old broad, eh?" Marta said.

Two men suddenly appeared to her left, and instinct told Marta to roll. She hit the ground as a hail of automatic fire ripped the air above her. She regained her feet a few meters away and lashed the men with the last of her clip. It was enough to send both of them spinning to the ground, shrieking as they fell.

Marta speculated that she had dispatched all of the men except one, and that the women were not inclined to give her any trouble. So she allowed herself the luxury of one deep breath and a brief feeling of security as she changed clips. Then she set about to hunt down the speaker at the fire. The one they called Uli, the rapist!

Slowly she circled the pit, thinking he might be hugging the ground opposite for cover. The fire was banked high, the flames reached even higher, and the pig skewered on the spit hung still higher. He could be hiding there, she thought.

After circumventing the pit, Marta turned to face the perimeter beyond the fire. The dense undergrowth, foreboding and primeval, loomed in the darkness. The wind rippled through the foliage while firelight flashed shadows on the swaying fronds. There was movement everywhere.

"Whachu lookin' at, *wahini?*" The female voice, launched from across the fire, seemed to strike Marta in the back, and she froze. "There ain't nothin' out there but da trees."

From over her shoulder Marta heard the distinctive click of a handgun cocking. She glanced down and saw that she had forgotten to pull back the bolt on her own weapon after changing clips. "Shit," she sighed at her own stupidity. But then she thought of how lucky she had been up till then, and about how well her training, though rusty, had served her. Something was bound to happen, sooner or later, she thought.

"So, how do you like our Hawaiian boys, *haole* whore?"

Marta seethed under the sting of the girl's words, which conjured up nightmarish visions of humiliation and pain. Her rage built with each degrading image that flashed through her brain until her fury erupted in a volcanic impulse. Without even thinking she spun and cocked the Uzi all in one motion. She heard the metallic snap of the spring jacking a round into the barrel, then felt the webbing between her forefinger and thumb press against the handle safety. Her finger tightened around the trigger and squeezed as she came out of her spin.

The young girl was courageous but unprepared for Marta's move. Though she did manage to overcome her astonishment and get off a shot at the last instant, the round careened wildly off into the bush. The spray from the Uzi found its mark, and the girl reeled backwards, twitching and jerking to the ground.

Marta approached the body cautiously. She was shocked by the young woman's beauty, forever frozen now into a wide-eyed mask of oblivion. At first she felt a mixture of guilt and pity, but those two emotions finally gave way to the sweet solace of revenge. "Whore, huh?" she said.

The sounds of the night triggered Marta back to the reality of her own danger. She revolved in a slow circle to scout her immediate perimeter. The girl had surprised her, and Marta wanted to make sure that such a shock didn't reoccur. She completed her slow pirouette and saw no one. She was glad to be overtly unthreatened, yet she understood that it was always the hidden ones who posed the most danger.

She was disappointed that the man called Uli was nowhere around. In the worst way, she wanted this man on his knees, begging her for his life. Yet another part of her recognized that she was lucky to be standing. After all, she had counted coup on five men and one woman and was still breathing. Oddly, she was surprised that it was the lone female who had almost done her in. The girls back in D.C. would get a hoot out of that one, she thought with a smile. She forced herself to look at the bodies strewn about her and, with a mixture of exhilaration and horror, concluded she had done enough damage for one day. She decided to withdraw while the option was still available.

Marta carefully approached the stepvan, turning in all directions as she moved. She found her shoes, then produced the guard's car keys from her dress pocket and climbed into the cab.

She tried what looked like an ignition key, and the engine fired up. She had to scoot forward on the seat, stretch her legs, and point her toes to reach the foot pedals. She ground the gears until she found reverse. She switched on the headlights, eased out on the clutch, and the wide van jerked backward out of the grove.

Marta slammed into a few trees before she got the big box turned around and pointed down the one-lane dirt road toward what she hoped would be civilization. The beams from the headlamps strafed the rain forest.

She steered left around a curve and saw light flashing off the trees at the end of a long straight stretch. She hoped it came from traffic on an intersecting road, but she could not be sure. Exhausted, she no longer trusted her senses. She feared she was feeling some side effects from the drug that had been injected into her earlier. She could even be hallucinating for all she knew. Still, for the first time since her ordeal began, she dared to believe in the twin possibilities of security and comfort. She pressed hard on the accelerator.

Suddenly she felt something slip over her head and lace about her throat. At first she thought she was imagining things, and she wondered what sort of drug the Hawaiians had given her. Then she conjectured that stress and exhaustion had teamed up to play tricks on her. She had heard of such a response, though she had never experienced anything like it. She was amazed at how physically realistic the manifestation felt. It was as if someone had twisted a cord about her neck and was gradually pulling it taut, but she was so exhausted she could no longer tell.

Then she felt a strange sensation, like a hot breath on the back of her neck, and she looked in the rearview mirror. There, directly behind her, appeared the twisted reflection of the man called Uli grinning over her shoulder like a deranged barracuda. She looked directly into his cruel eyes and saw that his smile widened just before he jerked the cord.

Marta had no time to scream, though that is what the horror she felt dictated. She gasped as the cord pulled her head backward so that she was looking directly up into Uli's face. Her hands were locked on the wheel. She would not let go for fear the van would crash. Then she thought how stupid that reaction was. She was being choked to death by a crazy son of a bitch who had already raped her, and she was worried about the possibility of a car wreck.

As if she were someone else, Marta watched Uli's face contort into a chilling grimace just as he put all of his strength behind the cord. She could feel her windpipe collapsing under the force, and knew that she had to do something, anything, or die right then. At that moment, Uli bent down and kissed her full on the mouth. It was a kiss of humiliation, contempt, and cruelty. It was a kiss of death.

Marta's soul screamed out her indignation. She let go of the wheel, grabbed Uli by the hair, and pulled forward with all of her remaining strength. The movement put her foot within reach of the brake, and she stomped on the pedal as hard as she could. The nose of the van dipped as the front wheels locked, and the momentum of the vehicle continued forward. The motion pitched Uli over Marta's shoulder and launched him toward the windshield. The glass cracked when his head hit it, then shattered as his body tore through the jagged opening. Marta heard a shriek just before she struck the steering wheel.

She couldn't be sure whether she had been knocked unconscious or just momentarily dazed by the blow. She lifted her hand and felt the warm sticky blood trickling from her forehead. Then she looked forward and saw Kanina's feet hooked over the dashboard. She got out of the truck and walked around to its front. Kanina was draped over the vehicle's snout like some animal that had been lashed to the hood as a trophy. She looked into the face of the man who had raped her. His features were locked in an expression that registered fear, pain, and surrender. Blood gushed from a gaping wound under his chin, and Marta realized the broken windshield had slashed his throat. The remainder of his body was sliced in several areas, and the discharge from the wounds had turned the hood of the van crimson.

She was surprised by the emptiness she felt. There was no sense of triumph, no feeling of revenge fulfilled. There was just a pervasive numbness and the relief she felt that the terror was finally over.

She looked once more into the distorted face that hung limp over the hood. Then she turned and, like a zombie, took a step toward the lights that flashed off the treetops in the distance. One step followed another until Marta recognized that she was walking alone down a darkened road cut out of the jungle. She should have been afraid, but she was not. Instead, she felt a certain pride that accompanied a sense of professionalism. She smiled faintly at the irony of that, then her smile widened with each footstep she took down that desolate road.

CHAPTER
FIFTEEN

Lieutenant William McKay stared across the fuselage of the Black Hawk and smiled. He watched Lee Warren turn several shades of green as the scientist bumped along through the clouds in the UH-60A helicopter. McKay thought he saw Warren gulp as if he were fighting back a wave of nausea. *Poor Doc*, he thought, *he made it all the way to San Francisco, then had to fly back to Hawaii.* McKay shook his head. Only Doc would have had the bad luck to deduce that any data as important as Project Dynamo would surely have a backup security system, and probably one as high-tech as the experiment itself. So he'd stopped off at the Army's Research Command Center in the Presidio while Gentry and his crew refueled the C-130 in San Francisco. He'd flashed his White House credentials, and come back with a special receiver programmed to pick up a homing signal from the missing disks. The system was so secret that not even General Ritter knew about it, though McKay later learned that documents explaining its existence were in a safe in the general's laboratory office. They were to be opened in case of an emergency. Unfortunately, they were invisible.

Warren peered over the notebook computer attached to the

receiver and fought his motion sickness. McKay looked out the window of the giant helicopter. Off to the east, the Marine could make out the faint pink of the coming dawn, and to the southeast the black outline of the Kona Coast. He had no idea whether Rogers would be within a hundred miles of the Big Island, much less Kona, but it was the only lead he had. He just hoped it would bear out.

McKay glanced at Sam Sloan, who sprawled on a pile of duffles in the rear of the ship. He was reading a dog-eared paperback. Probably Shakespeare, McKay thought, though he couldn't see the title from where he sat. He appeared to be taking Tom's predicament lying down, so to speak, but McKay knew that Sam was just as worried as he and Casey. After all, they'd become Guardians at the same time, though their circumstances had been different.

Next to Tom, Sam was the coolest of the bunch, McKay reflected. As a lieutenant commander, the Annapolis graduate had piloted the U.S.S. *Winston-Salem* to safety after much of the bridge and most of the officer contingent had been blown away during a missile attack in the Gulf of Sidra. The fact that a mere gunnery officer had executed this maneuver while fighting off several air and torpedo attacks helped to make Sam a national hero, a commodity the Navy sorely needed. So the brass set up the Missouri native as a public relations mannequin, and paraded him about the United States on a glory tour—until he got bored. That was when he chucked the high life and joined the Guardians.

McKay turned toward the cockpit and grinned. He saw that Casey Wilson had managed once again to talk his way into the pilot's seat. McKay didn't know if Casey was licensed to fly rotary-wing aircraft, but he knew the California Kid could pilot anything.

After all, it had been Lieutenant Kenneth C. Wilson who, in one day over the Gulf of Aden, had scored five kills, to push his total to seven, two more than anyone since the Korean War. This made him the Air Force's top ace among those still flying and the scourge of anyone stupid enough to climb into a MiG 23 and take to the skies against him. After his heroics in the Middle East, Casey was rushed home, where he did the parade circuit, and like Sloan got bored and sought another adrenaline rush. The Guardians Project sounded like it just might be it.

The copter banked as it started its descent into Kailua-Kona, and McKay glanced over at Warren to see what new color his face would add to the spectrum. But instead, what he saw was the flush of recognition.

"I think we got something here," Warren said.

McKay twitched. "Like what?"

"Two syllables! That's a new record for you, isn't it Billy?"

"Like what, goddamnit?" McKay roared, and Warren suddenly got serious.

"Like a homing response on the computer," he said. "Whoever's got the disks has them plugged in right now." Warren paused for a moment to study the coordinates on the screen. "And they're just east of the Kohala Coast."

"Where the fuck is that?" McKay snapped.

Warren checked the computer. "That's on the north shore of Hawaii . . . near the Waipio Valley." He looked at the Marine.

McKay consulted his map of the Big Island. "That's just seventy klicks from here." He returned Warren's stare.

"Do you really think it could be Tom?"

"If you didn't think it was possible, then why did you come all the way back from Frisco with that damn contraption?" Then McKay added, "Besides, have we got any other choice?"

Warren just looked at him for a moment. Then he shrugged. "No."

"Casey?" McKay bellowed into the headset. "Turn this thing around. Doc'll give you the coordinates."

"Will do, Billy," Casey acknowledged, and he banked the copter into a wide sweeping turn that circled the village below.

Then all hell broke loose. Within the span of a tenth of a second, McKay was blinded by a white flash that erupted somewhere within the fuselage, went deaf in the aftermath of an interior thunderclap, and damn near choked to death on a cloud of white smoke that permeated the ship. "Fuck!" he shouted. "What happened?" But a wicked case of dizziness told him all he needed to know. The helicopter was spinning out of control. "Casey!" he shouted through the headset. "Talk to me, babe."

After a moment, which seemed like an eternity, McKay heard a strained voice through his earpiece. "Billy?" came the choked response. "We got hit, and I can't hold it!"

"Can't you *do* something?" McKay was hoping in one hand and shitting in the other.

"I've run out of altitude, airspeed, and ideas," Casey rasped. "Hang on, man. We're going down!"

McKay was afraid of that. He just hoped that Casey's wizardry at the controls might pull something out of nothing and save them. He wanted to motivate the boy wonder to perform some last-minute magic, but decided the kid was preoccupied at the moment, and the best thing to do would be to leave him alone. So the Marine hugged the wall, tightened the cinch of his seat belt, and prayed he wouldn't lose consciousness upon impact. That was, of course, providing the machine didn't explode in a ball of flame when it crashed. Then he closed his eyes to lessen the dizziness, and rode the wild horse as it spun toward the cliffs below.

The first light of morning brushed the sky pink as Moheb Nazrullah approached the mouth of a small stream that marked the entrance to his destination. The rivulet cut a magnificent valley out of the mile-high Kohala Mountains that formed the *pali* coast beginning ten kilometers inland. The lush gap, bounded by 2000-foot cliffs, was checkered with taro fields and irrigated by majestic waterfalls that plunged 1000 feet to the canyon floor. The valley looked even more splendid now, Nazrullah realized, than when he first had gazed upon it from the mountains at midday. That had been several weeks ago when he had arrived to organize the mission.

He took a deep breath and inhaled the aroma of guava, ginger, fern, and *noni* apples, all accented by the salty tang of the sea air. It was sublime, he thought. Then he imagined how wonderful it would be just to stay there, to give the disks to the Bey's pilot, then nonchalantly row back into the river to live peacefully in the soft embrace of the valley. And perhaps, someday, even to die there.

But Nazrullah knew that could never be. The decision had been made, the signal sent, and the plane was on its way. Even the radio operator had congratulated Moheb on his success and told him that the Bey would be ecstatic when he heard the news. Nazrullah understood full well that his whole future rested in his shirt pocket, and as long as the disks remained safely there, that future was boundless. Then, he reasoned, he could return to the valley anytime. Hell, he could buy the damn thing and live like a king there if he wanted. It was truly tempting, but the valley would have to wait. After all, there was a world to conquer.

Nazrullah eased back on the throttle and dropped the anchor just beyond the reef. He would float there for a while and make sure it was safe to go ashore. There was much to do beforehand and he had plenty of time. He judged it would take the seaplane approximately ten hours, including a refueling stop somewhere in the islands, to fly from the mainland. That would give him time to scuttle the trawler, get ashore, hide the dinghy, and even grab several hours of much-needed sleep. Before the work began, however, he would spend a few minutes to enjoy his last Hawaiian sunrise.

Moheb stood on the deck and gaped as the clouds changed colors until they eventually bleached out in the full force of the sun's transparent light. It was all over in a few minutes. Then he went below to make a final inspection before he abandoned the trawler.

In the saloon, Nazrullah surveyed the expensive machinery there and thought what a shame it would be to destroy it. But the navigational, communications, radar, and sonar equipment had all done its work and was no longer needed. With the information provided by the disks, the Bey would surely conquer Maximov and afterward the entire world. Then he would have all the equipment he needed. Besides, the Defender of Islam could already buy or commandeer just about anything he wanted.

Moheb hated to ditch the laptop computer, though. With a forty-megabyte hard disk, the tiny Compaq had the memory of a desktop model at a fraction of the size and weight. He set up the machine just to marvel at the clarity of its full-sized screen one more time.

Then, on a whim, he decided to insert the invisible disks, partly to revel in his own victory and partly to reassure himself that they still contained the experimental data. He booted up a disk, and sighed his relief when the familiar heading appeared over a mass of numbers and Greek symbols. He studied the amber characters again, drawing on his education to decipher the figures. He discovered that most of his boyhood Greek had been pushed out of his mind, replaced by more modern codes and procedures that pertained to infiltrating the enemy's strongholds and stealing his most valuable secrets. He was really no more than a highly trained thief, he admitted. But he took solace and more than a little pride in the knowledge that he was perhaps the best thief on the planet.

He finally gave up trying to understand any of what appeared before him and glanced to the right of the screen. There he saw that same curious blip, the second cursor he had noticed the first time he had reviewed the disks. It was still there, blinking relentlessly at the top right of the screen. Again he wrestled with its significance, but he was still unable to interpret its meaning. He rifled through the computer training still lodged in his brain, but could come up with nothing that explained the phenomenon. Finally, he gave up and thanked whatever pagan spirit watched over spies—he considered it a sacrilege to invoke the name of Allah, here—that the second cursor was not his problem. Still . . .

He ejected the disk and placed it, along with its twin, in a plastic zip-lock bag and carefully sealed the top. Then he put it back in his shirt pocket. Next, he climbed down into the hull and opened the bilge cocks. He scrambled back to the saloon as seawater gushed in below. Then he grabbed the canvas rucksack, which contained a shaving kit, his prayer rug, and a single change of clothes, and returned topside.

He inflated the spare two-man raft, extended the telescoping oars, and lowered the dinghy over the side. Then he took one last look and climbed down into the raft.

As he cast off, he glanced at the broken mast and thought of Brubaker back on Oahu. He regretted having to kill such a worthy adversary. Even more importantly, the old warrior had met his death with courage and dignity without even flinching. Moheb mumbled a brief prayer in homage to Brubaker, then leaned into the oars.

He heard the surf crashing over his shoulder, and watched the trawler slowly sink in his wake. After Brubaker it had been simple enough to get past the dockhands. The Polynesian had reeked of marijuana, and the Caucasian was clearly a moron. All Moheb had had to do was affect a blithe attitude while he folded up the fuel bill as if he were saving it for his records. Then he had snapped orders, as if he had been eager to cast off, and the two fools had leapt to his aid, getting the trawler away from the dock in record time.

The dog, however, had presented a more difficult obstacle. In fact, Moheb remembered, the canine had proved much more intelligent than either of the two humans. Bonnie, he suddenly recalled her name, had been a pesky sheltie collie who was bright enough to figure out what had happened to her master but not bright enough to leave well enough alone.

She had evidently followed the larger of the two idiot dockhands off somewhere before the fight had started, a fortuitous circumstance for which Moheb was grateful. Otherwise, he knew she would have raised a commotion, and he shuddered to think of the dog barking incessantly and clawing away at the door while he and Brubaker fought in the office. He knew that would have drawn the attention of the dockhands, and *that* would have presented problems. You didn't have to be smart to fight, and while both men were imbeciles, they were also large.

Actually, Moheb had forgotten about the dog during the struggle, and didn't remember her until she reappeared on the jetty while he was piloting the trawler out of the bay. She raised enough hell there that he was sure she had attracted attention to him. He remembered that she had actually followed the boat, leaping and barking along the entire length of the 800-foot breakwater. He assumed the dog had returned to the office after the fight, managed to get inside, and followed the scent of her master's killer to where the trawler had been moored. Then she'd stalked the boat out of the harbor and into the damn bay, all the while yelping and bounding along the jetty.

Finally, Nazrullah could stand it no longer. He retrieved the Kalashnikov from its hiding place in the saloon and, with one round, nailed the bitch in the head. Considering that the dog had been in constant motion, Nazrullah regarded that shot as among the best of his life.

The trawler was almost under now. Only the bow remained above the surface. Finally, that too disappeared, going down in a surge of bubbles and spume. Moheb watched this with the same reverence he would display at a funeral. The old girl had functioned well and deserved his respect.

His moment of veneration was short-lived. The roar of the surf crashing over the reef suddenly captured his full attention. He turned for a quick look, and saw the swells burgeoning into breakers that flashed white caps as they marched toward the shore. The little raft dipped into a trough, then climbed a wall of water that flung it over the submerged coral. Terrified, Moheb clutched his breast pocket as if that would somehow protect the disks from the seawater. He cursed himself for using the last of the tape to bind the American. He'd intended to buy more at Haleiwa and use it to tape over the zip-lock seal of the plastic baggie. But, well, there had been some distractions.

He hung onto the raft, praying it wouldn't tip over as it bucked its way toward the shore. Finally, the surf dissipated into

tiny waves that slapped at the sand, and Moheb was able to step
into knee-deep water. But an unexpected wave, larger than the
others, caught him off guard while he was dragging the raft up to
the beach and knocked him to his knees. He caught himself with
his hands, and sprang up just ahead of a following wave which
would have soaked his shirt, breast pocket and all. He scrambled
onto the beach relieved and horrified at the same time.

Moheb paused for a moment to catch his breath and regain his
composure. Then he looked around for an appropriate place to
hide the raft, and eventually chose a copse of coconut trees on
the edge of the rain forest. He covered the gray rubber dinghy
with just enough palm fronds and fern branches to hide it without building a pile so large that it would attract the attention of
some idle passerby. That done, Moheb shouldered the rucksack
and walked the few hundred meters to the mouth of the stream.
He sat on a small sand dune overlooking the confluence and
rested.

For the most part, his work was finished. All that remained
was to wait as unobtrusively as possible for the arrival of the
Bey's plane. He decided he would do that at the City of Refuge,
an ancient Hawaiian temple in the valley. An appropriate
choice, he thought, considering that the temple had served as a
sanctuary for transgressors throughout history. Perhaps, he
mused, that spirit of refuge would also protect him.

He pulled the plastic bag from his shirt pocket and smiled at
the unbroken seal. He replaced it, then automatically reached
into his other pocket and withdrew the silver cigarette case. He
opened the hinged lid and extracted one of the dozen cigarettes
that remained. Then he reached for his pack of matches. They
weren't there. He patted down the remainder of his pockets,
then dug into them. No matches. "Oh, well." He shrugged. He
returned the cigarette case to his pocket and reflected on how
mysteriously Allah worked his will. It was a good time to quit,
he decided.

Moheb took a towel-sized cloth from his rucksack and carefully placed it on the sand facing eastward. He would have to
pray many times to make up for the missed prayers of the last
few days. Though the success of his mission was assured, there
was no point in tempting the Almighty.

He leaned forward onto his face in the supplicating posture of
the *salat*, and recited the sacred *shadada*. But as he proclaimed
Allah to be the one true God and Muhammad his prophet, he

couldn't help but compare that relationship in heaven to the one he would soon enjoy with Iskander Bey on earth.

Billy McKay opened his eyes, then wondered why he had bothered. The interior of the Black Hawk was still a cloud of smoke, and he couldn't see Doc Warren, who'd sat just a few meters across from him before the crash.

McKay remembered the impact, or thought he did. It hadn't been as bad as he'd expected, though it had been bad enough. There had been the instant stop that threatened to compress every vertebra on board, but there had not been the shattering breakup or a fire. At least, not yet.

He unclasped his seat belt and scrambled to his feet. The first thing he noticed was that the ship was canted toward the rear. Walking to the cockpit was reminiscent of climbing the aisles of parked C-47's, still used as "Puff" gunships in some parts of the world. He waved through the smoke as he clambered up the passageway, stepping over bodies en route. Then the ship lurched backward a few degrees further, and McKay froze and hung on. *What the hell?* he wondered. The copter seemed to stabilize, so he proceeded up the aisle.

Through the smoke he saw Casey slumped over the controls in the cockpit. For an instant he was paralyzed where he stood, dazed by the thought that the kid might be dead. But he forced himself to push beyond the fear and investigate. He tilted the young man's head back and wiped the blood off his expressionless face. McKay sighed when he saw that Casey was still breathing. Then he got a good strong pulse from the pilot's wrist and felt even better. He slapped him a few times until the ace reluctantly came around.

"Jennifer, baby," Casey moaned.

"Stop that shit, boy." McKay grinned. "I ain't Jennifer!"

Casey opened one eye, then the other, and stared up into McKay's face. "You sure as hell ain't," he said. "What happened?"

"I was hoping you could tell me," McKay groaned.

Slowly, Casey leaned forward. "I can't see shit," he said as he flipped a toggle on the control panel. A fan whirled somewhere in the cockpit and gradually sucked most of the smoke out. Then sparks showered the two Guardians, and Casey shut down the ventilation exhaust. "Don't want a fire, since we've evidently been lucky enough to escape one so far."

"No shit!"

"So where are we anyway?" Casey rubbed his head.

"I'm not sure. Let's have a look." Both men fanned at the remaining smoke, then peered through the plexiglass canopy.

"Tell me I'm hallucinating," Casey pleaded.

"Well, if you are, then we're having the same hallucination," declared the big Marine. "And I ain't believin' it." They looked straight ahead and saw what appeared to be the top of a copra plantation. In order to see the ground they had to look about twenty meters straight down! Now McKay understood why the Black Hawk hadn't broken up or burst into flames. He also figured out why it was tilted and why it had shifted suddenly. The damn thing had landed in the tops of several palm trees growing close together. "Jesus Christ!" McKay swore. "We're sitting in a goddamn tree!"

"I'll take it over the alternative," Casey groaned as he struggled out of the pilot's seat. "How're the others?"

McKay suddenly realized he didn't know. He couldn't see anything before, and he had wanted to check on Casey first. It was the big-brother syndrome, he guessed. He helped Casey up, then they started down the aisle. Just then the ship moved again, this time to port.

"Damn!" Casey said. "I guess we need to walk softly and *not* carry a big stick."

"One of us should wait here," suggested McKay.

"You go, Billy. I'm still a little wobbly."

McKay advanced carefully at a downward angle through the fuselage, checking bodies as he went. The flight engineer was dead, and he couldn't find Lee Warren. He continued toward the back of the ship to look for Sam. "Yo, hillbilly?" he called. "You still with us?" Nothing. "Sam, you all right?"

"Arrrggh." An animal-like moan came from the rear of the helicopter.

"Sounds like Sloan to me," McKay said, and he traced the moaning to a pile of baggage. He tossed away duffles as if they were pillows until he uncovered his partner. "Exposed again, eh, Sam?"

"It took you long enough," Sloan grunted. "I could have suffocated under all this stuff."

"Quit your bitchin', damnit! I got you out, didn't I?"

"Finally."

McKay reserved the duffle that rested on Sloan's chest for last. "I wasn't real motivated to find you. I was afraid you'd be covered in excrement, like the last time." McKay was referring to the Alaskan crash-landing of the StarVan back in the spring. After that wreck, he had found Sam unconscious in the orbiter's latrine.

"I've explained to you already." Sam was indignant. "That was an aberration."

"Maybe," McKay said, "but it smelled like shit to me!" He reached down for Sloan's hand and pulled the Guardian to his feet.

"So what's the deal, Neal?" Sam grinned.

"Jesus, you've been hanging around Casey too damn long. You're beginning to talk like him."

Sam stretched and twisted his six-foot frame to work out the stiffness and check for minor injuries. "Yes, Billy, I'm fine." He smiled sarcastically. "A few cuts and bruises, but no serious injuries. Thanks so much for asking."

"You're welcome," McKay snorted. "And to answer your question, well, you'd better see for yourself. Somehow, I don't think you'd believe me."

With McKay coaching on the delicacy of the maneuver, they crept to the center of the ship.

"Damn!" Sloan glanced out of the flight window at the tree-tops. "You're right, Billy. I never would have believed you."

"You two had better come over here," Casey said. "I found Lee."

McKay, worried, followed the sound of Casey's voice through the remaining smoke, and found the pilot kneeling over a crumpled body on the floor. "What's up, Doc?"

Sam and Casey groaned in unison.

"Glad to see that tragedy hasn't blunted your sensitivity, jarhead." Warren smiled weakly.

"I remembered your low threshold of disappointment, Doc, and I didn't want to push it." McKay returned his smile. "So how you feeling?"

"Not too well." He winced. "I think my leg's broken."

Casey nodded at Warren's right leg, and McKay saw that the tibia was protruding through the skin. *Damn!* he thought. With his training he could have set a less critical break, but a severed bone required the skills of a surgeon or at the very least the team's medic. And that was Tom!

"Shit!" McKay said out loud, and motioned for Casey to fetch the copter's first-aid kit. If his memory served, it should

contain an inflatable splint, which at least would protect the
bone and keep the leg relatively stationary. And more importantly, it would contain a generous supply of morphine to get
Lee through the evacuation. That in itself, McKay shuddered,
would be a nightmare.

Casey returned with the kit, and Sam volunteered to handle
the medical chores while McKay and Wilson retired to confer
on their predicament.

First, the two men checked the equipment lockers adjacent to
the cargo door, and found all the necessary material they would
need to operate the exterior hoist. There was even a collapsible
litter for Warren along with some rappelling gear.

Next, they searched through the debris for what McKay referred to as their "saddle" weapons. Under a seat he found his
Remington 1100 shotgun, which complimented the .45 automatic on his hip. He was sorry he hadn't brought the M60, but
escorting a body back from the islands was hardly the type of
mission on which he'd thought such power would be necessary.
He decided to let that be a lesson to him. From now on, he
vowed, he would take the .50-caliber to bed.

Casey's Ingram materialized behind the copilot in the cockpit, and they found Sam's Galil near its owner. Casey also discovered a .50-caliber machine gun in the weapons locker along
with several belt-drums of ammo and a box of grenades. He positioned the .50 on a special mount near the door, 'Nam-style,
and divvied up the grenades.

Then they set about to rig the litter onto the hoist while Sam
finished inflating the splint. Warren was out on two shots of
morphine.

"So what was it?" McKay talked while he worked. "An RPG
or what?"

"I'm not sure what the hell it was, Billy. I remember seeing a
contrail, though, and I banked sharply away from it. Whatever it
was, it blew the rotor right off the tail."

"A contrail, you say? Could it have been a missile?" McKay
asked.

"A missile?" Casey looked askance.

"Like a shoulder-mounted job. You know, a Stinger,
maybe?"

"Well, yeah, now that you mention it," Casey said. "It could
have been been a Stinger. But who would want to use one of
those on us?"

McKay continued to assemble the litter while he talked. "Maybe it wasn't us they were after. Maybe they thought it was someone else."

"Like who?"

"Well, the Army, I suppose," McKay conjectured. "The ship has Army markings, after all."

"Okay, I'll buy that," said Casey. "But since when is it open season on the Army?"

"Since the One-Day War. Where've you been, boy? Everybody hates the Army nowadays. We're the ones who blew up the world, remember. Besides, in Hawaii, they don't really need a reason," McKay explained. "It could be the Koreans who want to keep the skies clear for their drug shipments, or the Japanese who are trying to take over, or the Chinese who are thinking about taking over. Or maybe it's the Samoans who just want to kick some ass for the fun of it. I think it's the Samoans."

"Fifty bucks says it's the Koreans," Casey shot back.

"You're on, asshole." They shook on it.

"Yeah, well whoever it is," Casey said, "we'd better get out of here before they regroup and come looking for us. We spun out at an angle and landed a few kilometers away from where they fired at us. So that should have bought us some time, but not much."

"Maybe they think we're dead," offered McKay.

"I doubt it. There was no explosion."

"Yeah, you're right. We'd better hump it," McKay said. He finished assembling the litter, and all three Guardians carefully lifted the patient onto the rig. Then Casey engaged the auxiliary power and tested the hoist. It worked, though Wilson wasn't sure for how long. He lowered the cable, and McKay hooked it up to the harness. Then they all swung Warren outside of the fuselage. The helicopter didn't shift, so McKay gave the order to lower away.

Sam climbed onto the cable above the litter. Carefully, Casey worked the controls, and the hoist slowly began its descent.

Then it happened. Gunfire suddenly erupted from the jungle below and started hacking away at the canopy like an invisible chain saw. Casey immediately cut the power to the hoist.

"Perfect," McKay spat and lurched for his shotgun. "Casey, crank up that fifty. Our friends are back."

Casey rushed to thread an ammo belt into the machine gun. "Hook me up, Billy!" he barked.

McKay fired off a few double-aughts blind into the bush just to let the attackers know they weren't going to get to fuck around for free. Then he attached the snap-hooks of the gunning harness to the D-rings on the side of the special web belt already cinched around Casey's waist. "Let her rip, kiddo!" He backed away from the door.

Casey snapped back, then released the retracting handle and pressed the thumb trigger. The heavy-barreled Browning thundered in the doorway, spitting .50-caliber rounds at 500 per minute. They chopped at the foliage like a giant weed-eater on acid.

"Christ!" Sloan shouted. He was still hanging onto the cable a few feet to Casey's left. He looked down at Warren, who dangled in the litter just below and dangerously close to Casey's line of fire. "How about bringing us in," he shouted.

"Be with you in a minute," Casey yelled, as he hammered away at the ground.

"Heads up, Sam." McKay pitched over Casey's MAC-10. "Thought you might be feeling a little *nekkid* out there."

Sam one-handed the seven-and-a-half-pound weapon in mid-air and grinned his thanks. He wedged the submachine gun against the hoist cable to cock it, then held it like a pistol while he spewed out several short bursts at the ground. Though he wanted to get back in the ship, he knew there was no way they could stop firing long enough to get the litter aboard. They couldn't leave Doc out there alone. So he was stuck and he knew it.

McKay thumped away at the unseen enemy with his 12-gauge, and suddenly gained a renewed appreciation for his semi-permanent earplugs. In an odd moment of detachment, he noticed that he was surrounded by a hurricane of noise. Casey's .50 roared to his left, Sam's Ingram burped outside, and his own Remington pounded his hearing relentlessly. It was a miracle, after all his years as a soldier, that he could still hear at all. This reminded him to switch on his communications set just in case he needed to bitch at the boys. "Everybody plugged in?" he said, testing the system. Casey and Sam each responded that they were. Good, McKay thought. Everything was working okay. All that remained was to whip those bastards and go get Tom.

Then it happened. The ship moved a few degrees aft.

"Oh, shit," he heard Casey squawk through the earpiece. Then it shifted again, to port.

"I don't like this," Sam groaned. "We'd better do something, Billy."

McKay knew it had been too good to be true. The equipment was working fine, they had plenty of ammo, and they definitely held the high ground. What else could they possibly ask for? Well, that their platform didn't give way beneath them. It was time to make a move. Casey and Sam looked at the Marine like he was supposed to come up with something. *Well*, McKay thought, *that shit comes with the territory*. Then the copter shifted again. "Okay, that does it, boys. Let's get the hell out of here," he snapped.

"How?" Casey asked.

"Where?" Sam echoed.

"Rappel! Down!" McKay answered each question in turn. "What else you got in mind?"

"But . . . but . . . those guys are down there, Billy, and they're *shooting* at us!" Casey informed him.

"Fuck 'em," McKay roared. "We got no future up here." And as if to punctuate the obvious, the Black Hawk shifted again. "So here's what we're gonna do. First, Casey's going to get into a rappelling harness—now! Second, we're going to lower the hoist. Third, when I give the word, we're going to pop the pins on as many grenades as we can and drop 'em over the side. Fourth, Casey and I'll rappel down to give you covering fire, Sam, *if* all goes well. Got it?"

"Got it," Casey answered. He unfastened the gunning belt and moved for the equipment locker to retrieve the rappelling gear.

"Sounds good to me, Billy," Sam said. "I think."

"Well, Annapolis, if you've got a better idea, I'm all ears," McKay said as he took over the Browning.

"Let's do it!" Sam barked.

Casey squirmed into a harness while McKay blasted away with the .50. Then the pilot took over the machine gun while McKay hooked up. When everything was set, Billy tossed a bagful of .45 ACP clips to Sam and nodded.

"Ground floor, please." Sloan grinned, and Casey lowered the hoist. The two men watched as Sam and Warren, still oblivious in the litter, descended toward the canopy. When they reached a point just above the treetops, McKay motioned to Casey and they both ripped the pins out of a handful of grenades and dropped them over the side. Just as Sloan and Warren disappeared beneath the tree limbs, McKay saw flashes of orange and black on the ground, then heard the grenades go off, one by one. With each explosion the Marine winced, hoping that he had judged the timing correctly and that Sam and Lee weren't being ripped to shreds by his own miscalculation. Then the ship moved again, this time drastically to port, and McKay looked at Casey and yelled, "Geronimo!" The two Guardians dropped over the side.

When he slipped beneath the canopy, McKay immediately looked for Sloan and Warren. He spotted them almost at once, sinking slowly but steadily, a few meters beneath him. Perfect, he thought. Their gradual descent had kept them far enough above the jungle floor to avoid the shrapnel from the exploding grenades.

But just as McKay was congratulating himself on the plan, it started to unravel. One by one, muzzle flashes appeared in the bush below, indicating what McKay had feared all along, that the undergrowth was so damn dense that it had shielded much of the enemy from the fragmentation. *Shit!* he thought. *I guess we'll just have to do this the hard way.* He cranked off several rounds from the hip as he drew even with the litter.

He slowed to a pace that matched Warren's descent and fired to provide cover. Not that Lee cared, McKay noticed. While bullets buzzed all around him, Doc was actually snoring. *Ain't oblivion great?* McKay thought, as he pumped a double-aught slug into a bush that screamed. With tropical shrubs exploding all around him, he couldn't help but wonder how a horticulturist would take this scene. With catatonic frenzy, he figured. He chewed up more greenery. What he'd give for some Agent Orange about now.

McKay glanced beyond the litter and saw that Casey had arrived safely at the communal altitude, and was also contributing his best effort toward defoliating the rain forest. He was blasting away with Sam's Galil at every plant that moved.

The two men took up positions just below the litter and fired almost straight down, leaving the circumference of the killing zone for Sloan. The MAC-10 wasn't great for longer distances, but Sam had no choice. He couldn't shoot directly below for fear of hitting his two partners. Since he had no harness and needed one hand to hold onto the hoist cable, the small Ingram was the logical weapon. His main problem was that, at a firing rate of 750 rounds per minute, the MAC-10 was zipping through its thirty-three-round clips so fast that Sam was in danger of running out of ammo.

"For God sakes, Sam, take it easy!" Casey yelled. The Ingram was his weapon, after all, so he understood better than anyone how easy it was to run through a bagful of magazines. And Casey had watched Sam change the double loads, two clips taped together upside-down, twice since he had penetrated the canopy, and that seemed like just seconds ago. At that rate, Sam would go dry in about three minutes, including the period it would take to change the clips eight more times. "Slow it down!" Casey exhorted.

They were within a few meters of the ground, and their firing arcs had flattened accordingly. McKay looked to his left and saw a movement that materialized into a man. The Marine pivoted and fired from his hip just as he touched the ground. The 12-gauge slug caught the man in the abdomen, lifted him off the ground, and flung him backward several feet into a tree. McKay watched him hang there for a moment, propped against the palm trunk, his entrails gushing onto the ground. Then the man, who was distinctly Polynesian, slid wide-eyed beneath the undergrowth and disappeared.

"Samoan!" McKay barked into the miniature microphone taped to his larynx. "That's fifty bucks you owe me, Casey."

The entire team was on the ground now, even Sam, who had jumped the few remaining meters so that he could cushion the landing for Warren. Not that Lee would have noticed, but it was the thought that counted. Sloan eased the load down, unhooked the harness, and dragged the litter to the relative safety of the underbrush. "Who are these guys?" he whispered through his commo set.

McKay couldn't resist. "Ask Casey."

"Piss up a rope," Wilson snapped.

Then, suddenly, the opposing gunfire stopped. "Cease fire," McKay sub-vocalized. Then he ventured his head up and peered through the haze of gunsmoke at the surrounding jungle. Everything had become eerily still. "What's happening?" he whispered.

"You tell me," Casey replied.

McKay looked around some more, but all he could see was a dim, chewed-up rain forest. "Anybody know how many there are?" He took the silence as a negative. "Anybody know *where* they are?"

"I think they're all around us," Sam volunteered.

Then, from somewhere out in the bush, came a single voice. "Hey, soldiers? How ya doin'?"

Say what? McKay thought. *How are you doing? That's pretty polite for a guy who's been trying to kill us.* But then he figured what the hell. "We're doing okay. How about yourself?"

"I don't know, man," came the voice. "Not too good. You've killed a bunch of my friends."

McKay glanced to his right and, through the foliage, could barely make out Casey and Sam. They were squatting low around the litter several meters away. They both returned his look and shrugged. "Yeah, well, uh, you've been trying to kill us, pal. Why's that?"

"We were just kicking a little ass, man. We didn't mean no harm."

"See what I told you, Casey?" McKay whispered through his microphone.

"But now, we're pissed off," the voice continued. "And I'm afraid we're going to have to kill you."

"Fair enough, ass-wipe. Come and get it," McKay answered.

"Ass-wipe?" the voice was indignant. "Fuck you, main-lander!" And the jungle erupted in gunfire.

"Give 'em hell," McKay roared, and he poured buckshot in the direction of the voice. Casey and Sam added their automatic fire to the maelstrom.

Then a horrendous wrenching and snapping, louder even than the gunfire, cracked overhead. The battle suddenly stopped. Everybody looked up in unison and saw the jungle canopy twist and buckle above them. McKay crouched, momentarily paralyzed, and watched the treetops collapse under the weight of the black machine that came crashing through the branches. He looked over at Sloan and Casey, who had already grabbed the litter, one on each side, and were scrambling for safety. "Shit!" he heard himself yell. Then he bolted.

As he ran he could hear the screams of those who had reacted later than he and who knew they had no chance to reach the perimeter of safety. Worst of all, he could hear the crescendo of the crash, and measured his remaining life span against the escalating sound. He estimated the moment of impact and, at the last instant, dove like an Olympic swimmer. Then his world erupted in a tempest of flame and fury.

CHAPTER
SIXTEEN ——————————————

Tom Rogers rowed with his back toward the reef and snickered at the little man coughing in the stern. He watched as Jack, trembling violently, struggled with a crumpled pack of Camels. Finally, Jack succeeded in needling the last limp cigarette from the pack and fired it up. He took a deep drag, which launched him into a choking fit, and Rogers wondered at the ways people chose to commit suicide.

Jack hacked up something black and spat it over the side. Tom grimaced, knowing full well that Jack couldn't see his expression. Then he imagined how strange it must be for the little man to look right through someone to the beach beyond. The oars moving all by themselves, must have added to Jack's consternation.

Tom didn't have to turn around to see how close they were to the reef. He could tell by comparing the roar of the surf with the diameter of Jack's eyes, which widened as the dinghy approached the breakers. The little man's anticipation was better than a range finder, Tom mused.

He had been lucky to find Jack and the garbage scow still moored at Haleiwa. The commotion over the murder there had slowed their refueling process, he guessed, along with Hazel's blindness and Jack's indolence, of course. Tom had sneaked out of the dock office when the police had removed the body, and climbed back over the stack of cargo to the scow. There he had appealed to Jack's sense of intrigue and insatiable curiosity about extraterrestrials to persuade him to alter his course for the Big Island. Hazel still thought she was en route to Lahaina on Maui.

When they had first arrived, the beauty of the valley had struck Tom dumb. It was too bad, he thought, that he had discovered this paradise now. At a different time and under different circumstances, he would have loved to have shared it with Marta.

He was disappointed and worried that they had seen no sign of the trawler. If Nazrullah had come there, as Tom thought, then surely the boat would be nearby. Unless the Pashtun had scuttled it. That was a distinct possibility, and something he would have done in the same situation, Tom realized. Or it could be that Moheb was nowhere near the valley. After all, Rogers had only the matchbook to go on, and that was sketchy at best. Still, he had a gut feeling about the old warrior who lay headless in Haleiwa and about the message he had left behind. Besides, it was the only clue Tom had.

The wooden dinghy handled the surf easily, and the two men dragged the boat up onto the beach.

"Are you sure you don't need any help?" Jack asked a set of footprints in the sand.

"No, but thanks anyway. You've done all you can for me, and I appreciate it." Tom offered his hand, then realized Jack couldn't see it. "Shake?"

"Well, okay then. Good luck." Jack coughed, and extended his arm into empty space.

"Thanks." Tom grasped the small hand. "You too." He waited until Jack climbed into the dinghy, then he pushed the small craft off into the surf. "Are you sure you can handle it?"

"Sure!" Jack wheezed, then his eyes bulged as he glanced toward the reef.

Tom watched from the beach as Jack cleared the coral on his third try, and undulated toward the scow. Then the Guardian turned his attention inland and wondered how he was going to find his enemy.

He could search the valley undetected, of course. It was too large a job to complete soon, however, and he had a hunch that time was running out. As a reflex, he glanced at his right wrist to check his watch, then smacked himself on the forehead. "Dipshit!" Not only could he not see his watch, he couldn't even see his arm. He looked at the sun and estimated the time at about 1500 hours. It would be dark in three or four hours, so he had to think of something fast.

Though he didn't know Nazrullah's plans, he was certain that the Moslem would try to escape back to Spain, the location of the Bey's headquarters. That move would require transport, presumably an aircraft. Rogers couldn't imagine Moheb traveling by ship, not with the disks. He would be too anxious to return with his prize to endure such a slow mode of travel. *But would he leave the valley by land and rendezvous with a plane on the other side of the island, or would he arrange for something to meet him here?* Tom wondered.

He remembered the map Jack had shown him. Though ten kilometers long, the narrow valley had no airstrip large enough to accommodate a plane with the range to reach the mainland, where it could refuel and continue on to Europe. That meant that Nazrullah would have to leave the valley in order to catch his flight. So Tom decided to leave the beach and try to find some central place where the residents gathered and learn whatever he could. He didn't know what else to do.

Then a dark shape at the water's edge caught his eye. At first it looked like a piece of driftwood. Then something about it seemed familiar. Tom walked the forty meters to the tree-like object, looked around to make sure no one was on the beach, then fished the long, thin piece of flotsam from the surf. He recognized it even before he had finished dragging it up onto the sand. It was the makeshift cross-section of the mast from the fishing trawler. The pulley, containing some frayed rope fragments, was still fastened to the hook that Tom had rigged himself. The few strands of hemp were all that was left of the cord the Moslem had cut to plunge Tom into the inhospitable Kauai Channel.

So, Rogers thought, the Moslem was here after all. And he had scuttled the trawler, just like the KGB operations manual dictated. Tom wondered what else he could learn from the area. He scanned the beach but saw nothing more. So he decided to check out the edge of the rain forest, just like *his* manual instructed. Besides, he wanted to get off the beach as soon as possible. Even though he was invisible, somebody just might happen along and notice a set of footprints miraculously planting themselves in the sand. He didn't want a repeat of anything even remotely resembling his experience in Haleiwa. Besides, he was beginning to get the hang of this invisible stuff, and it would be stupid for him not to profit from his experience.

Tom found a set of footprints entering the jungle a quarter mile down the beach. About twenty meters into the rain forest he suddenly stopped. Off to his right was a hump of vegetation that seemed a little out of place. He approached the low pile carefully, then scanned the full circumference of the area. Nothing. He removed a few branches from the stack and discovered an inflated raft underneath. It was similar to the one Jack had found him floating in, though this one was not bright yellow. There was nothing about the raft that indicated it was from the trawler, but Tom was sure that it was. And more importantly, if the craft was Nazrullah's, why hadn't he deflated and buried it? Rogers could only assume it was because the Moslem intended to use it again. That meant that he planned to escape by sea, a development that Tom found surprising. Unless, of course, he intended to use a seaplane. *That must be it*, Rogers thought. It certainly made sense.

Then Tom noticed a buzzing sound from the sky. He looked up and saw a single-engine plane with pontoons circling the valley. That couldn't be Nazrullah's plane, he thought. Surely it was too small. Still, he replaced the branches and moved back into the bush.

He watched the pontoon plane fly along over the river until it disappeared beyond the trees. Then he settled in to review his options. He could follow the little plane to its mooring place, or even go into the valley and look for Nazrullah himself, but he might miss him when and if a larger seaplane arrived. If he stayed with the raft, and his hunch was correct about the seaplane, then he was pretty sure he would meet his old enemy again. And that was what the Guardian wanted more than anything else in the world.

It took several moments for William McKay to spot the aircraft after he had first heard the drone of its small engine. He wasn't accustomed to looking down for a plane, and picking it out against the background of the valley took awhile. He stood on the 1,500-foot rim of the lush canyon. The place was indescribably beautiful, he thought. He handed the binoculars to Sloan. "A floatplane," he said to everybody.

"Yeah." Sloan focused the instrument. "It looks like an old Maule fitted with pontoons. It's just circling, like the pilot's never been here before." He handed the glasses to Casey.

"Well, if he's looking for a place to land, there ain't but one," Casey declared. "And that's the river. Maybe he's trying to find the deepest stretch." He returned the binoculars to McKay.

The Marine, still fascinated with its beauty, scanned the valley one more time. He tried to trace the narrow, unpaved road that began at his feet and twisted into the ravine below, but lost it almost immediately in the jungle. Then he raised the glasses to look again at the end of the valley. "According to Doc's machine, this is the place. Right off the mouth of that river is where the signal came from." He looked at the others as if to ask: *Is this possible? Why would anybody trying to escape come here?*

"It's plenty remote," Sloan said, reading McKay's expression. "Maybe the Arab knew of the place and figured he wouldn't be hassled here?"

McKay let the binoculars hang from his neck. "Sounds good to me," he said, realizing they had no alternative. "Let's saddle up and see if we can navigate this goddamn goat path."

The men climbed into an open Toyota Land Cruiser, and Casey fired it up. With no muffler, the ancient four-wheel-drive sounded to McKay like a good candidate for Rommel's command car. They had liberated the vehicle from the Samoans back at Kailua-Kona after the Black Hawk came crashing down and broke up that savage little group forever. Only one of the shitheads had survived the explosion, and that was the one with whom McKay had parlayed in the jungle.

Though badly burned, the man had been able to direct the boys to Waipio and give them the keys to his Land Cruiser parked on a road less than a kilometer away. Because of his co-operative attitude, McKay had taken pity on the man and put a bullet in his forehead before they left the jungle.

Next, they had dropped Warren off at the local hospital and had made sure he was in good hands before they set out for the valley. McKay consulted his watch: 1509 hours. It had taken them over seven hours to accomplish all of that, he noted, and they had only gotten lost twice. He just hoped they wouldn't be too late to find Tom.

Casey rolled the battered vehicle up to the edge of the overlook and jammed the gearshift into low. The road dropped almost straight down into the valley. He looked at the others and gulped. "Ready, men?"

McKay peered through the windshield at the floatplane below and watched as it entered its glide path over the river. "Well, what are you waiting for?" He turned to Casey. "Let's slice this turkey!"

Casey slowly let out on the clutch, and the vehicle teetered for an instant before it plunged down the twenty-six-degree grade.

"Shit!" The cry came in three-part harmony as the machine disappeared into the valley below.

Marta Ryan pulled out of the steep bank to port, working the rudder furiously with her feet, until the Maule Star Craft leveled out directly over the river. She had to gauge the wind from the movement of the trees below since there was no other indication. The strong trade winds were relatively steady, so at least she had no severe gusts to deal with.

It had been a while since she had flown, but the rudiments had returned to her quickly enough. She was glad that her decision to get a pilot's license was finally paying off. But she had never operated a pontoon plane before. In fact, she had never even considered getting her water wings. Now she decided that if she survived this landing, she would change that.

Amphibious flying was fun, she concluded, though the pontoons were a drag, at least while airborne, and caused a dramatic increase in the ship's fuel consumption. She looked at the gas gauge and saw that the needle was hovering on empty. She had used up almost all of her remaining fuel circling the valley several times to screw up enough courage to attempt a landing. *That's an odd term*, she thought, her nerves working on her imagination. *Perhaps it should be called a "watering" instead?*

Her first pass had been devoted to searching for the fishing trawler that Uli had mentioned in his little speech the night before, and which she hoped would be anchored beyond the reef. She was disappointed that the boat was not there. The fuel situation left her no alternative. She would have to set the plane down now and worry about the trawler and the Arab, who was supposed to be on it, later.

As she eased back on the throttle and glided toward the surface, she momentarily flashed on her escape the night before.

She could see the lacerated face of the Hawaiian in the water below and shuddered at the hallucination. *The son of a bitch*, she thought, remembering the rape, *he got just what he deserved*.

Then she thought of how lucky she had been afterward to catch a ride on the main road that flanked the Hanalei River. She had spotted the floatplane moored several kilometers further on, and remembering Uli's reference to it, decided to commandeer it. Though she hadn't counted on having to wait several hours for the operator of the dock to appear so she could take on fuel, the delay had turned out to be profitable. The elderly dockhand had readily bought her story that she was to take the plane and meet Uli on Oahu, though it was obvious that she had never flown a floatplane before. She guessed that the hundred-dollar bill she had given him over and above the fuel cost had increased his gullibility somewhat. The fact that she had an Uzi slung over her shoulder probably hadn't hurt either.

The old man had given her directions to the Big Island, and located the Waipio Valley on the map they had found in the cockpit. The trip appeared to be an easy navigational exercise, a straight shot to her destination.

It had not, however, occurred to her at the time that she would find any major differences between the operation of a floatplane and one designed for ground landings. But the takeoff, during which she skipped along the river more times than she imagined she should, had educated her to the hazards of the upcoming landing. The old man had advised her that the ship had to be as level as possible so both floats would touch down simultaneously. Otherwise, the craft could pitch suddenly to one side and either roll or flip over.

She snapped her concentration back to the task at hand and summoned all of her coordination to work the flaps and rudder together. The plane descended to just a few feet over the water. Judging that it was as level as it was ever going to get, Marta cut the power. The Maule bounced off the surface and slewed to starboard. She hit the throttle, straightened the machine, then lowered it gently onto the water. The plane raced along the surface like a speedboat, then settled, as she powered back, into a slow, floating taxi. "Perfect," she said proudly, but she noticed she was trembling.

Marta pointed the aircraft toward an old wooden landing and throttled up against the current. Then she killed the engine and let the plane drift toward the dock. She looked at the Uzi on the seat beside her and wondered about taking it along. But she had no jacket or wrap so there was no way to hide it, and she couldn't see herself swaggering into an island village with a submachine gun. So she concealed the weapon in the cab and climbed outside the plane.

As she stood on the port pontoon and waited for the machine to float the remaining few meters to the landing, she inhaled the delicious fragrances and looked at the valley's scenery for the first time. *Magnificent*, she thought. Then she fingered the Semmerling automatic in her purse for reassurance and stepped ashore.

Moheb Nazrullah watched the floatplane disappear beneath the tree line. "Shit!" he spat, thinking surely that wasn't the plane they had sent for him. *That pissant craft wouldn't make it to Honolulu, much less Barcelona*, he thought.

He wiped the sleep from his eyes and checked his watch: 3:10. He had an hour and twenty minutes or so to wait for *his* seaplane to arrive. It was just as well, he thought, that the little plane had awakened him. Otherwise, he might have slept through his rendezvous.

He permitted himself one luxurious stretch, then tried to shake off the sleep hangover. Though he had been exhausted, his nerves had been stretched so taut that he had found it impossible at first to fall asleep. Even the wonderful bath at the waterfall had failed to relax him properly, though it had succeeded in cleaning off a few days worth of grime. When he finally had dozed off, he had crashed like the Hindenburg.

Nazrullah retrieved his rucksack and placed it on the low lava platform. It was a pity, he thought, that the black stones were all that remained of the once-sacred temple in an ancient city of refuge. This *heiau*, Kanina had informed him weeks ago, was estimated to be 1300 years old, and might even have been the temple in which Kamehameha the Great had received the mantle of power in 1782.

Moheb felt the spirituality of the place, and sympathized with Uli's passion for the history of his people. He was sorry that he'd had to use the Lono for his own ends. Nazrullah felt a kinship with the secular power of the place, and imagined that the authority of the great king of the Hawaiian Islands even now flowed through him.

He rummaged through his soiled clothing and wondered why he had bothered to keep the filthy garments. Habit from a destitute boyhood in his mountain village, he suspected. At the bottom of the pile, he felt the cold metal of the Sig-Sauer P230, checked the clip, and injected a .380 ACP cartridge into the chamber. He slipped the auto pistol into the back waist band of his fresh chinos.

He patted his shirt pocket and felt the disks. Then on reflex, he withdrew the silver case from his other pocket and unconsciously jammed a cigarette in his mouth. Then he reached for his matches. They weren't there. "Damn." He remembered. He had lost them. And then, of course, he had resolved to quit smoking. As the hour of his triumph neared, his nerves tingled, and he decided that he could postpone that act of will until this whole ordeal had been concluded. And, he rationalized, he deserved a cigarette. Besides, he was having a nicotine fit and if he didn't get a smoke soon, he was going to ram his head into the nearest tree.

Since it was time to start out for the raft anyway, Moheb decided to detour the short distance over to the hotel and grab a pack of matches. Though he had been careful to conceal his presence in the valley so far, it didn't really matter who saw him now. His plane would arrive in about an hour. Then he would be safely gone. And, he thought smugly, what could possibly happen in an hour?

CHAPTER
SEVENTEEN

Marta stood outside the Waipio Valley Hotel and stared in horror at her reflection in the window. Her own assessment was that she looked like a battered hooker. Her dress was ripped to mid-thigh, Parisian streetwalker-style, and the top three buttons of her blouse were missing. She was wearing no bra. Indeed, she had been unable even to find it the night before. And her wild hair, she thought, made her look like Little Orphan Annie after a session in a wind tunnel. She straightened herself up as best she could and thought: *What the hell, this is Hawaii.*

Once inside, she wondered why she had been so worried. She couldn't possibly look worse than the hotel itself. The place gave the term "rustic" a whole new definition. Oil lamps burned instead of electricity, and there was no hot water. In the whole establishment she counted five bedrooms, in which mosquito netting dominated the decor. Had she not spent the previous night being fucked by six men in the back of a van, she probably would have thought herself too good for the place.

Marta ventured into the heart of the hotel. It was one great room that served as lobby, dining room, and bar. In it were two men standing on opposite sides of the bar. Both looked at her as if they would like to rip the remainder of her clothes off. The one on her side of the bar, a customer, she presumed, shot her a particularly lascivious look. He was handsome with a slim muscular build and long black hair. His mustache gave him extra panache that she found especially attractive. At first, she thought he was Polynesian, like the one behind the bar. But after extra scrutiny, Marta decided that he looked more Middle Eastern. *My God,* it finally hit her, *he must be the Arab.*

She just stood there, nonplussed, and stared at the man who was the strongest candidate to lead her to Tommy. Failing that, he was the one who now possessed the Project Dynamo computer disks.

He suddenly flashed her a becoming smile, and she suspected that he mistook her shocked expression for one of dumbstruck, animal attraction. Or perhaps, she thought, her face expressed a mixture of both. She returned his smile with one of her own and started across the room. She purposely ignored him, walked up to the barman, and asked him if there was a phone in the house.

The Polynesian was indignant. "Of course, lady. What do you think this is, a barn?"

Marta decided to let that pass and just stared at the man until he pointed. She followed his finger to a pay phone near the door. She fished through her purse, found some money next to the automatic, and moved toward the phone.

"Dr. Connoly's office," a secretary answered officiously. Marta was surprised to find someone still there at almost 8:30 Washington time. She identified herself and waited for Maggie to ring on.

"Marta?" came the familiar, authoritative voice over the line. "Have you found Rogers?"

"He's alive?" Marta asked, the excitement bubbling in her voice.

"The Guardians think so," Maggie replied. "At least that's what they're reporting to the President."

Thank God! Marta almost blurted out. She then brought her boss up to date, leaving out the gang rape, of course.

"Nazrullah is there with you now?" Maggie was aghast.

Marta eyed the Arab at the bar. "He's sitting across the room as we speak." She recognized the name from Uli's remarks of the night before.

"He may very well have the computer disks," Maggie declared. "If he does, then you *must* get them! Understood?"

"Understood," Marta responded dutifully. Then she steeled herself for the critical question. "If I do find Rogers, what do you want me to do?"

After a pause, Marta heard the chilling reply: "Terminate the subject."

"Say again," Marta spoke slowly.

"Do it!" Maggie snapped.

The moment Marta had dreaded was finally upon her. She had assumed that she could handle the worst, if it came to that. But deep inside, she'd never thought that it would. Now that it had, she discovered that the very core of her had suddenly gone cold, and she was unable to speak.

"Marta?" the voice jabbed at her from 5000 miles away. "Are you still there?"

She wanted to say no, that she was not there, that she had never heard the command, and that after last night she never wanted to kill anyone, especially Tom Rogers, ever again. But instead, she mumbled, "Yes, Maggie, I'm still here."

"Do you understand what I said?"

All too well, Marta thought. "I understand."

"Do you have a problem with that?" asked Maggie, a hint of suspicion in her voice.

All kinds of problems, you stupid bitch, Marta wanted to scream. Instead, she whispered a simple no.

"Very well, then. Call me when it's done," Connoly ordered, and the line went dead.

Marta listened to the dial tone for what seemed like a long time, until a shrill scream exploded in her ear. It was the phone company's signal to indicate that the receiver had been left off the hook. Quickly, she hung up the phone. She took a moment to compose herself, then slowly turned toward the bar.

The first thing Marta noticed when she looked across the room was that the Arab was now gone.

Moheb Nazrullah strolled along the river on his way to the beach and looked at his wristwatch. The gold timepeace read 3:53. Thirty-seven minutes to wait for the plane, he thought, patting his shirt pocket. In a little more than half an hour, he would be on his way to glory.

He walked around a tight bend and saw a floatplane moored to a rickety dock along the riverbank. It must have been the same plane that had awakened him earlier, he assumed, the one he had seen dip below the trees. He wondered if it belonged to the woman at the hotel. "The Flying Whore," he said with a chuckle, then quickly lamented that he didn't have the time to enjoy her. A quick lay certainly would serve to take the edge off.

To Moheb, the woman had appeared outrageously disheveled, even for an American. In fact, she looked like she had just passed through the middle of Beirut during a rocket attack. And to think that she could actually fly a plane. *How odd*, he thought.

Still, there had been something alluring about her, and had he not been on his way to catch the most important flight of his life, he would have accepted her rather obvious invitation to play. She had a good body for a woman her age. A little skinny, perhaps, and she had no tits, but still she was firm. She was, of course, a vapid bitch, like most American females, but Moheb had never let a woman's mentality interfere with his sexual pleasure.

There also had been something spooky about her, especially the way she had turned slightly and looked at him while she was at the telephone. It was almost as if she had been talking about *him*. In any event, that look had made him paranoid and he had abruptly gathered up his rucksack and left. He knew there would be plenty of women to entertain him at his victory celebration once he returned to Barcelona. So he wiped the woman out of his mind, lit his second cigarette in as many days, and continued along the path to the beach.

Then, he felt something gnaw at his psyche. It was that same feeling that had rushed over him at the hotel, and one to which he had grown especially sensitive over the years. After all, he had survived the wrath of the Mujahadeen, the enemies of the Soviet Union worldwide, and even the KGB itself by heeding this particular intuition. He was not about to distrust it now. He reached under his shirt and drew the Sig automatic from its hiding place at the small of his back. Then he disappeared into the underbrush that lined one side of the path and waited for the object of his paranoia to appear.

Marta hurried along the path that bordered the river. She hadn't sighted Nazrullah and had no idea where he was going.

She had asked the barman at the hotel if he knew the Arab's destination. But the Polynesian merely had sniggered and said that he had never seen the man, who had walked in for a pack of matches. Then he had suggested that she try the beach, since that was why ninety-nine percent of the people who traveled to Hawaii came there in the first place. Marta had been in no mood for his sarcasm, and had whirled out of the bar before the man had even finished his remark.

She followed the path as it curved sharply with the river, and soon she arrived at the floatplane. She was glad that the Maule was still there. She had half expected to find it gone, stolen by the Arab. According to both Uli and Maggie, he probably had the computer disks and was definitely looking to escape the islands.

Marta considered fetching the Uzi from its hiding place in the cab of the floatplane, then decided against it. A submachine gun, though reassuring protection, would be a dead giveaway to the Arab. He was a trained, skilled, experienced, and dangerous field operative. Surprise, she decided, would be her best weapon. Still, she fingered the Semmerling in her purse as she continued down the path.

"Excuse me," came a sudden voice from behind her, and Marta spun around and looked into the handsome face of Moheb Nazrullah.

"I'm sorry. I didn't mean to startle you," he said politely. The Arab stood on the path with one hand cocked behind his hip and an unlit cigarette dangling from his mouth. "I just wondered if perhaps you might have a light."

Marta gaped at him for a long moment before she was able to reply. "Why, yes, I think I have a lighter," she said finally, with as much composure as she could muster. She reached into her purse and fumbled about, stalling for time. What should she do? she wondered. Offer him the lighter and continue to pretend, or pull her pistol and end the thing then and there? She still knew nothing of Tommy, and conjectured that perhaps the Arab might lead her to him. Then she remembered what the barman had told her,that the Arab had gone to the hotel expressly for a pack of matches.

"I know I have one in here someplace," she said, still fumbling in her bag, and she wondered what was the intention of his little ruse. Was he contriving a way to meet her for sex, or did he have something more deadly in mind?

Marta decided not to take any chances. She glanced away from the Arab for an instant to look into her bag. She wrapped her fingers around the cold steel of the Semmerling and released the safety. "Oh, here it is," she chirped. But as she moved to withdraw the weapon she looked back at Nazrullah and suddenly froze. He was wearing that same becoming smile she had first noticed back at the hotel. But this time his charm was accompanied by a pistol of his own, one which he now had leveled at her head.

"Perhaps, I could offer some assistance," Marta heard him ooze. Then she watched, mesmerized, as the dark mustache slid across his face in an arrogant smile.

CHAPTER
EIGHTEEN ─────────────────

Billy McKay hung on for dear life as the Toyota plummeted into the valley. With Casey at the wheel, the old Land Cruiser roared down the narrow road, twisting through hairpin curves, climbing downed trees, and jumping cavernous troughs cut by the runoff from heavy, tropical rains. Each turn brought a horrifying new entry for McKay's lexicon of off-road racing. Phrases like "This is insane," "We're going to crash," "Slow down, asshole," and "What the fuck am I doing here?" flashed through his frenzied brain.

"What's the matter, Billy?" Casey yelled over the whine of the rapidly overheating engine. "You look a little peaked."

"Never mind about me, hotshot," McKay snarled. "Just keep this goddamn thing between the ditches."

"Whatever you say, sir." Casey grinned, then he downshifted into low and jumped a log that McKay judged was bigger than the jeep.

"Christ!" McKay howled. Then the Marine decided to look at the scenery in an attempt to ignore the galloping approach of his own imminent death. He caught a quick glimpse of a majestic waterfall as the Toyota snaked through a series of S-curves.

"And, to your right, gentlemen," McKay quipped, "is the world's fastest waterfall."

"Where?" Sloan rubbernecked in the back seat.

"Whoops, you missed it!" McKay hooted. Then he closed his eyes and clutched the dash handle as the Land Cruiser thundered down the mountain.

McKay finally opened his eyes about an hour later when he felt the Toyota broad-slide for a distance that he figured was about twice the width of the road. "Damn!" he said as the vehicle came to rest. "Are we dead yet?"

"You betcha, Billy!" Casey grinned. "And we've just arrived at paradise."

McKay turned to his right and saw a sign that read "Waipio Valley Hotel" suspended over a porch. "Great!" he said. "I want a room with *two* maids." He lurched out of the vehicle.

Inside, the Guardians found a large room, empty except for a lone man working behind a huge bar.

"Six beers, mister!" Sloan swaggered up to the bar like an exaggerated Jesse James. The Polynesian appeared genuinely unimpressed as he drew the draughts. Then he set two icy mugs down in front of each man. "I assume you wanted two apiece?"

"You got it, amigo," McKay replied, then he killed one of the beers. He lifted the remaining glass and pressed it against his forehead. "Ahhh!"

"Say, pal?" Casey said, wiping the foam from his mouth. "You haven't seen an Arab-looking fella lurking around here, have you?"

"An Arab?" The man's brow wrinkled.

"You know," McKay piped up. "A raghead!"

The bartender rubbed his chin thoughtfully. "Could be," he fished, unaware that he had just said the wrong thing at the wrong time.

McKay turned red. "Oh, I get it," he rasped. "You've seen the guy and you'd be happy to tell us where he is right now—for a price. Right?"

"Right." The man smiled, obviously pleased with himself.

"Well, then." McKay drew his Colt .45 automatic and slowly placed it against the bridge of the man's nose. "Is this enough?"

CHAPTER
NINETEEN ───────────────

Tom Rogers sat with his back against a palm trunk and slapped at the sand fleas on his legs. It was hard to see the little critters against a neutral background. Of course, he could feel the tiny bites, which helped to narrow down the target area some.

Tom had been waiting for about an hour and had seen no one, either on the beach or in the bush. From his position a few meters beyond the hidden raft he could see only a forty-meter stretch of beach, but that was enough to keep someone from sneaking past him. And it was impossible for anything on two legs to approach through the jungle unheard.

Earlier he had swept the immediate area clear of footprints with a palm frond, just as the one who had hidden the raft had done before him. The Pashtun, he guessed. All that was left now was the waiting.

Tom fidgeted against the tree. He had never been much good at waiting, though he certainly had had enough practice over the years. In fact, he had spent an inordinate amount of his adult life alone, silently crouched in jungles, waiting for an enemy as silent and deadly as he to spring out of the night.

He didn't mind the solitude so much as the inactivity. Once he was certain that he had his shit squared away for a mission, there was really nothing more for him to think about, and that was when the boredom crept in. The tedium always set his brain to whirling.

He didn't care to think about Marta, for instance, which was all he could think about. He tried to concentrate on his invisibility. A condition, he presumed, that would capture the imagination of most of its victims. But oddly, he didn't think much about it. To be truthful, he didn't really care. After all, he had felt invisible long before the experiment had gone awry. He realized he had been basically formless ever since Marta had left him, so his present condition was really no more than an exterior manifestation of his interior self. Or in his case, he supposed that a lack of exterior manifestation would provide a more accurate description.

Why had she started the damn thing, he wondered, *if all she'd had in mind was to end it*? He pondered that question for a long while, covering every possibility on the spectrum, until finally he narrowed it down to a combination of a few probable answers. Then he decided that he had become insanely obsessive about the whole thing, and that no woman as unstable and self-absorbed as Marta was worth all this bullshit. *If she can do better, let her!* he decided, and vowed never to think of the skinny bitch again.

Instead, Tom forced himself to concentrate on Nazrullah, and visualized how he would squeeze the Moslem's head like a pimple. There was no way that he, Tom Rogers, Green Beret and Guardian, was going to be dumped overboard by a sleazy split-tail *and* a fucking raghead all in the same month—not for free!

He was lost in a fantasy, tripping through a personal repertoire of torture, when he noticed that the jungle had suddenly grown quiet. The stillness alerted him, as if he were a wild animal, to the approach of danger, and he immediately thought of concealment. Then it occurred to him that his camouflage was built-in, and permanent. He sat like a stone against the tree and waited for the inevitable sound of footsteps to rustle through the undergrowth.

When they came, Tom stiffened, all his senses alert. He turned toward the sound and watched for the jungle to reveal its secrets. He thought he heard the voice of a woman pleading, though he couldn't make out the exact words, and then the sound of a man telling her to shut up. *Oh, Christ!* he thought. A lover's quarrel was just about to blow his ambush. The footsteps, the ruffling foliage, and the voices all thundered through the undergrowth. Whoever the interlopers were, he thought with a chuckle, they weren't trying to sneak up on anybody. So he relaxed and watched for the break in the bush.

Suddenly, as if from a cannon, a woman shot out of the jungle and landed in the middle of the clearing. Tom was so surprised by this that he almost gasped out loud. But what followed rendered even that shock insignificant. A man with a pistol in each hand soon followed the woman into the opening and stopped at its edge. He stood there, like an arrogant prince, and lorded over the woman who lay with her face in the sand, weeping. Tom sat stark still, paralyzed in disbelief, as the loathing welled up from his core like lava in a volcano. He just sat quietly, trembling with hatred, and looked directly into the dark, piercing eyes of Moheb Nazrullah.

The Pashtun unshouldered his rucksack, placed the smaller pistol in one of the zippered compartments, and tossed the pack aside. Then he looked at his wristwatch. "You are in luck, whore," he sneered. "I have just enough time to give you the last, best fuck of your life." His mustache twisted into a malicious smile as his free hand moved to his belt buckle. "Get on your knees, bitch!"

Tom looked to the woman, prostrate in the sand, and for an instant flashed on the odd familiarity of her slender build and dark coloring. Whoever she was, she didn't deserve this indignity. Only a coward would treat a defenseless woman this way. *You won't have to endure this torture much longer, sweetheart.* He smiled, wishing that she could somehow hear his thoughts.

"On your knees, slut!" the Moslem roared, and the woman crawled slowly to all fours. She cringed there in the sand, offering her raised buttocks in a pathetic, trembling sacrifice. As the Moslem swaggered up to straddle her from the rear, she lifted her head to wail out one final cry of torment.

Tom Rogers gasped at the face that screamed in supplication just a few meters in front of him. The face had dominated his thoughts, had haunted his memory and twisted his guts inside out for far too long. Unable to move, unable to breathe, Tom just blinked into that tear-stained face that he both hated and loved with equal ferocity, and wondered if his obsession had finally driven him mad. He had to be insane, he concluded. How else could it be that he was looking directly into the quivering, stunned face of Marta Ryan?

Billy McKay stood on the planked landing with his back to the water and covered the shoreline with his shotgun. He cradled the Remington 1100 with affection, though he would have preferred his M60. The Maremont could cover a hell of a lot more riverbank than the 12-gauge semi-automatic.

Sloan surveyed the water from his position on the starboard float while Wilson poked around inside the cabin of the Maule M-7. "What have we here?" Casey chirped in that high, nasal, pure-Malibu tone. He stepped out onto the port float brandishing an Uzi. "Hey, Billy. Wanna buy a submachine gun?"

McKay had been around Casey long enough to expect almost anything. So he turned toward the cockpit with that "what now?" look on his face. But he came up short when he saw the Uzi. "Jesus, kid. Where did you find that?"

"Professionally stowed under the seat." He waved the weapon. "Practically in plain sight."

"Perfect!" McKay moaned, thinking that at least this time an amateur had had enough sense to leave the gun behind. "We'd better commandeer that in case the guy comes back. We don't want him to shoot *both* his feet off, now do we?"

McKay looked at Casey, who now was armed with the Uzi plus his usual MAC-10, enough firepower to waste Liechtenstein without changing clips. "Give me that damn thing," McKay said, pointing at the machine pistol.

Casey stepped onto the dock and offered the Uzi in his outstretched hand. Then he froze. "What's that?" He tilted his head, listening.

"What's what?" McKay asked, cursing his age and his earplugs at the same time.

"Aircraft," Casey replied, "from the northeast."

McKay strained in that direction. *How can he hear that?* he thought. *Goddamn young ears!*

"Over there." Wilson pointed.

McKay squinted into an empty sky. *Goddamn young eyes!* Then he spotted a silver glint low on the horizon and watched it inch toward him. The plane grew as it approached until it began to take on identifiable characteristics. Two engines mounted over the wings, a double tail, and drop-tanks near the wing tips.

"Whatever the hell it is . . ." McKay reached for his binocs. "It's carrying extra tanks."

"A Beriev," Casey piped, "Russian seaplane from the late sixties. And those aren't drop-tanks, they're floats."

McKay returned the field glasses to their pouch and just stared at Casey. "So what color is the pilot's hair, asshole?"

Casey studied McKay quizzically, then caught on and turned back toward the sky. "Blond," he deadpanned.

"Shit!" McKay shook his head.

"Sure are a lot of amphibious aircraft around here." Sam crawled through the cabin and out onto the bankside pontoon of the Maule. "What's the deal here?"

That was a damn good question, McKay thought as he watched the Beriev roar overhead. He noticed that slung under the wing tips were, indeed, small floats and not drop-tanks. *The little bastard was right again!* He was surprised by the aircraft's size. It looked to be about a hundred feet long. The plane was as big as a Herc, he thought.

He watched the ship pitch to port, fly a half circle over the beach, then disappear below the trees. The damn thing was setting down beyond the reef just like it had been here before, something that he doubted. "What's the range on that whatever-it-is?"

"You tell me, Billy." Casey grinned. "It's from your era."

"I was four years old, butt-breath. Now what's the range?"

Casey shrugged. "I'm not sure."

"Guess!"

"Well, let's see." Wilson thought out loud. "Two Ivchenko turboprops, about four thousand horsepower each; wingspan about equal to the ship's length; max speed about four hundred miles per hour, fuel tank capacity . . ."

McKay tapped his foot while Casey figured.

"I'd say about twenty-five hundred miles, give or take a hundred."

"Just far enough to make it from the mainland," deduced McKay. Suddenly he leapt off the landing and headed toward the beach at the double.

Sam and Casey stood on the dock and watched McKay, then stared at one another blankly.

"Well, come on, goddamnit!" The Marine barked over his shoulder.

"What's the deal, Billy?" Sloan shouted.

McKay stopped and turned around in the pathway. "It doesn't take an Annapolis degree to know that *that*"—he pointed to the sky over the beach—"is the Arab's escape vehicle!" He turned toward the beach.

Casey and Sam casually strolled over to the Toyota and climbed in. Wilson cranked up the starter. "I guess he couldn't wait for a ride, huh."

Moheb Nazrullah placed the pistol against the nape of the woman's neck, and that shut her up. She had been howling like some terrified schoolgirl instead of the hardened slut she obviously was. *Good God*, he thought. *She's behaving as if this has never happened to her before.* Then he lifted up her dress and saw that she was wearing no underwear, and that really gave him a laugh. He unzipped his pants with his free hand, and was making ready for his fun when he heard a large plane thunder overhead. He looked up through the tress and saw the seaplane pass over and veer toward the sea beyond the reef. "Goddamnit, they're early!" he snarled. But if he hurried, he could still finish before the plane landed. He turned back toward the girl to resume his pleasure, but something grabbed his wrist and tried to wrench the gun from his hand.

"Great God!" Nazrullah gasped at the unseen force that threatened to break his arm. "What the . . .?" But then he knew. Instantaneously he knew. It was the only logical explanation. It had to be the American! "Rogers?"

"You remembered," came a voice from above the Moslem's wrist, now bent back against its own forearm. "I'm flattered."

"Tommy?" the woman squealed.

What is going on here? Moheb thought. *They know each other?* Though stunned and confused, Nazrullah still managed to hold onto the pistol, but he was pointing it at himself, and that hardly qualified as an advantage. The pain was now excruciating. "But you're dead!" he gasped.

"Then think of me as a ghost." The pressure increased, and Moheb was certain his wrist would snap at any second. "The ghost that has prepared a place for you in paradise."

Nazrullah's desperation grew with his pain, and he knew he had to do something and do it now. He judged by the sound of the voice where the American's body was likely to be and launched a kick straight up.

"Shit!"

It connected.

Moheb's hand was suddenly freed, and the pain in his wrist lessened. But he could no longer use that hand, so he switched the gun to his left one. He knew that the pistol would be of questionable use against an unseen target, but if the American knew the girl, then she could provide him with a visible one. He saw the slut frantically crawling bare-assed toward the edge of the clearing, and scrambled toward her. He caught her by the ankle just as she reached the undergrowth, and dragged her to him until he cradled her neck in his forearm. He put the muzzle of the pistol against her temple. "I will kill her, Tom Rogers. You know this."

Nothing.

The invisible grunting ceased, along with the American's pain, Nazrullah assumed. Rogers was lying still, hiding behind his own silence. "I said I will kill her," the Moslem repeated, "if you don't show yourself."

"That's gonna be hard." The voice came from the middle of the clearing, and Nazrullah whirled and fired twice in the general direction of the sound. One bullet kicked up a mist of sand. The other didn't. Instead, there was a moan, but it was too soft for Moheb to get a directional fix. Within a few seconds, however, he realized he didn't need one.

Just beyond the center of the clearing Nazrullah focused on a bizarre sight. There, a faint nimbus formed slowly, like an aura steadily growing about a dim silhouette of a human being. "Allah be praised!" Nazrullah whispered. "I've got him now." And he leveled the Semmerling at the figure's head.

The Guardians stood on the beach and watched the rafts disembark from the Beriev. Two rafts, five men each.

"Well, at least the odds are even." McKay snickered, looking at his two colleagues. "How far do you figure the seaplane is from here?" He turned to Sloan.

"About eight hundred meters," Sam replied.

"Too far for the grenade launcher, huh?"

"About twice too far, Billy. You know that."

"But not too far for the rafts, college boy."

Sam smiled. "That's downright murder!"

"You bet your ass." McKay grinned.

Sloan loaded up the 40mm shape charge into the M203

launcher slung under the barrel of his Galil. "Should I wait until they cross the reef?" he asked.

"Yeah, why not," McKay answered. "Maybe they'll flip over in the surf, give us a good laugh."

"You're cold, Billy." Casey smiled.

McKay shielded his eyes from the sun. "Yeah, but I'm consistent."

Then two shots in rapid succession rang out. To McKay, they sounded like pistol shots, but he couldn't tell. He looked at the others. Sam shrugged, but Casey pointed down the beach. "Four hundred meters that way," he said.

McKay thought immediately of Tom and wanted to hustle toward the shots, but the rafts had cleared the reef and were approaching within five hundred meters of the beach. *One fight at a time*, he reminded himself. He uncased his binoculars while Casey crouched in the sand, just in case Sam was a little off.

At four hundred meters the naval commander opened up. McKay watched the first grenade fall thirty meters short, but it sent up a hell of a plume and showered incandescent copper in all directions. "That got their attention." McKay laughed. He could see the eyes bulge on the boys in the rafts through his field glasses. "Try another, Sammy."

Sloan thumped off another round, and McKay watched it explode within a few meters of the first raft. The concussion flipped the small boat, and the white phosphorous starburst burned through the Hypalon-coated nylon and burst the raft like a balloon. Black-suited bodies plopped in the surf afterward, but the water couldn't extinguish the phosphorous that burned through to their bones.

"The odds are looking even better," McKay remarked as the shrieks died down from the surf. "Send out another, Sam. With any luck they won't get a shot off."

But just as Sloan touched off the next round, the five men slipped over the side of the remaining raft.

"Damn!" McKay snorted. "I guess we'll have to fight after all." He turned to Sam. "Hit 'em one last time, Commander. Maybe you'll boil a few!"

Sloan held the weapon almost level for the final shot of about a hundred meters. When the round exploded, a man was catapulted up with the column of water and slapped the surface a few seconds later, screaming. The other four men had disappeared.

"Fan out, boys," McKay ordered. Casey took the right flank, thirty meters down the beach, with the MAC-10, and Sam the left with his Galil. McKay held down the center with his newly acquired Uzi. They all crouched low in the sand.

The four invaders, clumped just a few meters apart, sprang out of the surf simultaneously, their muzzles flashing at McKay.

"Shit!" The gunfire bit at the beach all around him, and the Marine tried to bury himself in the sand. "I think I found 'em, boys," he strained into his throat mike. "I could use a little help here."

Casey and Sam instantly reacted, spewing out lead as they converged on the center. McKay saw two of the attackers, one on each end, spin into the surf. He concentrated his aim on the middle. But all he got from the Uzi was a sharp click. "Damn!" The sand had fucked up the firing mechanism, he thought. He reached for the Colt .45 on his hip with one hand and the K-Bar sheathed to his chest with the other. Then he flattened out on the sand. He looked up just in time to see the two remaining attackers, less than thirty meters away, leave the water in a crouch and head straight for him. "Oh, shit!"

He let go of the K-bar for an instant to cock the .45, but knew the handgun was no match for automatic weapons. Still, he might get lucky. He started to aim the Colt when a burst of gunfire punched the beach just inches in front of him and lashed his eyes with sand. "Fuck!" He couldn't see anything. *I don't believe this shit*, he thought. *I'm going to die here blind because I'm looking for somebody who can't be seen. Perfect!*

McKay cringed there in the sand, waiting for the fatal shot to strike, when a maelstrom of fire ripped the air above him. Shouts of rage and pain interlaced the shooting, and McKay covered his head with his arms and tried to visualize the firefight.

Then a black silence dropped over the beach and hung there, trembling. The echoes of combat vibrated through the air so that McKay wasn't quite sure where the fighting ended and the stillness began. For a moment he wasn't even sure whether he was alive.

"Hey, Billy?" It sounded like Casey. "You all right, man?"

McKay moved his head, felt no pain or blood, then raised to his knees. Unable to see, he peered in several directions with a dazed look on his face.

"It's over, dude," Casey chirped. "We won."

"That's nice," was all McKay could say.

"Look!" Casey pointed beyond the reef. The big seaplane was roaring down its liquid runway toward a takeoff. "Guess they've had enough, huh?"

"Yeah, and it looks like we walked away from another one, Billy." Sam extended his hand and helped the Marine to his feet. "Don't take it so hard."

McKay pawed at the sand in his eyes. The granules felt like jagged boulders grinding into his pupils. He eventually cleared the grit away. Finally, he was able to see four blurred bodies floating in the surf, and he was happy to note that none of them were his. He took a deep breath and remembered the two shots that had come from the jungle before the firefight. Then, without a word, he grabbed the MAC-10 out of Casey's hands, jammed in a fresh clip, and stalked off down the beach.

The second bullet rammed his left shoulder with the force of a mule kick. Tom Rogers reeled but willed himself to stand. The wound blazed like fire. He wanted to cry out, but he let out a soft moan instead. He had been shot several times in his life, but each new wound still thrust him into an unexplored province of excruciation. *My God!* he screamed in his brain as the shock settled in.

He knew he should have kept his mouth shut, but instead he had popped off at the Moslem, and that had given his position away. And the raghead had gotten lucky with his second shot. Tom realized that he had become too confident and comfortable with his invisibility, and had forgotten the first rule of survival: A little paranoia is a good thing. The hatred he felt for the Moslem plus the surprise of seeing Marta again had just been too much, even for Tom Rogers.

Then suddenly, he caught a flash of movement right in front of his eyes, just as he moved his arm. He moved again and saw an even stronger image. He held his hands in front of his face and watched in horror while his limbs materialized before him. The one thing that he had hoped for was now happening, and he couldn't have been more unhappy about it. *The timing sucks!* he thought.

He could see the bones in his fingers now, like in an X ray, and for the first time in days, he had feet under him. But if he could see himself, could the Pashtun? It was a desperate and stupid question, he knew, but what the hell. He looked at

Nazrullah across the clearing and saw his worst fears confirmed. The Moslem's smirk told Rogers that he had lost his advantage, and the pistol leveled at his head told him that he had once again become a visible, tangible target.

Then there was Marta. *What the hell was she doing here?* he wondered. *She looked like she had been rode hard and put up wet.* He searched her eyes and tried to read beyond the fear. He thought he saw something behind her glaze, a spark of concern. But then that was something he had wanted to see all along, and so he disregarded it. This was no time for wishful thinking. There was a more perilous enemy to deal with first.

"How nice of you to make an appearance," Nazrullah snickered. "I've been wanting to see you for some time now." He steadied the gun. "Funny, you don't look like I imagined at all. I thought you'd be bigger."

Rogers glanced down and saw that all five feet, eight inches of him had rematerialized, jumpsuit and all. "Sorry to disappoint you."

"No apology necessary. I'm just happy you *showed up*." Nazrullah's laugh was like a bray. "I thought I'd lost you, *old chum*."

"Oh, I get it." Rogers smiled. "Too bad the sharks didn't."

"Yes, that was unfortunate. How did you escape?"

"Allah was with me," Rogers sneered.

Nazrullah's face became a black cloud. "There is no end to your blasphemy, eh, infidel?"

"I can't think of any, raghead."

"Then I shall have to end it for you." The Moslem's arm straightened as he sighted down the barrel at the Guardian's unflinching face.

There was nothing for Tom to do now. He was caught in the open with no weapon and was too far away to rush Nazrullah before he could get a shot off. He flashed one last look of defiance at his enemy, then closed his gun-metal gray eyes for what he knew would be the last time.

But instead of a pistol shot, there came the thump of a grenade from several hundred meters up the beach. Tom opened his eyes and looked at Nazrullah. The Moslem was staring in the direction of the new sound instead of paying attention to his prisoners. As Tom started to bolt, the Sig automatic steadied again at his head.

"Don't move," Moheb snapped. "That sound you hear is

made by my colleagues who have come to collect me, and it won't alter you're fate in the slightest."

"I hate to argue with you, shithead, but that sound you hear is coming from *my* colleagues who have come for *me*, and that's going to alter your fate about a hundred and eighty degrees."

"Bullshit!"

"You think so?" Tom smirked, trying to keep the conversation going. "Have your boys got grenade launchers? And if so, who are they shooting at and why? Think about it, asshole."

The Pashtun scrunched up his face and looked down, mulling over what Rogers had just said. He relaxed his grip around Marta's neck while he thought, and that was all the cue she needed. Marta lunged upward, grabbed the Moslem's arm, and sank her teeth into the flesh just above his wrist. The gun went off, firing wildly into the bush. Nazrullah howled like a pig and cracked Marta over the head with the butt of the pistol. Rogers used the diversion to cover the ten meters that separated him from certain death and dove for the gun. He vaguely noticed that Marta's limp body rolled out of the way. He grabbed for the pistol and was wrenching it free when Nazrullah managed to fling the weapon across the clearing.

Finally it was down to just the two of them, Tom thought. No magic, no weapons, just training, cunning, determination, and most of all, hatred.

Tom straddled the Moslem, pinning him against the sand at the edge of the clearing. The Guardian's left shoulder throbbed, and blood saturated his sleeve and dripped into Nazrullah's face. The pain was too much for Rogers to use that arm, so he pushed with his right hand against Moheb's upturned chin. If only he could use his other arm, he thought, he could snap the Pashtun's neck.

Nazrullah struggled to breathe against the American's hand. He clawed desperately at the fingers covering his lower face, but couldn't wrench them free. The Guardian had the strength of a bulldog, he thought, spitting away the mixture of sand and blood that clogged his mouth and stung his eyes and nostrils. Then he gathered all of his strength for a series of short, stiff jabs at the American's shoulder. He fired off three sharp blows at the open wound, then pushed off the sand with all his strength.

Tom wailed out his pain in a long, jagged roar. He was pushed backward and landed on his hurt shoulder. The combined jolts paralyzed him with agony. He rocked from side to side in pain for a few seconds before he could struggle to his knees. He crawled around in the direction of the Moslem and saw the man rummaging furiously through a rucksack on the other side of the clearing, stealing furtive glances back at the Guardian.

Tom scanned the area in a flash, looking for the Sig. He couldn't find it, saw Marta still sprawled unconscious, and quickly looked back at the Moslem. Then he remembered the Simmerling that Nazrullah had stowed in the pack earlier, and charged headlong across the clearing. He butted the Pashtun between the shoulder blades and sent him sprawling into the bush. Rogers scrambled into the jungle after him and grabbed an ankle as the Moslem regained his feet. Tom jerked hard, and Nazrullah pitched forward into a tree, slashing his head against the trunk. Stunned, Moheb tried to rise to his knees, but collapsed instead.

The pain and exertion had exhausted Rogers, and he couldn't take advantage of the Moslem's momentary lapse. Tom struggled to his knees, but could get no farther. He knelt there in the bush, gulping lungfuls of air, and fought to regain his strength.

For the first time he noticed the steady rattle of gunfire from the beach. Each round that popped in the distance announced the arrival of the Guardians. Tom had known that they would find a way to cut through all the bullshit and trace him.

He knew they wouldn't have given up. For more than two years the Guardians had been his family, and family doesn't forget or take no for an answer. Especially Billy McKay. Although the stubborn Marine managed to piss Tom off about ninety percent of the time, Rogers knew he could count on McKay to be there when the shit came down. And it was coming down in buckets now. So naturally, Billy was just a quarter of a mile away. *That should be close enough*, Tom thought.

Rogers changed his mind the instant he looked up. What he saw was a blurred Nazrullah in the middle of a whirling roundhouse kick. Next came a tight close-up of the man's foot followed by a galaxy of stars. The blow connected with devastating force and sent Tom reeling backward into the clearing. The last thought that ricocheted through Rogers's brain was hope that somehow his head would manage to stay on his shoulders.

Tom swam through a sea of darkness, breathing cold liquid

*as if it were air, and watched the sharks as they wafted by. One
that passed within inches of him carried Nazrullah on his back.
Both beast and man turned and sneered at him, bearing razors
for teeth. Another, with Marta in its mouth, floated right up to
him, and the leering woman reached out and slapped Tom over
and over again in the face. "Wake up, pig!" she snarled. "Wake
up, you worthless slanderer of God!"*

"Wake up, infidel." The blow stung Tom's cheek, and he
opened his eyes to a vision of Nazrullah sitting on his chest and
slapping him repeatedly in the face. "I want you awake for
this," the Moslem hissed.

Tom tried to move, but discovered that his arms were pinned
under the Pashtun's knees. Then he focused on a pistol that
flashed just a few inches in front of his eyes. It was the
Simmerling that Nazrullah had retrieved from the backpack
while Tom lay unconscious.

"Awake, now? Good." Nazrullah smiled, and his mustache
stretched tight, like a thin greasy line, across his bleeding face.
"You put up a valiant effort, Tom Rogers, but you were simply
no match for a soldier of Islam. Like on the trawler." Then he
punched the Guardian in his wounded shoulder, just to heighten
the American's awareness. "Still with me?"

Rogers writhed in pain but fought back the impulse to
scream. He would not give the Pashtun that satisfaction under
any circumstances.

"And now, it is your time." Nazrullah placed the pistol
against Tom's forehead and, with the same greasy smile, released the safety. "Good-bye, old chum."

The shot reverberated through the clearing, echoing off the
trees in waves of sound, and Tom felt a splattering of cranial
goo strafe his face. The moment that it took for him to understand that the scream he heard had been his own seemed like a
lifetime. Through the gore that splayed over his face, Tom could
barely see a pair of dark brown eyes roll up white toward the
black and red cavity that was once the Moslem's forehead. Then
Nazrullah, already in paradise, pitched forward and landed in
Tom's face.

"Shit!" The Guardian scrambled out from under the oozing
skull and rolled in the sand, choking on the blood and brains of
his enemy. Every heave reinforced that he was still alive,
though a few moments before, he had resigned himself to his
own imminent death. He finally turned over and, wiping the

sludge from his eyes, looked across the clearing. There with the smoking Sig-Sauer held in her outstretched hands, knelt a trembling Marta Ryan.

The man and woman just stared at each other across the empty space. Tom didn't know what to say, and Marta appeared too shaken to speak. Finally, Tom broke the silence. "I wanted to see you one last time before I died. There for a while, I thought that was all I was going to do, just see you."

Marta's expression hardened. "That's about all you are going to do, Tommy." She moved the pistol to her right until it covered the Guardian's head.

Tom returned her stare with a look that was a mixture of confusion and sadness. "So that's why you're here," he rasped.

"Yes." Her answer was almost a whisper.

"Don't tell me, let me guess." He glanced at the sand. "Maggie?"

Marta nodded.

"Uh, huh." Tom's smile was mirthless. "I'll try to remember in the future never to trust Maggie Connoly." He shook his head. "Or Marta Ryan."

It was Marta's turn to look away, and her evasive glance confirmed that, for Tom, there would be no future.

"Before you pull that trigger, I have a few questions for you."

"Don't, Tommy . . ."

"No." He held up his hand in protest. "You have to grant the condemned man his last request. It's a point of honor, something I don't expect you to understand, but just take my word for it."

"Please, Tommy, this just makes it worse."

"Not for me it doesn't." His eyes narrowed into bullets of disgust. "First of all, why did you do it?"

"Do what?"

"Start the whole thing."

"You mean *us*?"

"You know that's exactly what I mean," he strained.

"Tommy," Marta bristled, "you're acting as if *you* have the gun."

"Fuck the gun," he bellowed, "answer the question!"

Marta jumped at his sudden explosion and, for an instant, Tom thought she might jerk the trigger.

"Answer the question," he repeated evenly.

She looked away for a second while she thought, then said, "I was bored, and you were someone new, someone outside the same old Washington crowd."

"Fresh blood?"

"I suppose." Her reply was so soft that Tom could barely hear her.

"I see." Tom shook his head. "And the ending?"

Marta's pause was uneasy. Finally, after a few false starts, she spoke. "Our life-styles were incompatible. There was no way we could be together."

Rogers looked at her as if she had two heads. "Incompatible life-styles! That's it?"

"Well, frankly," she added, "you didn't exactly have your life together."

Tom just looked at her and smoldered. He was not a cosmopolitan man, and so could not offer Marta the cleverness that she mistook for sophistication. He understood all too well what he was. A simple warrior, a loner in the hard places of the world. He was not as proud of that as he once had been, yet it was still what he was. He couldn't change it, though for Marta he would have tried. He understood now that he would have to remain what he had always been, a man who walked the edge between life and death. Marta was right, of course. He didn't have his life together. But then, did anyone? And most of all, did she?

As he stared at the woman he once loved, he was suddenly struck by the strangest sensation. The longer he looked at her, it seemed, the more she began to fade, as if her image were disintegrating gradually before his eyes. Finally, he imagined that she vanished altogether, and all that remained of her was a gun.

"So," he said, "you left me because our life-styles are incompatible, and now you're going to shoot me because I don't have my shit together? I've heard of adding insult to injury but never the reverse."

She almost smiled at that, but caught herself at the last moment. "I don't want to hurt you, Tommy, but I have my orders."

"Orders from Maggie, huh?" he scoffed. "You two make a good pair."

Marta frowned, and the pistol quivered in her hand. Tom could see that he had made a dangerous remark, but he no longer cared. "Don't you want a drink first?" he pushed.

Her quiver turned into a full-fledged shake, and Marta flushed with rage. "You son of a bitch!" she snarled.

Tom didn't flinch. "Go on, Marta, shoot. You'll be doing us both a favor."

She straightened her arms to steady the weapon. For the third time that day, Tom stared at his own death down the muzzle of a gun. This time he vowed he would not close his eyes. He would watch the end come with the same detachment as a scientist observing an experiment. More importantly, he would force Marta to look directly into his eyes. Maybe she would see all they had once meant to each other. It just might work, he thought. For one protracted moment, he was sure he saw a tear glisten in Marta's right eye as she sighted down the barrel.

But Tom would never know for sure. Because at that instant, the clearing erupted in a blistering staccato of gunfire. One long, jagged burst caught Marta at the waist and sliced her up the center. A blade of .45 slugs split her open at the sternum and tore away her mouth in one swift, crimson slash. Her small body left the ground, then jerked and flopped about in midair like a rag doll suspended in a storm of metal.

This can't be happening, thought Tom. He felt each bullet as if it were tearing away his flesh instead of Marta's. The fact that it was either him or her was momentarily lost on the Guardian. All he knew was that the only woman he had ever loved was being shot to pieces.

Finally, the fusillade ended, and the accompanying crash rolled away like distant thunder. All that was left was the sting of cordite that hung in a gauze over Marta's riddled body.

Tom turned toward the perimeter and blinked at the imposing figure of Billy McKay. The Marine stood there at the edge of he jungle with a MAC-10 cradled in his elbow and stared back at his friend with eyes of stone. "Fuck her," he said, his voice as dead as his eyes. "She was trash."

CHAPTER
TWENTY ——————————

Dr. Marguarite Connoly sat on the edge of the bunk and stared at the institutional-green walls. A wool blanket, dotted with moth holes, covered the bare mattress and scratched her thighs. The light blue shift, stenciled with a number just below the shoulders, was too short to cover the back of her legs when she sat. She hated wool, even in the winter. The harsh cloth was unbearable during summer in Washington, D.C. The smell of stale urine that permeated everything in the cell was enough to make her gag with each breath. *Jesus Christ*, she thought. She stared at the seatless toilet just a few inches from her bunk.

Three sharp blows rapped off the iron door and echoed like gunshots through the concrete room. The sudden noise startled her. She jumped off the bunk, cupped her hands over her ears, and scurried into the corner. The heavy door slid open, then closed with a bang. For what seemed like a very long time, she stood there, facing the corner, trembling. Finally, she heard a male voice speak to her from across the cell.

"Maggie?" the man said softly. "Are you all right?"

She forced herself to turn around. First she saw the gleaming cordovan loafers, then the khaki slacks, the pinpoint cotton shirt neatly pressed and open at the neck, and finally, the freshly shaven face of Jeffrey MacGregor.

"Are you all right?" he repeated.

Incredulous, she just stared at him. "How do I look?" she said.

"I've seen you look better." He motioned to the bunk. "Mind if I sit down?"

"It's your prison, Mr. President. Help yourself."

He settled onto the bunk and tested the mattress with his palms. "A little on the firm side, huh?" He forced a smile.

"Firm?" she glared. "Try petrified!" She moved a few steps, turned, and leaned back against the wall. "But then you always did have a fondness for euphemisms, Jeffrey."

He forced another smile. "You still blame me, don't you?"

"Humph," she snorted. "You put me here. Who else should I blame?"

"You ordered a murder, Maggie," the President reminded her. "You're lucky I didn't have you taken out to the Rose Garden and summarily shot!"

"You're the one who ordered the murder, Jeffrey, or have you forgotten? Does the line 'Who will rid me of this turbulent priest' ring a bell?"

MacGregor stood up. "I was referring to the whole goddamn situation, not specifically to Rogers, for crissakes!" His face flushed, and his voice rose steadily until he was almost shouting. "Your all-encompassing arrogance led you to misconstrue the remark. Then you took it upon yourself to act on that misunderstanding. Why didn't you clarify it with me first?"

Connoly saw that both his fists were clenched and that the veins bulged in his neck. "I . . . I thought . . . I . . ." she stammered.

"Go on, Maggie, say it," MacGregor yelled. "You thought you could do anything!"

"No," she hissed, "I thought I was doing what you didn't have the *balls* to do!"

"Is that what it was? I thought it was Maggie Connoly playing President. It's the role you've always coveted, isn't it?" He turned and walked toward the door.

"Where are you going?" she asked, frantic.

"Why, to the White House, of course. Isn't that where Presidents usually go?"

"Jeffrey," she pleaded, "surely you're not going to leave me here?"

"Yes, Maggie, I am." He stepped through the opening, and the door slammed shut behind him.

Connoly rushed to the door and pressed her face against the bars of the small window. "Jeffrey!" she cried. "For God's sake, why are you doing this to me?"

The President stopped and turned back toward the cell. "Because you deserve it, Maggie." Then he turned and walked away, his footsteps echoing down the long concrete hall.

EPILOGUE

McKay set the tray down on the beach and distributed the drinks to the cripples on either side of him. "Doctor, your Mai Tai," he chimed to Lee Warren, "and a Hurricane for you, Lieutenant Rogers." He served the cocktails with a flourish, like a European waiter, but was careful to avoid Warren's encased leg or cause Rogers to move his bandaged shoulder. It was obvious that the crusty Marine rather enjoyed his uncharacteristic display of deference and civility.

Warren, propped in a lawn chair, looked at McKay quizzically. "Your behavior is beginning to scare me, Billy. What's the deal?"

McKay flashed a toothy grin. "I'm warm and sensitive, Doc, didn't you know?"

Rogers cut his eyes at the Marine.

"For all the years I've known you, McKay, that particular part of your personality has managed to elude me," Warren said.

"Well," sniffed McKay, "we all have many sides." He stretched out on a large towel to soak up what remained of the late afternoon sun.

As he lay there, caressed by the trade winds, he thought of

MacGregor and how all of this was the result of an Executive Branch guilt complex. The President had arranged the all-expenses-paid vacation for the Guardians because of a "misunderstanding" within the White House. McKay shook his head. That misunderstanding had almost cost Tom his life and had cost Marta Ryan hers. And now Maggie Connoly was in jail. He smiled at the thought of Iron Maggie cooling her heels in the slammer. *That ought to give her an attitude adjustment.* He snickered. *Thank you, Mr. President.*

He sat up to watch Casey cut didos in the surf, hanging ten on the nose of his fiberglass board and crouching in the curls. Then, just beyond, he saw Sam hiked out in a trapeze harness, his toes gripping the raised pontoon of a planing Hobie Cat. Both men resembled teenagers cavorting in the water.

McKay was content to stay on the beach and check out the action closer in. He had set up their "base camp" to be perfectly positioned between the water's edge and the Banyon Tree Bar behind the old Moana Hotel. From this vantage point, he could properly scrutinize the female population. And as usual, Waikiki was teeming with cooz. Sculptured golden asses, trimmed in string bikinis, sashayed by like undulating gifts of flesh. McKay fired up a cigar, adjusted his Ray-Bans, and settled back to watch the show.

"I still don't understand all of this invisibility stuff," Rogers said, out of the blue. They were the first words McKay remembered him speaking all day.

"I'm not sure I do either," said Warren, applying sunscreen to the tip of his nose. "And neither do the Army scientists. Not altogether, anyway."

"What do they think?" Rogers asked.

"The general consensus is that the Magnetic Enhancement Device altered the molecular makeup of your cells, and the shock of the gunshot wound acted as an antidote," explained Warren.

"How?" McKay was curious now.

"Well, the way I understand it," Warren continued, "the magnetically enhanced realignment of your cellular structure, which is what caused the invisibility, required an inordinate supply of oxygen to sustain the condition. One reason you were chosen for the experiment, Tom, was because you've got a heart like an adolescent bull and an aorta the size of a fire hose. You've never smoked, so your lungs are still cherry. Anyway, the hemorrhage from the wound and the resulting shock cut back the blood, and thus oxygen supply, which in turn reversed the condition."

"Then what about the people killed at the laboratory?" McKay asked. "Surely they were in shock too."

"Good point, Billy," Warren said. "I must say, I'm surprised at your acumen."

"Piss up a rope, Doc!"

"That's more like it." Warren smiled. "But to answer your question, those killed at the laboratory remained invisible because they continued to be exposed to the lingering magnetic bombardment that caused their realignment in the first place. All of those bodies reappeared within hours after they were removed from the scene."

Rogers frowned. "But that doesn't explain my clothing."

"Well," Warren continued, "the current theory there is that when your body changed back, so did the magnetic field immediately surrounding it. And that encompassed your jumpsuit."

"What about the building?" asked McKay.

"It's still invisible," Warren said. "And nobody knows why."

"Hum," Tom snorted. Gripping his shoulder, he rose carefully and walked away.

For a long moment, McKay and Warren just watched Rogers drift down the beach. Finally, Warren said, "There he goes, the last of a vanishing breed." Then he turned to McKay. "Have you two got it squared away yet?"

McKay shrugged. "I don't know, Doc."

"Don't you think now is as good a time as any to find out?"

The Marine and the scientist looked at one another. "I suppose you're right," McKay said. He got up and started down the beach after his friend.

It took McKay about a hundred meters to catch up and fall in stride with the Green Beret. A few meters farther the Marine spied a pair of approaching young lovelies and leered as they wafted past. "Oh, Jesus!" he moaned, turning to watch them from a reverse angle. "A couple of strong bodies there, huh?" He studied Rogers for a reaction. Nothing. "You did notice them, didn't you?"

Suddenly Tom stopped and whirled on the Marine. "What do you want?"

"I guess," McKay said, looking down, "I want to know if you're all right."

"No!" Rogers glared. "Does that do it for you, or is there more?"

McKay pawed at the sand with his foot. "There's more. I just wanted to say . . . well . . . that I'm sorry."

Tom looked at McKay with eyes filled with pain. "I know," he said.

Some faint music from the back of the beach drifted down to where the men stood at the water's edge. Someone had brought a portable disk player and had set it up on a picnic table. People began to congregate there, listening to the music and watching the sunset. McKay recognized the song, an old Jimi Hendrix tune from the sixties, one that his mother used to play when he was a small child, *Castles Made of Sand.*

The colors shifted as the sun sank, and the clouds reflected a show of resplendence in the sky. "I don't know if I can do it anymore," Tom whispered.

The Marine reached out and put a hand on his friend's shoulder. "I know," he said, and the two men stood in silence and watched the sun disappear in the ocean.

Suddenly, Tom winced, "Damn! That's my bad shoulder."

McKay recoiled. "Jesus, I didn't know."

"Of course you didn't," shouted Rogers, "you ignorant, fucking jarhead!"

"Now wait just a goddamn minute, greenie beanie!"

"Wait for what?"

"Wait till you get well, then I'm gonna kick your ass."

"Oh, yeah?"

"Oh, yeah! And another thing, shithead . . ."